Lady Blue

Helen A Rosburg

Medallion Press, Inc.
Printed in USA

DEDICATION

I must confess I wrote this book for myself.
It was the most fun I've had in ages.

Published 2009 by Medallion Press, Inc.

The MEDALLION PRESS LOGO
is a registered trademark of Medallion Press, Inc.

Typeset in Adobe Jenson Pro
Printed in the United States of America

ISBN: 978-1-60-542063-9

10 9 8 7 6 5 4 3 2 1
First Edition

her western ideas of love and marriage. Most heart wrenching is the decisions that Cecile faces and the bitter agony in her journey to find love. **Call Of The Trumpet** is not your conventional historical romance, but Helen Rosburg goes to great length to pull the reader into the world and culture of this strange society."

—Tracy, Historical Romance Writers

<u>*Previous accolades for* **Blaze of Lightning, Roar of Thunder**</u>

"Helen A Rosburg delves deeply into the subtleties of the mountains and desert and into the deepest recesses of the human heart. **Blaze Of Lightning, Roar Of Thunder** is a compelling novel of loss and renewal, of revenge and redemption; a credible, inspiring tale of lasting love and its power to endure, to flourish, to heal wounds deemed not healable. A one-sit read."

—Vicki Hinze, www.vickihinze.com

". . . Blaze is full of strength and beauty, and her ability to grow after such horrific trauma is captivating."

—*Publishers Weekly*

"Ms. Rosburg is a gifted storyteller, creating a compelling tale, sucking the reader into the pages to become part of the story. As each page turns, the reader experiences the West as it was in the days of hostile banditos and bounty hunters."

—Lauren Calder, *Affaire de Coeur*

"Rosburg captures your attention with a riveting prologue and doesn't let go until the gut-wrenching climax. She delivers strong, motivated characters, attention to detail, a well-drawn backdrop, and a story as old as the West. This is truly a memorable read."

—Kathe Robin, *Romantic Times BOOKreviews*

Lady Blue

Helen A Rosburg

Chapter One

$\mathscr{L}$ife, as Harmony had known it, was over.

With a heavy sigh, she stared into the small square of mirror hung over the scarred dresser top. Had she really become so pale in so short a time? The ocean voyage had lasted scarcely a week.

Before that, however, there had been the weeks spent at her mother's bedside, and the sleepless nights, grieving in advance of the inevitable. Then the funeral, and the long, dark days of mourning. No, it had not been a short time at all. It was simply far longer than she remembered. So long, in fact, she could not recall the last time she had sat astride her favorite mount and loped across the meadow grass in the shadow of the majestic mountains. It was no wonder the honey tone had vanished from her skin. Even her flame-colored tresses seemed to have dimmed. She had not seen the sun in a long, long time. Harmony wondered if she would see it ever again.

A painful ball of grief replaced the area her heart and lungs had once occupied and then burst, sending shards of agony throughout her entire body. Perhaps the pain she felt was so much greater because she mourned more than the loss of her beloved parents. Gone, too, were sunlit days under impossibly blue skies, the wind in her face, the smell of horse and fertile earth in her nostrils, the feeling of freedom as she galloped across the plains of tall, dry grass.

A single tear slipped down Harmony's cheek, and she quickly swiped it away, afraid that if the dam broke she would never be able to stop crying. The life she had left behind was gone, perhaps forever. She must learn to live with the knowledge, no matter how painful. Her life was in England now.

"Miss, are you in there? Hello?"

Startled, Harmony whirled toward the door. The cloudy dream of her former life evaporated as if it had never been.

"Yes? What is it?"

The maid offered a brief curtsy. "Your sister, miss. She asked me to fetch your bag and tell you the coach is waiting."

"Thank you. I'll be along in a moment." Harmony watched the girl leave with the single bag she had taken up with her for the night then glanced around to make sure she had left nothing behind. It was easy to see, in the sparsely furnished room, nothing personal remained. All that was left was her lingering disappointment in Agatha's welcome.

Harmony had enjoyed her building excitement as the ship on which she had voyaged made its slow, stately way up the Thames to the London docksides. For a time the sun had come out from behind the cloud cover of homesickness. The bustling river traffic had distracted her and the scenes along the riverbanks quickly piqued her interest. Like it or not, this was her new home. She should get to know it. When the teeming streets of the fabled city came into view, Harmony found her fingers curled tightly around the deck railing. Her heart pounded and she began searching the crowded wharves for a glimpse of her sister.

Never in her life had she seen so many people. She studied their apparel curiously then glanced at the skirt of her sapphire blue suit and exhaled a quiet sigh of relief. She was appropriately, even smartly clad, based on her measure of the most well-dressed ladies and gentlemen in the throng.

Harmony briefly pressed her knuckles to her eyes to suppress the sudden hot sting of tears. The suit, along with several other lovely gowns and accessories, had been purchased on one of her infrequent trips to New York with her mother and father before her father, a successful and wealthy cattle rancher, had passed away.

The memories were precious and bittersweet.

And they were a part of her past. Her future was in England, with her sister, Agatha. Harmony forced her hands away from her face back to the rail and let her gaze once again scan the crowd. Her heart seemed to skip a beat and she drew in a sharp breath. Was that Agatha?

The years had not been kind. The woman in the black dress and hat looked old beyond what Harmony knew her age to be. And then there was no more time for thought as Harmony was bustled aside to make room for the crew laying the gangway. Upon learning all passengers' luggage would be assembled on the dock, she gathered her skirts and stepped carefully onto the shore planking.

On the docks, excited passengers reuniting with loved ones swarmed past her and Harmony was carried along in the stream of humanity. Inevitably, she drew close enough to Agatha to open her arms to her sister for a welcoming embrace. In the fleeting instant before her sister's response, Harmony felt a rush of warmth. Perhaps everything was going to be all right after all. Maybe the long years of separation and infrequent communication were not, in the end, going to matter. Despite her fears and homesickness, maybe Agatha and England were, indeed, going to be "home."

Heart brimming, Harmony stepped forward and

enclosed her sister's thin frame in the gentle circle of her arms. And felt Agatha stiffen.

"Agatha," Harmony whispered near her sister's pearl-bedecked ear. "Agatha . . ."

The older woman's only response was to back away, stiffly, from Harmony's embrace.

"Harmony," Agatha said sharply. "Decorum, please. We are in public."

The first barb had been delivered; Harmony felt it keenly. It remained as it had been when they were children, before Agatha turned nineteen and received a substantial inheritance from a recently deceased great-aunt living in London. Though the two had never met they had corresponded over the years. Their communication, and the inheritance, apparently persuaded Agatha to forsake her home and her family and move to Britain.

On the long voyage across the Atlantic, Harmony had had ample time to ponder the changes time must have wrought upon her sister. She had hoped the years might have softened her. She had hoped in vain.

"I apologize, Agatha," Harmony offered, hoping to pacify her sister before the situation was blown out of proportion as had happened so often in the past.

In response, Agatha gestured to a nearby liveried footman and said, "Indicate your bags, please, Harmony, so Charles may stow them in the carriage."

Harmony gratefully moved away to study the neat rows of baggage unloaded from the ship's hold. A moment later she obediently pointed out her brass-banded trunk and single carpetbag.

"Well," Agatha sniffed. "I can only hope you packed appropriately. You certainly packed *enough*. We will be leading a quiet life in the country, Harmony. I hope you don't expect to put on airs with a fancy and expensive wardrobe."

Though she had to bite her lip, Harmony wisely refrained from comment. Thanks to their mother's fine taste, her wardrobe was smart and contemporary, hardly "fancy." Agatha, however, would undoubtedly find the lovely clothes worthy of the harshest criticism.

"Put the trunk on top, Charles," Agatha ordered, "and the smaller bag inside." To Harmony, she said, "Due to your ship's arrival so late in the day, we will spend the night in a hotel and proceed to the countryside in the morning. I assume you packed efficiently enough that your carpet-sided bag will suffice for the night."

It would have to, Harmony mused, a bit of the sting of her sister's greeting mitigated by the thought of dinner and an evening in what would surely be a posh London hotel.

The carriage ride through the busy city streets was a silent one, a blessing for which Harmony was profoundly grateful. The long trip had exhausted her,

Agatha's greeting had saddened her, and homesickness seemed to have a grip around her throat, making it difficult to swallow, much less speak. Though the edifice was less than imposing, Harmony was glad when the coachman drew his team to a halt in front of the hotel.

"I will meet you in the dining room in one hour sharp," Agatha commanded regally and sailed up the narrow staircase to the left of the entryway, a hotel maid scurrying in her wake with her bag. Harmony followed a second maid to another room at back of the hotel's first floor.

The paucity of furnishings and lack of ambience hardly mattered to Harmony. At least she was alone. For a time. Dinner hour arrived all too soon.

The fare served in the dining room was as plain and unimaginative as the hotel itself. The only spice was Agatha's conversation.

"I trust your journey was pleasant," Agatha commented while slicing into a thin, gray slab of meat slathered in an unappetizing, brown, gravylike substance. "I'm certain our late mother's solicitor provided adequately for your journey out of the trust I maintain on your behalf until your majority."

"The voyage was very nice, thank you, Agatha." Harmony speared a small potato after ascertaining the pale tuber had not touched anything else on her plate. It appeared pristine and she popped it in her mouth.

"Do not think," Agatha snapped, "that you will be seeing any more monies out of your trust until you have come of suitable age. I am not of a mind to spoil you as our parents have done."

The potato turned to dust in Harmony's mouth. Shortly thereafter, braving her sister's displeasure and disapproval, she excused herself and fled to her room. Sleep was long in coming and a blessing when it finally arrived.

And now it was time to get back into a closed coach with Agatha, drive to her home in the country, and spend the next three years, until she attained majority, wondering why her sister resented her so deeply. She could hardly wait. With another long sigh, Harmony pulled on her gloves and left the room. She willed the painful memories of her former life to stay behind along with the ghost of her brief presence in the unwelcoming space. If they accompanied her, she feared she would not be able to bear her prison sentence at all.

Chapter Two

*I*t's about time," Agatha snapped when Harmony appeared in the hotel's small foyer. She took in her sister's appearance in a single, brief glance, turned on her heel, and marched out the front door.

Agatha noted, with approval, the alacrity with which her coachman moved to open the carriage door. She did not, however, deign to give him the slightest notice as she climbed inside. Familiarity of any kind with the lower classes was anathema. He did his job and he got paid for it. There the relationship began and ended. Agatha sat back in her seat and smoothed the black folds of her skirt. She stared straight ahead as Harmony ducked through the doorway, averting her eyes when her sister sat down opposite her.

Agatha clasped her hands in her lap and tried to hold back the wave of resentment that threatened to wash over her. She had no desire to live in a constant state of annoyance for the next few years.

It seemed, however, that was exactly what was going to happen. Their mother's will stated explicitly that Harmony was to live with her until she turned twenty-one, and Agatha was to exercise discretion over Harmony's inheritance as well. At least their mother had made one sensible decision. Agatha sniffed audibly.

As for her sister's appearance and manners, well, what could she expect? The girl was scarcely civilized. She had lived in the West, for heaven's sake, with cowboys and Indians. She had been allowed to ride a horse wherever she pleased like an uneducated heathen.

But she could be trained, Agatha consoled herself as the coachman cracked his whip and the carriage rolled forward. It might well be a long, difficult task, but it was possible. And there was no time like the present to begin.

"I find that color entirely unsuitable," she said primly. "You should be in black, Harmony. *Black* is the color for mourning."

"It's dark blue," Harmony responded. "It's close enough."

"As I said, black is the appropriate color for mourning."

Agatha's tone was obdurate. There was not a trace of sympathy or emotion in the angular lines of her thin, pinched features. Harmony did not expect there ever would be. If, after a six-year separation, she had not had a single kind word to say in greeting, she doubted the future held much better. She had not yet even expressed any sympathy for their mother's passing. Mother. The dearest, sweetest human being Harmony had ever known. It was suddenly more than she could bear, and her simmering anger boiled over at last.

"What would you know about mourning?" she said bitterly. "I can understand why you didn't come all the way to America when Daddy died. It was so sudden and unexpected. But Mother was sick for a long time, Agatha. You could have come to see her before the end. And if you didn't want to see her, you might at least have come to the funeral. You would have had such fun gloating over her grave."

"Harmony!"

The way Agatha had spit her name at her was like a slap and Harmony recoiled. She could not imagine what had possessed her to say such an ugly thing, until she saw Agatha's lip curl, actually curl like a snarling dog, and the caustic acid of resentment burned her once again.

"It's true and you know it," Harmony spat back. "All you ever cared about was money. The only times you wrote were to ask for more."

"Stop your vile tongue this instant!"

Harmony bit back the next words that longed to tumble from her lips. This was not what their mother would have wanted. Furthermore, Agatha obviously harbored her own resentments, and fueling her sister's fires was not the smartest thing to do on the first day of a very long stay with her.

Trying to relax back in her seat, Harmony consoled herself with the thought that at least she had not had to spend the last six years with Agatha around. They had never gotten along, and it had been a relief when Agatha had decided to move to England, the birthplace of their now deceased maternal grandparents and great-aunt. Victorian England, as Agatha had informed her family, was more suited to her moral temperament and standards. Knowing she had never been happy on the wild, vast sprawl of the Simmons ranch, their father had willingly financed Agatha's move, and had, despite Agatha's inheritance, continued to subsidize her until his death. At that time Agatha had inherited another very comfortable sum. But it hadn't been enough. It was never enough.

Harmony's eyes narrowed as she gazed once again at her sister. What was wrong with her? Was she so empty inside that she tried to fill the void with material things?

She was only twenty-seven, but looked forty, Harmony mused. Was it because there was no laughter, no gaiety, no joy in her life? And was that what Harmony was now condemned to as well?

The thought made her shudder. What had her

mother been thinking, to put her younger daughter's inheritance under the control of the elder until Harmony turned twenty-one? How could her mother have done it to her?

But even as she wondered, Harmony knew. She had said as much near the end of her life. She had wanted the sisters to try and find their way back to each other. They would be left with only each other. But would it work? Had their mother been wise or merely blissfully foolish?

As she continued to look in her sister's direction, Harmony doubted their mother's plan, if that was what it was, would succeed. But she was willing to try. It was what Mother had wanted, and it was the last thing she would ever be able to do for her.

Harmony could almost feel her mother's long, thin, elegant fingers squeeze her hand for the final time. Her flesh had felt papery thin. Harmony could barely see the rise and fall of her chest beneath the white muslin gown.

"Promise me, Harmony," her mother had breathed. "Promise me you'll try. Agatha . . . hasn't known the love and warmth of family as . . . as you have. Help her. Please . . ."

Tears rose in a warm rush to Harmony's eyes and she turned her head so Agatha wouldn't see them. But who were the tears for, she wondered? Harmony dashed them away and gazed out the window.

Were they for her mother? Herself? For Agatha, perhaps? As hard as she tried to think they might be, however, Harmony was unable to feel any compassion for her hard, unloving sister. Agatha had left the ranch and her family of her own accord. She had freely chosen to live elsewhere and Harmony felt no sympathy for her. Yet she had promised their mother . . .

Harmony pulled a handkerchief from her reticule and dabbed away the evidence of emotion on her cheeks. It would no doubt bring a stinging reprimand from her sister and weaken her resolve to fulfill the promise to their mother. Replacing the handkerchief she turned her attention to the passing scenery. This was her world now. It would be well to take note of it. To try and take it into her heart and get to know and love it. It would make the passage of time less painful if she could come to love the land where she lived.

London's teeming avenues had been left behind and they entered a pleasant, green landscape. It was similar to, yet different from, countryside she had seen in America. Harmony drew her elegantly arched brows together thoughtfully.

"The scenery here is so . . . so tame," she said abruptly in an attempt to reach her sister in whatever distant place she had gone in her mind. "So orderly and neat. Back home it seems more . . . well, primitive,

I guess."

"Exactly," Agatha responded promptly. "It pleases me that you are able to note the difference. *Everything* here in England is more orderly and less . . . primitive, as you say. It is the essential reason I chose to reside here."

"Yes. I can see how it would suit you," Harmony said without sarcasm. "It's beautiful. Still, I miss the ranch. The mountains, the wide open spaces, fields of tall grass bending in the wind."

Harmony cut herself off before the memory could summon back her tears. Agatha stepped immediately into the silence.

"The ranch is being held in trust. You can return to it at your majority. Though I don't see why, once having experienced true civilization, you would want to."

No, Harmony thought. Agatha wouldn't.

"You are going to learn to lead an entirely different kind of life here," Agatha continued with mounting enthusiasm. "A godly and righteous life. No more galloping about on horseback like a wild Indian. Chasing after cattle. Or shooting a gun." Agatha grimaced in distaste.

"What's wrong with knowing how to ride and shoot?"

"You can't be serious, Harmony!" Agatha appeared dumbstruck.

"Mother and Daddy thought it was fine," Harmony replied calmly. "Why don't you?"

An unbecoming blush crept up the crepelike skin

of Agatha's neck to her cheeks. "I will not deign to answer such an ignorant question. In the future, mind your insolent tongue. I won't have it."

Harmony stared at her sister in disbelief. Despite her desire to control her temper, and knowing it would further worsen her lot, the embers of her anger fanned into a flame.

"You should mind *your* tongue, Agatha, before you cut yourself with it."

Agatha gasped then seemed to recover herself. Her already rigid spine straightened another notch. "You will learn not to speak to me like that," she said in a curiously flat, quiet voice. "You will learn a great many things, sister dear, not all of them pleasant. I would suggest you not taunt me again. *I* am in control of your life now."

The retort died on Harmony's lips. A harsh, cold light shone from her sister's pale gray eyes, and a sliver of fear worked its way into Harmony's breast. "I . . . I'm sorry, Agatha," Harmony forced herself to respond. She really did not wish to antagonize her sister. A joyless, boring existence was one thing. To have to endure Agatha's animosity for the next three years was quite another. She was wrong to have provoked her. "My remark was uncalled for."

"Yes, it was," she said tartly. Somewhat mollified, Agatha relaxed back into her seat. But Harmony, apparently, was not done bedeviling her. "*Now* what are you doing?"

"Opening the window, Agatha."

"I can see that. Close it at once."

Harmony ignored her. She cocked her head, as if listening. "Don't you hear that?"

"Hear what?"

"Hoofbeats," Harmony replied. "Coming up from behind us."

"Close that window, I said!" Agatha brushed at the heavy black material of her skirt. "The dust will ruin our clo—"

Agatha was abruptly silenced by the roar of a gun. She screamed as Harmony slammed the window shut. The carriage lurched to a halt, nearly unseating both women.

Chapter Three

*H*armony was the first to right herself. She helped her shaken sister back into her seat. And heard a shout. A strange thrill ran up her spine.

"Dear Lord," Agatha whimpered. "Dear Lord, what was that?"

"I don't know. But I'm going to find out."

"Don't open that door, Harmony! Don't go out there! What are you doing?"

"Stay where you are, Agatha. And please . . . be quiet." Harmony opened the coach door and froze.

It wasn't possible. She was in Victorian England, not in America's wild and only half-tamed West. Yet there he was before her, like a figure from the cover of the dime novels she loved.

The kerchief was pulled up just below his eyes. A casual, open-necked white cotton shirt was tucked into a pair of tight buckskin breeches. He sat easily, almost lazily, astride his horse and waved his pistol first at the coachman, whose trembling arms were raised to the sky, then at the women inside the coach.

"Good morning, ladies." Gun held steady, he slid from his mount and approached the carriage. "If you would be so good as to step outside, please."

A mewling sound issued from Agatha's throat.

Harmony merely stared. A jumble of strange emotions warred within her breast, effectively preventing coherent thought.

Never had she seen such black, black eyes. Almost as black as the long, straight, silky hair that glinted with auburn lights where it fell across his shoulders. For an instant, she had the insane desire to pull the kerchief down and see the rest of the face below those alarming eyes.

"If you please, ladies. I haven't got all day." As casually as a gentleman might wave a glove, he gestured with the gun.

It wasn't possible; it couldn't be happening. It had to be a dream. That was it. She had fallen asleep in the carriage and this was happening only in her subconscious.

But if so, why did she suddenly feel fingers around her wrist? And why did Agatha's piercing shrieks actually hurt her ears?

The answer sent a chill through her entire body to the very marrow of her bones.

Then the hand clasping her wrist gave a tug, and without further delay, Harmony stepped from the coach. She pulled the quaking, whimpering Agatha behind her. She'd grown up with guns. She knew what they could do.

"Thank you, ladies. Now, if you would throw all your valuables on the ground in front of you."

Time came to a standstill. Something was wrong. Very wrong. Harmony almost laughed out loud at herself. Of course there was something wrong! But, perhaps she had misheard?

No. The black eyes snapped merrily, perfect accompaniment to the amusement she had heard in his voice. She glanced quickly behind her and saw her sister, pale and shaking, remove her gloves and hurriedly tug the rings from her fingers.

"Wait, Agatha. Stop."

Agatha made a choking noise. The gunman raised his eyebrows.

"Get back in the carriage," Harmony commanded.

Terror-stricken, Agatha moved to obey. The bandit once again leveled his gun.

"I wouldn't do that if I were you."

Harmony stepped in front of her sister. "Get into the coach, I said. He won't shoot an unarmed woman."

Puling, Agatha climbed into the coach. Harmony concentrated all her attention on the lean figure in the close-fitting deerskin breeches, heart thudding erratically. From the corner of her eye she saw the terrified coachman perched on the edge of his seat, arms still raised, and knew what an enormous risk she was taking.

Yet now that the initial shock was over and her nerves had calmed, she was certain she intuited no threat from the man with the gun. She felt nothing but an odd sense of excitement. These were things she knew, things she was familiar with. A beautiful, well-cared-for horse and a well-oiled gun.

The pistol moved one more time. It was pointed straight at Harmony's heart.

"All right. Have it your way. *You* throw down your valuables."

Reacting only on instinct, feeling nothing but the strange, urgent stirring in her breast, Harmony stepped forward. "I'm sorry. But I have nothing to give you."

"Does this mean I have to search you?"

From inside the coach, Harmony heard her sister's gasp. She ignored it. Defiantly, she stared straight into the snapping black eyes and lifted her arms.

"Please. Be my guest."

For a long moment the two stood and stared at one another. Only Agatha's uncontrollable whimpering disturbed the silence. Despite the sounds of fear, the very situation itself, Harmony knew that the gunman smiled beneath his mask.

Abruptly, the bandit stepped back and lowered his pistol. "All right, young lady, but I'd like you to remove your gloves anyway, and then we shall see what we shall see."

"This is unconscionable," Harmony snapped, then immediately had to smile. She had sounded just like her sister.

"You have the most beautiful smile I've ever seen," the laughing-eyed bandit said.

Harmony abruptly sobered. What on earth was she thinking, playing games with a man holding a gun on her? She wasn't surprised to hear Agatha make a sound like she was being strangled.

Now she was certain the gunman smiled. His eyes not only sparkled but crinkled at the corners. A measure of her bravado returned until he cocked the pistol and aimed it at her midsection.

"Gloves, please. Now."

"Harmony!" Agatha yelped.

She tugged at the fingers of her left-hand glove and pulled it off, then removed the other as well. A genuine sliver of fear worked its way into her breast and a deep feeling of regret formed a painful lump in her throat. The sapphire ring was small and held no sentimental value, being an heirloom from some unknown, distant relative, but the larger diamond had been a beloved gift from her father. She made no move, however, to remove either ring until the gunman nodded toward her left hand.

"I think I'll take that one," he said. "A token, we'll call it. A sapphire to remind me of the courageous little lady in blue. And her sapphire eyes."

Harmony held her breath, scarcely daring to hope. Slowly, she worked the ring from her finger and handed it to him.

The bandit continued to stare at Harmony over his mask. The ring lay on his open palm. Abruptly, he closed his fist and shoved the gem into his pocket. He backed toward his horse and flourished his pistol at the driver.

"Turn around and pick up the reins," he ordered. "As soon as this little lady is back inside, you continue on, nice and slow, to wherever you were going." Eyes still on the driver, he gathered his horse's reins and, with one smooth, graceful motion, sprang astride his mount. "Go on and climb inside, young lady."

Harmony did as she was instructed. She heard the crack of the coachman's whip the moment she had closed the door behind her and sat down quickly as the carriage surged forward. By the time she was able to open the window and look outside, the bandit had disappeared. The incident was apparently over. She and Agatha had survived and she had even, miraculously, come away with her diamond ring. Breathing a deep sigh of relief, her sister's sudden attack took her completely by surprise.

"How *dare* you?!" Agatha hissed. "How dare you endanger our lives by conducting yourself in such a brazen fashion?"

Harmony could only stare, mouth agape, at her sister.

"Don't you realize that dreadful man could have killed us both? Don't you?"

Harmony gripped the edge of her seat with white knuckles as the coach swayed and jolted down the road, finding it difficult to believe such a thin and shriveled body could contain so much venom.

"Agatha, what's the matter with you?" she asked incredulously. "Not only did he not harm us, he took only a single ring, my sapphire, when he could have taken—"

"Shut up!" Agatha screeched. Eyes straining from her head, she leaned forward threateningly, as if she might fly at her sister's throat. "You dare to defend that . . . *criminal*? You try to tell me just because, by the grace of God, we were released uninjured, this was only a little excitement?"

"I said no such thing!" Harmony snapped, incredulity turning to anger. Even as she said the words, however, she realized how close to the truth Agatha was. She might have smiled then, despite her fury, remembering the amused black eyes above the mask.

But it appeared her sister was going into a swoon.

Alarmed, Harmony watched Agatha sink limply back into her seat. Her eyelids fluttered closed.

"Agatha!" Harmony clasped one of her sister's pale, dry hands and chafed it.

"Don't you touch me!" Agatha recoiled violently and snatched her hand away. "Don't touch me, you brazen hussy!"

Eyes wide, Harmony shrank away from her sister.

"And don't you give me that innocent look! I saw the way you behaved, daring that man . . . *daring* him to touch you! As if you *wanted* his filthy hands all over you!"

"Shut up, Agatha!" Harmony flared at last, pushed over the edge by her sister's perverse tirade.

"Dear Lord, protect me." Agatha squeezed her eyes tightly shut and folded her hands as if in prayer. "Protect me from this devil's child."

Harmony took a long, deep breath and tried to calm the war of emotions in her breast. What was wrong with her sister? Why such overreaction?

She wasn't sure she wanted to know the answers. Something very dark lurked at the edges of her thoughts. She wanted to cast no light on it.

The coach made a sharp turn to the left and Agatha's whimpers began anew. "Home. Oh, thank God, we're home." She pressed a handkerchief to her nostrils and sniffed loudly.

The menacing darkness returned to cast its pall over Harmony as she turned her attention to the scenery outside the coach. The open, sunny parkland had disappeared and they had entered a thickly wooded area that stretched away on either side as far as the eye could see. So dense were the ancient, twisted trees Harmony could not even see any light between them. She felt as if they had arrived in an alien world.

Nothing stirred in the dark hush of the forest. The only sounds were the clatter of the coach and the rhythmic thud of the horses' hooves on the hard-packed dirt road. Sadly, Harmony realized how fitting it was that her sister lived in a place like this.

The carriage slowed, passed through a break in the trees, and turned into a wide, gravel drive. A vague chill shivered down Harmony's spine as an immense, sprawling stone house loomed into view. Its cold gray walls were almost completely obscured by encroaching ivy. Two massive stone lions stood sentry on either side of the front steps, as if there to guard the virtues, as well as the property, of their prim, virginal mistress.

The robbery attempt seemed years away, almost as if she had dreamed the incident entirely, so overwhelming was the oppressive atmosphere that now surrounded her and pressed on her as if it had living weight. She tried to revive the memory of the bandit, tried to hold on to something that was real, and warm. But she could grasp and hold nothing.

The morning's event was likely the most exciting thing that was ever going to happen to her again. The black-eyed bandit was probably the last real man she'd ever see.

The three years stretching in front of her seemed an eternity. She had not come to a green and fertile island nation and the arms of a loving, if long lost sister, but to a parched and barren desert of grief, hostility, and loneliness.

Chapter Four

"My name is Mrs. Rutledge."

Harmony looked up from the hard, straight-backed bench on which she had perched. Though older, and gray, Agatha's housekeeper looked astonishingly similar to her mistress. She had the same thin, dry appearance; her face was long and her features small. Her expression seemed perpetually disapproving. Harmony remembered her manners and rose to her feet.

"I'm Harmony Sim—"

"I know who you are. Follow me, please."

Harmony was completely put off by the housekeeper's manner, and had half a mind to say she'd stay right where she was. But when she glanced around again, she decided that following Mrs. Rutledge was, by far, the better idea.

The parlor in which she had been told to wait, while a nearly prostrate Agatha was escorted to her room, was dank and airless. Even in the near dark she could see that everything, aside from the ponderous mahogany furniture, appeared to be maroon, from the faded oriental rug to the thick velvet drapes pulled snugly across the tall windows. It was the most cheerless space she had ever been in and she wondered, grimly, what her own room would look like. Reluctantly, she followed the retreating housekeeper.

From the parlor they re-entered the black-and-white-tiled entrance hall. A large and elaborately carved circular table stood at its center. A tarnished suit of armor leaned against a far, paneled wall. Heels clicking sharply, Mrs. Rutledge left the foyer and disappeared into the dimly lit corridor, the walls painted an unhealthy-looking dark green shade, above mahogany wainscoting. The wall color reminded Harmony of mold growing in some dark and airless place. Like a dim and dying forest, perhaps. Or her sister's home. Harmony shuddered.

Only an occasional candle sconce decorated the halls, and only a few of the candles were lit. The pale light flickered eerily on the walls and on doors to rooms unseen. Then Mrs. Rutledge turned left and started up a steep, narrow stair. It was so dark at the top, Harmony could see nothing, and she hurried so she didn't lose sight of the housekeeper. If she did, she feared she might wander forever in the shadowed corridors that appeared to wind on forever.

The second floor was much like the first. Mrs. Rutledge finally stopped in front of a door identical to all the rest and opened it with a key that hung from a ring attached to her belt. The housekeeper gestured her inside and Harmony stepped over the threshold.

"This is your room. The bell rope is next to the dressing table. I will bring your lunch shortly on a tray. If you require anything in the meantime, you've only to summon me."

Harmony did not miss the faintly grudging tone in the woman's voice. "I'm sure I won't need to . . . disturb you. And I don't care for any lunch either, thank you."

Mrs. Rutledge responded with an almost imperceptible lift of her sparse, nearly white eyebrows, as if she had been warned what to expect and was not in the least surprised. "As you wish." Without another word, the housekeeper left, pulling the door closed behind her.

Harmony turned slowly, inspecting the room that was to be her prison cell for the next three years. Like the rest of the house, the room was dark: dark, heavy furniture, dark and heavy fabrics. There was a huge armoire and a dressing table that might double as a desk. A large Turkish carpet covered most of the wood floor, and her trunk had been placed at the foot of a high, wide, canopied bed. Everything smelled slightly moldy and damp. Disheartened, Harmony crossed to the window and peered between the tendrils of ivy that sought to block out any ray of light that might try to find her.

Woods stretched for as far as she could see into the distance. Nothing moved. Not the whisper of a breeze to disturb a leaf, or the silky flash of a squirrel's tail. No bird rustled in the branches. It was exactly as a prison was supposed to be: colorless, lifeless, cheerless. Harmony turned from the window. And caught movement out of the corner of her eye.

By the time she whirled back to the ivy-covered glass, whatever it was had vanished. The woodland had returned to its uncanny stillness.

Yet Harmony was gripped by the most peculiar sensation. Someone, something, was watching her. She could not escape the notion that a pair of eyes spied upon her from within the shadowed shelter of the trees.

Harmony's fingers tightened on the dusty windowsill as a vague chill shivered through her limbs. Unbidden, the memory of a dark-eyed thief swam before her eyes. She shook her head.

She must not, she chided herself, allow her imagination to run wild. It was too easy in a place like this. She didn't need to add to her woes. The bleak vision of her immediate future was as much a burden as she could bear at the moment.

Nor did she need to dwell on the fantasy of a chance encounter with a lighthearted bandit at the side of a lonely, country road. She had more important things to think about. Like how to endure the next three years. Determinedly, she turned from the window and began to unpack.

Even as she pulled her clothes from the trunk, however, Harmony found herself remembering the way he had looked at her when he had asked for the ring . . . to remind him of the lady in blue with the sapphire eyes . . .

Harmony jumped, nearly falling over a pair of shoes, when Agatha burst, unannounced, into the room. She sniffed and eyed the clothing strewn over the furniture.

"I trust you are planning to tidy up this mess?"

"I was unpacking, Agatha."

"At least you weren't idling away your time." Agatha smiled tightly. "Just be quick about it. I've sent for the authorities and they'll arrive shortly."

"The authorities!"

"Of course the authorities. Why are you acting so surprised? That dreadful man stole a valuable sapphire ring, did he not?"

"Agatha, that ring wasn't terribly valuable. It's hardly something to bother the authorities about, especially since nothing else—"

"Hussy!" Agatha spat as she backed from the room. "I'll not stand here and listen to you defend that criminal!" The older woman stepped into the hallway and slammed the door. A moment later, Harmony heard the sound of a key turning in the lock.

"Agatha!" Harmony flew to the door and tried to open it, but the latch turned uselessly in her hand. She heard the rapid thud of footsteps fade down the hall. "Damn you," she whispered. "Damn you, Agatha!"

Her curse evaporated into the dank and heavy silence of the chamber.

The short, round, and entirely bald man who represented the law in the nearby village of Millswich shifted uncomfortably on the hard, horsehair sofa. Agatha eyed him with disapproval from where she sat, rigidly erect, on a chair of similar fabric and contour. If the situation hadn't been so grim, Harmony would have laughed out loud.

When he appeared to have found the position of least discomfort, Mr. Henry cleared his throat and returned to the question he had asked Harmony moments earlier. "You said, um, let me see." He glanced at his notes. "You said the thief then got on his horse and simply rode away?"

"After I'd gotten back into the coach, yes," Harmony replied quietly. She glanced quickly at Agatha to see if she would have an amendment to this response, as she had to all the others before it. But her sister remained silent this time. Mr. Henry continued.

"Now, Miss Simmons, if you don't mind, I'd like you to try and give me a more complete description of this individual."

"I don't mind at all, Mr. Henry. Except the man wore a kerchief over his face. Therefore, I can give you very little detail."

Agatha cast her sister a withering look. "My sister's memory seems to have been affected by the . . . horror . . . of the experience," she said in a scathing tone. "Actually, Mr. Henry, there's quite a bit I can tell you about the young man's appearance." Agatha's glare slid from Harmony back to the constable and transformed into a smile. "And I'd like to be as helpful as possible."

Flustered, Mr. Henry glanced between the two women. "Well, please, go on then, Miss Simmons."

It was Harmony's opportunity, and she seized it. She pushed to her feet.

"I think I've told you all I can, so if you don't need me any longer, Mr. Henry, I—"

"Sit down," Agatha ordered.

Harmony ignored her and concentrated her most fetching smile on Mr. Henry. "I'm sorry, but this has been a very trying day. If you don't mind, I'd like to return to my room."

"By all means, Miss Simmons." Mr. Henry rose with stiff politeness, oblivious to Agatha's furious motions for Harmony to remain where she was. "I only hope my questions haven't tired you excessively."

"Oh, no, Mr. Henry. But I do have a headache. So if you'll excuse me . . .?" With a sweet, sad smile, Harmony exited. Her smile vanished.

She had absolutely no intention of going to her room. Her cell.

Harmony recalled the sound of the key turning in the lock, and her blood heated. The only thing for it was to take a walk. She needed to cool her temper and gather her thoughts. Life with Agatha simply could not go on like this.

The massive front door swung inward with a groan and Harmony winced. But no one was around to notice, apparently. Distantly, she heard her sister's shrill voice whining away to Mr. Henry. She stepped outside into the cooling shadows of the summer dusk.

The immediate area surrounding Agatha's home was only slightly more enticing than the interior of the house. All around stood the grim, dense woodland. To the right of the house, also covered with creeping vines, was a low, stone stable. Remembering the coachman, and not wishing to be seen, she went to the left and followed a narrow, pebbled path that seemed to lead to the back of the house.

Overgrown weeds plucked at Harmony's skirt as she continued along the path. She rounded a corner and saw what had once been an undoubtedly lovely formal garden, but what was now merely a tangle of wildflowers and long, sharp-bladed grasses. Beyond the edge of the garden the wood began again.

There was nowhere else to go. There were no gardens to stroll, and there was certainly no refuge in the forest. Besides, Mr. Henry would be done with Agatha soon and her sister would surely discover Harmony was not in her room. The thought of enduring another of Agatha's tirades was simply too overwhelming. She'd had enough for one day. She was tired. Maybe she'd take a bath and change out of her blue traveling suit.

As Harmony turned on her heel, however, she heard the unmistakable click of a door latch. The sound seemed to have come from the terrace doors off to her left. She automatically stepped back out of sight and, a moment later, heard her sister's voice.

"There's no one out here, Mrs. Rutledge. You must have been mistaken."

Harmony held her breath. Should she run around to the front, slip in the door, and hurry to her room before they discovered she wasn't there? Her dilemma was solved an instant later.

"All right then, Mrs. Rutledge. Lock all the doors. If she's not in her room, it will serve her right having to beg to be let in. Or she just might spend the night in the stable. It would do her a world of good. Maybe then she will learn to follow my orders and appreciate my hospitality."

The terrace doors clicked shut. Harmony's hands balled into fists at her sides.

The thought of spending the night out of doors in this gloomy, forbidding place was nothing compared to the anger she felt toward her mean and shrewish sister. She would not give her the satisfaction of knocking on the door and asking to be let in. Nor would she sleep in the stable. She would not now, or ever, do anything Agatha wanted or expected. And that included spending the night outside.

The village of Millswich couldn't be too far away. She'd march herself into town and find herself a bed for the night. An inn, perhaps, that would take payment on the morrow. Or a kindly family. Then let Agatha explain why she had locked her only sister, come only the day before, all the way from America, out of her house.

Courage and determination bolstered, Harmony picked up her skirts and hurried along the path back to the front of the house. She glanced at the windows, saw no one, and ran into the trees along the side of the road. She was soon lost among the shadows.

Harmony knew that if she followed the drive back to where it had left the main road, she must eventually run into the village. Barely aware of the now rapidly advancing darkness, she started on her way. She was careful to keep her distance from the road in case someone came along.

But the way seemed a great deal longer on foot than it had seated in a plush carriage. Nor were her narrow shoes, so perfectly matched to the dark blue suit, made for walking any distance. Brambles and bushes plucked at her skirts, and her soft-soled shoes turned on every pebble. When she feared she could not go another step, she let herself sink to an area of leafy ground, back propped against the bole of a tree. The eerie stillness of the forest closed around her at once.

Even the faint rasp of Harmony's breath sounded loud to her, so quiet was the darkened wood. A tremor of fear shivered through her torso.

Maybe it wasn't such a bad idea to spend the night in the stable after all. Wincing at each small sound she made, Harmony pushed to her feet. And heard a distinct rustling in the undergrowth behind her.

Heart in her mouth, Harmony whirled. But she could see nothing, and heard no other sound. Only the thundering of her heart came to her ears.

It was probably only some harmless forest creature, she told herself. She would, however, make her way back to the road at once and return to the stable.

But even as she turned, Harmony realized she had become disoriented. She no longer knew in which direction the road lay. Concentrating totally on which way to go, she heard nothing, saw nothing, until a hand snaked out of the darkness and clamped over her mouth.

Chapter Five

The world ceased to exist. Stark terror reigned. The ebon stillness of the forest was as nothing compared to the void into which Harmony fell. It was as if her body, her senses, had shut down completely. There was no sight, no sound, no touch, no smell. Only fear. Paralyzing, heart-stopping fear. Then animal instinct took over and she began to fight for her life.

Wildly, Harmony clawed at the hand pressed over her mouth. It was becoming difficult to breathe, and the more she struggled the tighter the hand's grip became. Harmony felt herself being pulled closer and closer to a lean, hard body.

Suddenly the pressure of the restraining arms relaxed. The grip eased steadily, and now the hands that held her were gentle. She felt herself being turned, slowly and carefully, in her captor's arms.

She saw the black eyes first. They flashed at her in a pale shaft of moonlight that had found its way through the trees. As her heart pounded frantically against her rib cage, Harmony lowered her gaze to the rest of the face she had only been able to imagine. The straight, aquiline nose. Shapely lips that might have been drawn by an artist's hand, the bottom fuller than the top. Even as she watched, they curved into a smile.

Harmony gasped, a belated reflex. The hold on her arms tightened, though not painfully.

"Sssshhh." He pressed a finger softly to her lips. "Come with me," he whispered. "And don't say a word."

Reality was instantly suspended. Harmony was not the properly raised American girl living with her prim sister. She was not the well-bred child of a wealthy family. If she was, she would have to kick and scream and attempt to escape. But she did none of those things, so she must be someone else. Rather than call for help, she held on to the stranger's hand and followed him as he picked his way through the trees.

Farther and farther they wound their way through the woods and still went on. Where the sharp branches of the undergrowth would have pulled at her skirts and torn at her flesh, the stranger held them aside for her to pass, never letting go of her hand. And when, exhausted, she stumbled, he swept her into his arms and continued on at a more rapid pace.

After what seemed quite a long time, the stranger slowed. Harmony was unaware she had closed her eyes until she felt herself lowered to the ground. Vaguely disturbed by the fact she had lain so comfortably in his arms, cradled against his broad chest, she opened her eyes wide and looked about her. Looked anywhere but at the handsome stranger.

They had come to a small clearing. A tall, big-boned chestnut mare grazed a few feet away. The animal looked familiar. It was, in fact, the very horse she had admired when the gunman had held up the coach. If she had entertained the slightest shadow of a doubt that her captor and the bandit were one and the same, it was banished as effectively as the moon behind a passing cloud.

"What . . . what's going on?" Harmony whispered. "Why have you brought me here? What do you want with me?"

"First, allow me to introduce myself. Anthony Allen, at your service."

Anthony Allen. Harmony repeated the name to herself. It was beautiful. But maybe she had fallen asleep against that tree trunk and was dreaming all of this.

It was simply not possible she had been carried off into the woods by an incredibly handsome stranger, the man who had earlier stopped their coach, and who now introduced himself as casually as if he were an elegant gentleman in a London parlor.

Yet he had. And just as she had not been asleep and dreaming in the coach, she was not asleep and dreaming at the present. For lack of anything better to do, Harmony responded.

"Anthony," Harmony murmured, tasting the name on her tongue. "But why . . . why have you brought me here, Anthony?"

"Why . . . because I'm kidnapping you, of course."

Stunned, Harmony felt as if a bucket of cold water had just been dumped over her head. She drew herself up a little straighter.

"You can't . . . you can't *do* that."

Anthony shrugged, smiling. "I already have."

Harmony's natural sense of spirit and rebellion surfaced from wherever it had gone into hiding. She cast about her for a break in the trees, a place to run.

"I wouldn't try that, if I were you. You'll never find your way back in the dark. And I wouldn't want anything to happen to you now that I've gone to so much trouble to find you again."

Anthony smiled, a brilliant, slightly crooked smile, and, to her horror, Harmony felt a trembling weakness in her knees. She was suddenly reminded of the sensation of being watched that afternoon as she stood at her window.

"You followed us, didn't you?" Harmony demanded.

"I found out where, and who, you were. Yes."

"So you could kidnap me." It was a statement, not a question. "But why?"

"Because you have a wealthy sister who will, no doubt, pay a great price to get you back."

Harmony took a moment to savor the irony of her captor's statement. Agatha, doubtless, would pay him, but not to get her back . . . rather to keep her hostage.

Puzzled both by his hostage's silence and the faint, enigmatic smile curving her lovely lips, Anthony cocked a single brow. "Besides, how else to get to know the lady in blue . . . the girl with the sapphire eyes?"

Like a debutante at her first ball, Harmony felt a blush rise to her cheeks. But she was neither a debutante nor in attendance at a ball. She was in a dark forest, evidently in the middle of the night, with a man who had kidnapped her and was going to demand money from her sister for her return. She looked away self-consciously. Shouldn't she be running? Screaming? Something?

"You can't possibly get away with this," Harmony said at length, in lieu of taking physical action.

"Well, we'll soon find out, won't we? Now, I think it's time we got going."

Anthony turned his back and tightened the chestnut mare's girth. Over his shoulder, he asked, "Are you coming?"

Harmony hesitated. She told herself yet again she

should turn and run, take the chance of getting lost in the woods, anything but meekly succumb to her captor. But it was as if she had been hypnotized.

Harmony had to force her thoughts away from the present, her bizarre circumstances, and think about her sister. What *would* Agatha do when she learned she'd been kidnapped? Would she worry? Would she feel guilt over the things she had said to Mrs. Rutledge? Or was her first reaction the most accurate? Might Agatha actually be glad she was gone?

The answer to every question nearly overwhelmed her, as if a flood of cold, dirty water had swept her from her feet and sucked her under to drown. Flailing mental arms to bring her back to the surface, Harmony envisioned Agatha standing in her dark, unwelcoming parlor, muttering to Mrs. Rutledge that the kidnapping was: "Good riddance to bad rubbish."

Heartsick, she knew her imagination was undoubtedly, and sadly, not far off the mark. If she could not go back, however, at least she could go forward, even into the unknown. Sniffing back tears, Harmony realized the terrible irony of the situation. Going along with her kidnapping was preferable to trying to return to a sister who apparently despised her. Decision made, she sidled up next to her captor.

Without apparent effort, Anthony lifted her to the front of the saddle, then slipped his foot into the stirrup and swung up behind her. He put one strong arm around her waist and his heels to the mare's sides. They walked from the clearing into and through the trees until they reached the forest's edge where a moonlit meadow stretched before them. Anthony kicked the mare into a gallop.

Harmony was thrown against Anthony's chest. She remembered how it felt when he had clasped his hand over her mouth and pulled her back against him. He was hard and broad and she found herself wondering what it would be like to run her hands across his chest. Would he have long, silken hair there, like that which fell over his shoulders? Or would his flesh be smooth, with only the definition of his muscles over which to run her fingers? Harmony closed her eyes.

And why, oh why, was she thinking such thoughts?

To keep them away from Agatha and reality, an inner voice whispered. But she felt guilty nonetheless and tried to turn her attention to other things.

The mare's gait was mercifully smooth. Harmony tangled her fingers in the animal's mane anyway, and hung on tightly. The ground beneath the thudding hooves fairly flew past. Harmony could smell the rich odor of the moist earth and green, green grass the horse's shoes tore up in her passage. She tried to focus her attention on that, instead of the muscular man at her back.

Time as well as reality lost its meaning. The ride seemed to go on forever. Harmony had no idea how much time had passed when she finally saw a road in front of them and a light beyond it in the distance. Anthony pulled the lathered mare to a walk when they reached the road.

"Now, in case anyone comes along," he murmured in her ear, "we're man and wife, returning from an evening with friends. All right?"

Harmony was only able to nod. They continued on in silence until they reached the source of the light.

The inn was rustic and quaint, filled with the sounds of Saturday night merrymaking. Anthony slid to the ground and tied the mare to a rail in the courtyard. He turned and held out his arms to Harmony.

What else was she going to do? She edged around until she had both legs on the left side of the horse, let herself start to slide, and found herself once again in Anthony's arms. They held her close against him, and she fancied she could almost feel the beating of his heart. Her own heart was behaving oddly and she tried to pull away. Anthony held her fast.

"Before we go in, Harmony," he whispered in her ear, "I want you to forget any foolish notions you might have about trying to get away. These people here are my friends."

He released her abruptly and Harmony stood,

trembling slightly, as he withdrew something from the pack on the back of his saddle.

"Here, put this on. Keep the hood up. Please," he added. He draped the dark cape over her shoulders and drew the hood up himself. "Once seen, no one would be able to forget those eyes and that hair."

Harmony clutched the edges of the cloak closed over her breast and adjusted the hood. At a gesture from Anthony, she preceded him through the door he held open.

"Tony, me luv!"

An immense, jolly woman with apple cheeks crossed the room with surprising alacrity and enveloped Anthony in a bear hug.

"I was beginnin' t'think ye wasn't comin' t'night after all." She released him only to clasp him firmly by the shoulders. She nodded, with a huge smile, in Harmony's direction. "But now I see what ye've been about, I s'pose I kin fergive ye."

Harmony ducked her head, blushing furiously. She heard Anthony chuckle.

"So now that you know I've a beautiful lady to tend to, you won't mind if we, uh . . . excuse ourselves . . . will you?"

The woman laughed heartily. "'Course not, luv. Y'go right on up. Yer room's ready an' waitin'. Me finest sheets, too."

"Thanks, Maggie. You're a good girl." He swatted her generous backside, which brought forth another peal of raucous laughter. "I'll bet you kept my dinner warm, too, didn't you?"

"'Course I did! I knew ye'd be about some hungry business or other." With a wink and a sly nod in Harmony's direction, Maggie burst once more into laughter and headed off into the kitchen.

"Come, my dear." As if he were about to guide her onto the dance floor, Anthony crooked an arm and held it out to Harmony. "I think it's time we sought some privacy. In spite of all that wrapping, you're attracting far too much attention."

For the first time since they had entered, Harmony glanced around her. The low-beamed, smoky room was filled with men, almost all of them regarding her with prurient interest. One of them raised his mug in salute and winked lewdly. Harmony grabbed Anthony's arm and let him lead her quickly from the room and up a steep, narrow stair.

The entire building was constructed of wood, and a pleasant woodsy fragrance filled Harmony's nostrils. The corridor, she noted, was more well lit than the hallways of her sister's home.

Anthony paused in front of one of the doors, inserted a key in the lock, and turned it. When it clicked, he pushed the door open in front of him.

"After you, my lady."

Although she wasn't cold, Harmony realized she was shivering. She stepped across the threshold.

The room was large and homey. Worn, but comfortable and sturdy furniture was strewn about, including a cozy sofa covered in bright chintz. A colorful hooked rug lay in front of a cheerfully crackling fire. Beyond a partially open door to her left, Harmony glimpsed a wide bed. Her legs were suddenly so weak she had to grab the back of a chair to steady herself.

Anthony was at her side in an instant. "Are you all right?"

Harmony found she was incapable of speech. She couldn't take her eyes from the bed. Anthony followed her gaze. Then he looked at her quizzically.

"Is there something wrong with our bed?" he inquired casually.

"Our . . . our bed?" Harmony breathed.

Anthony nodded, smiling broadly. It was the last thing Harmony saw before her world went black.

Chapter Six

*H*armony regained her senses swiftly. She opened her eyes to find she was, yet again, cradled in Anthony's arms. Before she could protest, he laid her gently on the sofa. Eyes wide, she shrank away from him.

Anthony made a clicking sound with his tongue and planted his hands on his narrow hips. "Now, now, now," he admonished. "Don't go getting any foolish thoughts in your pretty little head. I've brought you here to extort money from your sister . . . not to rape you."

Harmony could not even bring herself to look in his direction. She sat upright, tried to smooth away the wrinkles in her skirt in order to have something to do with her hands, and prayed for a hole to open in the floor so she could throw herself into it and vanish forever.

"I think I might have the cure for what ails you," Anthony went on mildly. He pulled a stopper from a crystal decanter and poured a deep amber liquid into two petite crystal glasses sitting side by side on a silver tray.

The subtle symbolism was not lost on Harmony, but she could not keep herself from looking up through lowered lashes to watch what Anthony was doing. The obviously expensive tray, decanter, and glasses seemed somewhat incongruous in a place like the inn. But perhaps the proprietress kept such things around for her more special guests.

An instant later Harmony caught herself with an inward gasp. She was speculating on niceties when she'd been kidnapped for ransom by a stranger and was alone with him in his private chambers?

"Here you are." Anthony handed one of the glasses to Harmony. "It'll do you good. Help you to relax." Following his own advice, Anthony sipped delicately from his glass and sprawled in the chair opposite the sofa. "There's no reason why you shouldn't be as comfortable as possible for as long as you're here."

Still reluctant to look Anthony in the eye, or think again about her situation, Harmony decided to stall by tasting the liquor. Feeling no guilt whatsoever—how could she when drinking an alcoholic beverage seemed like the least of her worries?—she brought the glass to her lips.

"Go on," Anthony urged. "It'll make you feel better about all this. Also, I promise that if you get a little tipsy, I won't take advantage of you."

Did he mock her? A spark of indignation ignited

in Harmony's breast. She threw her head back and tossed half the contents of the glass down her throat. An instant later Anthony was on his feet, pounding her on the back while she choked.

"What . . . what *is* this?" Harmony managed to ask when the coughing had subsided to a mere sputtering.

"A rather fine brandy, actually," Anthony replied as he returned to his chair. "I apologize if you didn't find it to your liking."

"No, I . . . I do like it, as a matter of fact." Harmony stared into the depths of her glass and felt a welcome warmth spread through her midsection, loosening the grip of her anxiety. The burning on her tongue turned into a pleasant aftertaste. She took another sip.

"That's it. After you've had dinner and some wine, you'll feel even better."

Anthony rose and refilled their glasses, and Harmony found herself in an increased state of wonder and disbelief. She had been kidnapped, and was now being served an excellent brandy from the hand of her kidnapper. They were going to have dinner and a bottle of wine. It wasn't real. Couldn't be happening. She was definitely asleep.

Right. Like she had fallen asleep in the coach, and with her back against the tree.

But it seemed better to treat the situation as if it were a dream. Reality was simply too much to contemplate at the moment. If she forced herself to dwell on the details of her current circumstances, she might very well do what she should have done in the woods and run away screaming at the top of her lungs.

Then Anthony's fingers brushed hers as he held the bottle over her glass and Harmony had a whole new problem to worry about.

The sensation at the origin of the touch was like the first taste of the brandy on her tongue. It burned. Then it went on a flaming journey through her body. She tried to take a deep breath without appearing obvious. It was impossible. Instead she took another sip of brandy.

No, she silently and adamantly protested. A stranger's touch simply could not have such power over her body. And yet she could not take her eyes from his.

He moves as gracefully as a cat, Harmony thought to herself as she watched Anthony return to his chair. He hung both legs over a padded arm and raised his glass to her in salute.

"Here's to you, lovely Harmony. To the time you'll spend as my hostage, as well."

Was she really a hostage? The thought came to her with sudden clarity despite the fuzziness beginning to cloud her thoughts. What would he do if she really wanted to leave? His behavior was so gentlemanly, she found it difficult to believe he might actually try to physically restrain her, or harm her in any way. He would probably, she mused, apologize for the inconvenience and offer to take her home.

Harmony felt a smile touch her lips. To her horror, she giggled, then raised her glass in response to his toast.

"Thank you," she whispered, and drank.

❦

The fire had burned low and the chill of the late summer's evening had crept into the room. But Harmony felt warm. She stared into the dying flames and tried to concentrate on their hiss and crackle. It wasn't easy.

It was becoming increasingly difficult to remember that she was, indeed, a captive. Anthony, no matter how charming, was a robber and a kidnapper. He was going to extort money from her sister. Moreover, she was, for the first time in her life, alone with a man. In a room at an inn. Drinking spirits. And, apparently, becoming affected by them.

The warmth deepened to a flush Harmony felt rise from her breast to her cheeks. She was in a situation too racy even for the dime novels she read. And she was enjoying every moment.

Again unable to look in Anthony's direction, Harmony stared into the dregs of her glass. She tilted it to watch the last golden drop run from the bottom to the side. Anthony, alert to her every need, misinterpreted her action.

"You've run dry. A fine host I am," he drawled as he unslung his legs from the arm of the chair. He stood and reached for the decanter.

"Oh, no, no," Harmony protested. "I've had quite enough, thank you."

"A few more drops," Anthony urged. "To make one more toast."

"Well . . ."

Anthony poured a finger into each of their glasses. "With these last drops, I make my final toast." He touched his glass to Harmony's. "To a very lucky encounter."

Harmony watched Anthony over the rim of her glass and wondered if he meant that the luck was in meeting her, or in the prospect of obtaining some of her sister's money. Perhaps it was only the brandy, but she wanted very badly for it to be her.

"Why did you really do this?" The words were out before she could stop them, her tongue loosened, no doubt, by how much she had had to drink. Her parents had warned her about such things.

Grief and guilt momentarily threatened to overwhelm her. Then she remembered her sister, and what Agatha would have to say about the situation. The thought was abruptly sobering.

"You mean, why did I kidnap you?" Anthony said, pulling Harmony from her reverie. He looked faintly surprised. "I told you. Because, for one night's work, I'm going to make enough money to retire. For a few weeks, at least."

Harmony made a valiant effort to keep the disappointment from showing on her face as her spirits plummeted to her feet. She felt a welcome spark of irritation as well.

"But why do you have to steal at all to make a living? Surely you could find some better, easier way. An *honest* way."

"My dear, this *is* an easy way for a man like me to make money." Anthony turned from Harmony to stand in front of the fire. "Or were you expecting me to tell you that I do this because I am a pitiful child of poverty, stealing only to feed my aged mother and starving brothers and sisters?" He uttered a short laugh. "Sorry, but I'm afraid I steal because I am simply too lazy to make a living any other way. And the . . . adventure . . . shall we say, appeals to me."

"Yet you . . . you're obviously an educated man!" Harmony protested, though not entirely sure why.

"Why, thank you, my dear." Anthony bowed low from the waist. Long, dark, shining hair fell forward, as if in a caress, across his shoulders. He straightened and brushed it back nonchalantly. "But I see no reason why the educated, as well as the ignorant, shouldn't be allowed to steal. Do you?"

It occurred to Harmony that it was ridiculous for her to agree. Yet she did.

"Besides," Anthony continued, "having acquired all the gentlemanly attributes will only make it that much easier for me to take my place in society when I have finally amassed enough money to retire."

"Is that your purpose in being a thief? To buy your way into society?"

"At least until I can think of something else I'd rather do." Anthony looked amused. "Why do you ask? Don't tell me you're worried about the morals of the man who's just kidnapped you?"

Harmony winced and quickly looked away. She was making a fool of herself and she knew it, questioning Anthony as if he were an intimate acquaintance instead of the man who had stolen her in order to extort money from her sister.

"I . . . I'm sorry," she stammered finally. "I certainly didn't mean to be so personal."

The smile, all traces of amusement, vanished from Anthony's features. He placed his glass on the mantle over the hearth and crossed to the sofa.

"No. *I'm* the one who is sorry," he said quietly, and sat at Harmony's side.

Harmony stiffened as her heart started to pound.

She continued to stare into the fire, completely unable to look at the man beside her.

"Please," he said, voice softly urgent. "I'm sorry. I was teasing you and I shouldn't have."

It felt like her heart was going to burst from her throat. Harmony forced herself to turn her head and look Anthony in the eye. She was faintly alarmed to note his brow was furrowed and his eyes had narrowed. Though he looked at her, his attention seemed inwardly directed, as if he fought some inner battle. He leaned forward, bringing his face mere inches from hers.

"Perhaps, Harmony," he whispered, "I said what I did because I'd like to think you might . . . you might care what happens to me, if only a little. In spite of what I've done."

He was too close, too near. She stared at his lips and licked her own. The pounding of her heart had heated her blood uncomfortably. In a nervous gesture, she played with the heavy chignon at the nape of her neck. Her finger caught in one of the pins and pulled it loose. Her hair tumbled free.

The indrawn hiss of Anthony's breath was the only sound in the room besides the dying crackles of the fire. He stared at the red satin curtain of hair that ran like a cascade of bright water over her shoulders and breast to pool in her lap. With it unbound, he was able to see the myriad of colors in it, light reds and dark, and strands the color of teak. Unable to help himself, he reached out to touch it, and it was as fine as he had imagined it would be. He raised his eyes to her face, captured at once by the stunning, gemlike blue of her eyes. He longed to touch the tip of her small, feminine nose, the shallow valley beneath it, the cupid's bow of her upper lip and its generous, pouting partner . . .

"You're the most beautiful woman I've ever seen."

And you are the most handsome man, Harmony sighed silently. She no longer cared about the details of her circumstances. And her dim and dismal future seemed very far away. She cared about nothing except that his lips were coming nearer, and nearer still. Her lids grew heavy and her own lips parted in anticipation. Her entire being was concentrated on the sensations she would experience in the next moments, when their flesh touched at last . . .

"Damn!" Anthony swore softly at the sound of a knock.

He rose slowly from the sofa and Harmony had to force herself to try and breathe normally. Especially when she gazed up at the deerskin-clad figure standing right in front of her.

She had, apparently, had the same effect on Anthony as he had on her. Except that the results of his arousal were far more apparent.

Harmony's very blood and bones turned to water

as she stared at the impressive bulge at the crotch of Anthony's breeches. Oblivious, he looked toward the door.

"A fine time Maggie chose to bring our dinner."

Maggie. With a jolt of alarm that brought her sharply back to her senses, Harmony wondered if it was, indeed, the inn's mistress. What if it wasn't?

"Wait, Anthony," she found herself saying. "What if it isn't Maggie? What if . . .?"

What was she saying? How could she even think to protect this man? Before she could begin to answer, Anthony had moved to her side. Softly, briefly, he touched her cheek.

"You're a very special lady," he whispered. "Thank you for answering a question I had a little earlier."

The knock was repeated. When Anthony turned to answer it, Harmony ducked behind the door to the bedroom. It wouldn't do for the jolly landlady, with her repertoire of winks and nods, to see such a betraying flush on the cheeks of the woman Anthony had in his room.

There was a babble of conversation, the clinking of glassware, and the ring of pewter plates being set on a table. Enticing aromas drifted to Harmony's nose. Her stomach rumbled. Moments later Anthony peered around the edge of the door.

"You can come out now." He grinned and crooked

his arm to lead her to the table that had been set in front of the fire. He held her chair. "Make yourself comfortable, my lady, and with my own hands I shall serve you."

The meat pie steamed when Anthony dug into it. More delicious aromas swirled into the air.

"I'm sorry this isn't Chateaubriand," he apologized without a hint of remorse. "But it *is* the best that Maggie has to offer. Here you are." Anthony set a plate in front of Harmony. "Here also is the inn's best wine, a rather nice claret, though personally I prefer the wines of Bourgogne."

Harmony watched him pour a ruby-colored liquid into a clear glass goblet. Chateaubriand. Wines of Bourgogne. Excellent brandy and cut-crystal decanters. Impeccable manners and educated speech. She looked at his hands.

Not a callous, nor a speck of dirt. The nails were neat, almost as if they had been manicured. His hair, though long, appeared well cut and cared for.

"Why are you frowning?" Anthony inquired, pulling Harmony once again from her reverie.

"I . . . it's nothing. Nothing. I'm sorry. This is a very nice dinner."

"Thank you, but my part in it was small. I merely had to arrange for your company. Maggie did the real work."

There it was again, the reminder of his plan: kidnap and ransom. All she was to him was a prisoner, nothing more. This was not a romantic assignation and she was not free to leave.

Dinner, however, was delicious. The wine was a perfect accompaniment and went down so very easily. It wasn't long before Harmony felt the hazy golden glow enfold her once more.

"I feel compelled to make one more toast," Anthony said quietly, filling the comfortable silence. "To the girl with the sapphire eyes. And the most pleasant evening I believe I've ever had."

Did he mean it? Did he? And why, oh why, did she find herself wishing the night would never end?

Chapter Seven

The dish that had contained the meat pie was empty. The loaf of bread was gone. The wine bottle held only dregs. Harmony rose from the table gratefully, glad to unbend and be able to take a deep breath. It caught in her throat when Anthony walked right up to her and put his hands around her waist.

"Not an inch bigger, by golly. Where'd you put all that?"

A giggle erupted from Harmony's lips. Anthony's grin widened. Then, suddenly, the two of them found themselves caught in the throes of helpless laughter. They fell onto the cushions of the couch, holding their sides and gasping for breath. Anthony was the first to recover.

"Damn. You're not only the prettiest hostage I've ever taken, or the most sweet-natured, but the best humored, too. Maybe I won't give you back after all."

Harmony sobered abruptly. She had managed to forget for a time that she was, indeed, only his prisoner.

That time was over.

"Harmony," Anthony said, grin faded, "what's the matter? What's wrong?"

"Nothing." Harmony shook her head. "Nothing at all."

But it was something. Something very big. The words tumbled out before she could stop them.

"Nothing's wrong, that is, except I'm your prisoner. You kidnapped me. For money. Yet here you sit, plying me with wine, flattering me—"

"Harmony!" Before she could move away from him, he captured her hands and held them tightly. "Harmony, please. I didn't mean for this to happen." When she turned her head from him, he took her chin with the fingers of one hand and gently turned her face back to his. "Won't you at least listen to me? I didn't—"

Anthony stopped abruptly. He let go of her and crossed his arms, as if afraid he might reach for her again.

"Never mind. You're right."

Feeling a chill that had nothing to do with the temperature, Harmony watched him cross the room to stand in front of the fire.

"You're right," Anthony repeated, voice a monotone. "I kidnapped you because I saw an easy way to make money. Because you are a beautiful, intensely desirable woman, I also found myself attracted to you. I would have seduced you if I could. You're very sensible to turn away from me."

Harmony was shocked at the intensity of the pain that stabbed into her heart.

"I can't even apologize," Anthony continued, arms still folded across his breast as he stared into the banked embers of the fire. "I can only promise to return you safely at the time I specified in the note I left."

"You . . . you left a note?"

"Yes. Shortly before I . . . abducted you." Anthony smiled ruefully. "It was all very carefully planned."

"I see." The chill in her heart seemed to have affected the tone of her voice. It was icy. "And just what do you plan to do with me between now and the time you return me?"

Anthony cleared his throat. "I, uh . . . I think, to start with, you should get some sleep." He gestured toward the bedroom. "If you don't mind?"

Harmony remained motionless and Anthony raised a hand to ward off her silent accusation.

"You have nothing to fear. I promise."

Numb and wooden, Harmony rose from the couch. She walked into the bedroom and stood staring at the bed. She did not turn around until she heard the door close behind her. Fully expecting to be alone, a cry escaped her lips when she saw Anthony.

He smiled sadly. "I know I can no longer convince you that I have no intention of touching you, but would you please get into the bed anyway?"

Harmony felt a sickening lurch in the pit of her stomach. But she was helpless. She moved toward the bed. Anthony crossed to the other side.

"Go on. Get in," he ordered gently.

An attempt to flee at this point would be useless, Harmony knew. Nor did she think her weak and shaking legs would carry her. How quickly had a dream turned into a nightmare!

The dark blue silk of her skirt made a rasping sound as it slid across the bed's faded yellow quilt. Under her weight, the feather mattress conformed to the shape of her body. Her heart beat so painfully she feared it might break itself against her ribs.

The mattress bent again, this time to accommodate Anthony's form. Their bodies just touched. Harmony closed her eyes.

How sweet it might have been. How horrible it had become. Harmony waited for the inevitable.

"Please don't be afraid, Harmony," Anthony breathed into the darkness. "I only want to make sure that if I fall asleep, I'll know if you try to get up and leave."

Silence fell again. The only sound was of their steady, rhythmic breathing. Anthony did not move so much as a muscle and, after awhile, Harmony felt herself begin to relax. Her muscles were simply too tired to remain taut any longer. She seemed to sink a little deeper into the mattress.

It was warm where his body pressed against hers. His faint, clean, masculine odor was strangely reassuring. She wasn't even aware when her eyelids closed and she crossed the threshold of consciousness into the peaceful abyss of sleep.

❧

Harmony awoke abruptly. It took a moment to orient herself, then she remembered where she was. And why. She remained very still.

The man at her side snored softly, lips barely parted. His long black hair was spread across the pillow. It had the gloss of a raven's wing.

"Anthony?" she said in a voice scarcely a whisper. "Anthony, are you awake?"

He didn't stir. Cautiously, Harmony touched his arm. Still no response.

It would be so easy to leave. She could quietly slip away. Everyone else at the inn was undoubtedly asleep as well. She could slip away and return to Agatha. He had wanted her only for the money he would gain by his efforts. She was merely his prize. One, moreover, he had lavishly tried to seduce. A bonus, probably. It would be so easy to leave the inn in the darkness while he slept.

Yet for a time he had been so kind, so gentlemanly, so happy. Nor could she deny that she was powerfully attracted to him. As he had been to her.

He had not touched her, however, even when he had such ample opportunity. He had not forced her. He had responded to her only when she had practically handed him an invitation. Harmony felt her emotions torn in two as she gazed at the man asleep beside her.

A thief. An unusually scrupulous one, to be sure, but a thief just the same. Only by an accident of fate had they met. Nothing more. There *could* be nothing more.

To be certain he was asleep, Harmony touched Anthony's shoulder. "Anthony, can you hear me?"

He didn't even sigh.

Harmony swallowed back the unexpected lump in her throat and eased from the bed. Slowly, carefully, she inched across the mattress. She halted and held her breath when Anthony suddenly moved. But it was only to roll into the warm indentation her body had left upon the mattress. Then she saw his lips move.

Had a dream disturbed his sleep? Curious, Harmony bent down to hear what it was Anthony whispered. She heard only a single word.

"Harmony," he breathed. The faint shadow of a smile touched his mouth.

She was completely unaware of the tear that slid

down her cheek. She was only aware of the need to move more carefully so she would not waken him. She breathed a sigh of relief when she was once again snuggled to his side, his warmth touching and enfolding her.

Harmony was nearly asleep again when she felt something stir at her side. She tensed until she felt the fingers curl around her hand. With a smile of her own, she let herself drift into the sweetness of her dreams.

Chapter Eight

The first faint light of dawn touched the distant hilltops and crept across the meadow. An elegant copper beech shone briefly in the advancing sunlight, and its dew-studded leaves seemed to tremble. The side of a low, whitewashed cottage came alight, its thatched roof casting awkward shadows as the sun continued to climb. Daybreak had arrived.

A dog barked as someone scolded. A laden cart rumbled noisily along a peaceful road. Directly below her, Harmony heard the jingle of a curb chain on a bridle and the resounding stamp of a metal-shod hoof on the cobblestone courtyard. She looked down and saw Anthony saddle a handsome gray mare. The chestnut, already tacked, tossed her head with eagerness to be out into the crisp, clean morning air. It was almost time to go.

Harmony stepped back from the window. There was a cracked mirror over the dresser and she turned to it. But there was really not much she could do about her reflection. She ran her fingers through her hair and left it hanging over her shoulders and down her back. She tried to brush some of the wrinkles from her rumpled blue skirt, but it was a waste of time. Finally she shrugged into the black cloak and left the bedroom. She tried not to look at the bed where she had awakened, head nestled against Anthony's neck, arm thrown possessively across his chest.

Harmony could not, however, stop the memory of Anthony breathing her name in his sleep. Or how, when she had opened her eyes, it was to see him leaning up on one elbow, smiling down at her as if they had been lovers . . .

Foolishness. Insane foolishness. Harmony hurried on through the sitting room and into the hall. She shut the door firmly behind her and headed for the stairs. She did not look back.

Maggie was mercifully absent when Harmony passed through the common room. It smelled of stale smoke and spilled ale and she walked out into the fresh air of the courtyard gratefully.

Anthony looked up from a stirrup he adjusted. "Well." He grinned.

Self-conscious about her tousled appearance, Harmony reacted as if she had been stung. "What's the matter?" she asked defiantly. "Do you find something amusing?"

Crinkles appeared at the corners of Anthony's eyes as his grin broadened. "Not at all, no. In fact, you're the first woman I've ever spent the night with who got up looking better than she did when she went to bed." Chuckling, he handed her the gray mare's reins. "May I help her ladyship mount?"

Was he making fun of her? Or did he really mean it? Irritated and short of temper, Harmony grabbed the reins from Anthony's fingers and led the mare to the mounting block. But the skittish animal refused to stand still and shied sideways each time Harmony tried to fit her foot into the stirrup. Anthony watched the whole performance, arms folded, grin undimmed.

"Damn you!" Although she knew better, her temper and humiliation got the better of her and Harmony gave a sharp, angry tug on the reins. It was the wrong thing to do and she was immediately sorry, but she preferred to die rather than ask Anthony to help her.

The mare responded by rearing. Harmony was pulled off her feet and nearly off the block. Anthony roared.

"Damn you, too!" she shouted, and whirled on him. Anthony laughed harder.

The right thing to do was what she had grown up doing, gentling horses with gentle voice and gentle hands. However, there was another part of her and another way. Harmony could also ride a bronc until it stopped bucking. Once she had even drawn a gun on a coyote she saw sneaking out from behind the barn stalking her favorite barn cat. She almost always wore her holster with the two Colts, one on each hip, even when riding a bucking horse, and it had served her well that day. Despite the violent motion, she drew a bead on the wily old coyote and blew him into the next Sunday, saving her cat. That side of Harmony's personality, egged on by Anthony's laughter, took over and shoved good sense aside.

Teeth gritted and eyes flashing, Harmony pulled on the mare again. And again the animal sidestepped. This time, however, Harmony was prepared. She leaped from the block in the direction of the mare's sideways movement and miraculously managed to land astride. Anthony broke into fresh gales of laughter.

"Now what's so funny?" Harmony demanded. Her fury mounted as Anthony bent double, holding on to his sides.

It took a few moments for Anthony to regain control of himself. "It's just that . . . that . . ." He had to pause to wipe the tears from his eyes. "I *was* going to ask you sometime if you were ever frightened when I pointed my pistol at you. Now I realize what a foolish question that would be. You're not afraid of anything, are you?"

"What do *you* think?" she retorted.

"I wonder how I ever managed to kidnap you at all. I guess you must have let me, huh?"

Harmony allowed herself a tight smile. "Perhaps. And perhaps someday I'll have the opportunity to show you how good *I* am with a pistol and find out if you're ever frightened."

Anthony's laughter erupted anew. It was brief.

"Hey, where are you going? You're supposed to wait for me!"

Anthony vaulted into the saddle and gathered his reins even as he kicked his mount into a gallop. It was several minutes before he managed to catch up with the gray. Eventually, with a smug smile, Harmony pulled her horse down to a walk. Anthony cleared his throat.

"I, uh, realize I'm only the kidnapper, but would you mind heading to your left, toward those hills over there? Even though I warned your sister in the note not to call out the *gendarmes*, she didn't much look like the type to be trusted."

Without response, Harmony turned off the road into the direction Anthony had indicated.

"Thank you," he said dryly. "Now, would you mind if we rode at a little faster pace? Where we're going isn't far, but I'll feel better when we get there."

Harmony urged her mare at once into a swift gallop and left Anthony temporarily behind again. When he had caught up with her they continued, side by side, to lope across the wide meadow that stretched away on either side of the road. They slowed to crest the line of low hills, and when Harmony saw what lay beyond them she was pleasantly surprised. She pulled her mare to a halt and gazed down at the tree-lined streambed.

"Is that where you're taking me?"

Anthony nodded. "It's nice and secluded and not too far from your sister's home so I can take you back as soon as it's dark."

"Are you anxious to get rid of me?" Harmony bit her tongue, but the words were already out.

Anthony cocked an eyebrow and resisted the urge to smile. "Let's just say I made a promise to return you. And I never break a promise."

Before Harmony could wonder at the reply, Anthony turned his horse and started down the steep, narrow path that led to the stream below. Harmony followed and urged the mare to a faster pace as Anthony disappeared behind the thick, hanging branches of a weeping willow. She rode right behind him into the cool, green shadows.

A frog plopped noisily into the water and a frightened hare darted into a hole along the stream bank. The mare dropped her head to drink and Harmony slid from her back. She found herself standing to her knees in soft, fragrant river grass.

Anthony joined her when he had tethered the horses then stretched out on the bank with his arms folded behind his head. When his eyes drifted closed, Harmony allowed her gaze to caress his long-limbed form.

Sunlight filtered through the branches of the willow and dappled the smooth skin of his face and forearms. He looked so handsome, so innocent, a half smile on his lips. Harmony felt a little guilty for the hard time she had given him that morning. She felt guiltier as she let her eyes slide a little further down his body.

Anthony had crossed his legs at the ankles. His tight black boots and even tighter breeches accentuated his muscular thighs. And something else. Something that had made her knees weak and her head spin last night. It was doing so again. In a desperate effort to turn her attention elsewhere, she picked up a pebble and tossed it into the stream.

Anthony rolled over and supported himself on one arm. "Would you mind answering a question?"

Curious, and glad he had spoken at last, Harmony shook her head. "Go on."

"Tell me what a beautiful young woman is doing locked away with her ugly sister in an even uglier old tomb of a house."

Harmony couldn't resist her smile. "As a matter of fact, I hadn't lived there very long. You . . . abducted me on my very first day."

Anthony looked surprised. "Your very first day. Well. I'd heard from my . . . sources . . . that you'd recently come off a ship from America. But I had no idea you'd only just arrived." He shook his head. "What prompted you to leave your country and come to England's fair shores?"

Harmony's smile faded. "My parents died," she replied quietly. "I had nowhere else to go."

"I'm sorry." Anthony, too, had quickly sobered. He sat up with his arms clasped around his knees. "Then what happens, but on your first day in England you're robbed and kidnapped." He rose abruptly and walked a few paces to stand at the edge of the stream.

Harmony, however, had seen the look in his eyes before he turned away. "Are you trying to tell me," she inquired softly, "you're sorry about that, too?"

Anthony hesitated, then turned to meet Harmony's gaze. His smile had returned. It was gentle.

"Let's just say . . . I'm not sorry I got to know you."

She had absolutely no idea how to respond. His warmth and sincerity had taken her completely by surprise. She wasn't sure she could have replied anyway, for the uncomfortable lump that had formed in her throat. She tried to swallow it away. And saw something moving fast out of the corner of her eye.

Before Harmony could react, it had brushed her lips

and landed on the left side of her nose. She screamed.

"Harmony!"

"Get him! Get him!" she shrieked, and whirled as the insect buzzed around her head. "Get it away from me!"

Startled and off balance, Anthony took a blind swing. His boots slipped in the mud and he toppled over backward. There was a loud splash.

Horrified, Harmony stared at the spot where Anthony had disappeared beneath the water. Until he came up, sputtering and spitting and loudly cursing. Then she laughed. Laughed until tears ran from her eyes and it became difficult to breathe. And she felt her own feet begin to slip from beneath her.

"Oh, no . . . Anthony! Nooooo!"

"Laugh at me, will you?" Maintaining his grip on her ankles, Anthony pulled Harmony into the water with him.

"Anthony!" Harmony gasped for air and pushed the hair from her eyes. "Anthony, how *dare* you?!"

"Very easily, my love." Anthony laughed and dunked her again.

This time Harmony did not scramble for the surface. She kicked to free her feet from the hindrance of her petticoats and dove for the bottom. She closed her eyes to the mud-riled water and felt for Anthony's feet. Then she tugged. Hard.

Anthony slipped back into the water, arms flailing as he went under. Harmony surfaced and pulled herself onto the bank. Laughing, she waited for him to emerge.

Anthony came out of the water and onto the bank in a single motion. He shook his head and spattered droplets of water in all directions.

"Well, I guess that teaches me, once and for all, not to mess with you, Lady Blue." He jumped to his feet and tried unsuccessfully to brush the dirt from his wet breeches. They had now become so revealing Harmony had to look away.

"How about a bottle of wine to keep us warm while we dry out?"

Harmony looked back in Anthony's direction, trying to keep her eyes on his face. "For breakfast?"

Anthony glanced up at the sun. "No, for lunch. How about some of that, too?"

Dismayed, Harmony realized it was noon already. Where had the time gone? She watched him unpack his saddlebags. He certainly was well prepared, she mused. Almost as if he had kidnapped a young lady before. Had he? She was surprised at the stab of jealousy that accompanied the thought.

"Here you are, *mademoiselle*." Anthony leaned over, bowing, to hand her the metal cup of white wine. "I'm sorry I couldn't find more elegant stemware, but

Cook broke it all in a fit of rage."

Harmony laughed as Anthony sprawled in the grass beside her. As he had on the evening before, he raised his glass in a gesture of salute.

"To a lovely day," he said softly. "To a lovely, perfect day, my sweet, sweet Harmony."

Their cups clinked together in the silence.

Though the wine was making her head swim, Harmony felt compelled, out of pride, to drink to Anthony's last toast.

"Again," he said, touching his cup to hers, "let us drink to your masterful horsemanship."

"Thank you." Harmony ducked her head, feeling a blush flood her cheeks.

"May I ask how and where you learned to ride?"

The entire situation was so unreal Harmony was grateful to grab onto something solid and comforting: her past. Nestling her cup in the grass to keep it upright, she sat up a little straighter.

"Before . . . before I came to England, when my parents were alive, we lived on a ranch in the American West."

"A ranch!" Anthony exclaimed. "Cattle or horses?"

"Both."

"Excellent. And the breeds?"

Did he really care? Harmony had to admit a fire had lit in his gaze when she had mentioned the livestock.

"My father started with Longhorns, but shortly before he died he imported a Hereford bull and a couple of heifers."

"Aha. Sturdy English stock from the hills of Herefordshire."

There was genuine warmth and excitement in his tone and Harmony couldn't help but respond to it.

"Yes, indeed, and they proved to be extraordinarily sturdy. My mother and I continued to breed Herefords after Daddy died because we were so impressed by the efficiency with which they convert their feed to beef. We even did some crossing with the Longhorns, and the results were amazing."

Anthony wondered if he had just actually felt his heart do a flip-flop in his chest. He reached for Harmony's hand and squeezed it.

"Let me guess. Higher quality steaks with better marbling?"

"How on earth did you—?"

"I . . . I, uh, have a keen interest in livestock," he said, reluctantly releasing Harmony's slender, delicate hand and turning away. "What about the horses?" he continued. "Did your family breed them as well?"

"Not initially. We purchased our working stock

from other ranchers. But then Daddy became interested in harness racing."

"The new sport that's taken your country by storm?"

"Exactly. Don't tell me you know all about Standardbreds as well."

"Why shouldn't I? Wasn't that breed founded by another English animal?"

Harmony was truly impressed. "Yes, the great Thoroughbred racehorse, Messenger. I believe the trotters, Standardbreds, were begun with a cross between Messenger and a Narragansett Pacer."

"You're so right. And your knowledge is impressive."

"As is yours," Harmony replied, returning the compliment. The conversation, she suddenly realized, was as heady as the wine, and she momentarily pressed cooling hands to her cheeks.

It wasn't that she'd never had a conversation with a member of the opposite sex before. There had been ranch hands with whom she was casually friendly, and they certainly had a lot in common to talk about together. And there had been young, well-educated men of good families she had met while traveling with her mother and father. But never before had topics in common, education, and good looks been all wrapped up in a single package.

Furthermore, as long as she was being honest with herself, Harmony had to admit that the "bad boy" element, the hint of danger, was even more titillating in real life than in the dime novels she loved to read.

More curious, and compelled to draw Anthony out even further, Harmony regarded him with a quizzical expression, right forefinger lightly tapping her upper lip.

"Tell me, Anthony," she said slowly. "I'm curious. How did you come to find out about harness racing and the Standardbred breed? Have you an interest in horses?"

If she only knew, Anthony silently mused. But that was the point. She didn't. And it had to remain that way. Still, however, he knew he should give her an answer.

"It avails a man to be well mounted, does it not?" he replied at length. "Especially a man in my position."

It was not exactly the kind of response she was fishing for, but Harmony wisely let the matter drop.

Mere moments later, Anthony abruptly stood up and brushed off the seat of his breeches. "May I get you anything else?"

Harmony gazed at the remains of their picnic lunch and shook her head. "No, thank you. If I eat any more I'm afraid I might pop and you'll have nothing to return to my sister."

The reminder was sobering. To both of them. It struck Harmony as absurd, however, that she felt dismay at the thought of returning to Agatha. She had been kidnapped. Robbed and kidnapped. She was absolutely mad to sit in the willow's pleasant shade and pretend she was having a picnic and polite conversation with an attractive gentleman from the upper echelons of society. He was a common thief! Surely she should wish to end her ordeal and go home. Shouldn't she?

Home.

The very thought made her shudder.

Harmony pictured the dimly lit corridors; dark, dusty drapes; and heavy furniture. How could that ugly stone house be preferable to this fragrant green sanctuary beneath the drooping willow limbs? It wasn't. Nor was Agatha's acid-tongued company preferable to the presence of the handsome, charming, and apparently intelligent man at her side. Thief or not.

No, it was not absurd to want to remain where she was. Her only dismay was in the fact the day had so swiftly waned, bringing her unlikely idyll to an end. As stars began to wink overhead and Anthony gathered his scattered belongings, Harmony brushed a tear from her cheek.

Chapter Nine

*S*ummer twilight drained the light from the valley. Dusk settled softly over the green hillsides and stole the definition from the feathery branches of the willow. Birdsong had faded away and the only sound was the rushing of the river against its banks.

Harmony's heart had squeezed as she watched Anthony, intent on memorizing every feature. She would undoubtedly never see him again as long as she lived. The thought constricted her throat.

What a strange day it had been. What a strange man Anthony Allen seemed to be.

There were a good many things Harmony found unusual and incongruous about Anthony Allen. An interest in, and knowledge of horses was one thing. But how had he come to know so much, and care so much, about cattle? Surely that was not the usual area of interest for a common thief. Harmony, however, strongly suspected that Anthony was not merely a common thief.

While pondering her handsome abductor, Harmony realized the darkness had deepened and a crescent moon now rode in the sky. Somewhere in the hills a fox yipped and howled. "It's getting late. I guess I'd better saddle up the horses."

"Yes," Harmony replied dully. "I guess you'd better." She watched him hold out his hands to her.

His grip was strong and firm and warm. Harmony let him pull her upward. He did not let go of her hands. His expression was sober as he gazed into her eyes.

Harmony didn't know whether to cry or to give in to the shivering arousal she felt being so close to Anthony. Nor did she know what she wanted. Why did he look at her with such intensity? Not knowing what else to do, Harmony closed her eyes. She was completely unaware of the parting of her lips, or her body straining forward, closer and closer to his. She was aware of nothing until she felt him release her hands and place his palms to her cheeks.

"No," Anthony groaned. "No, Harmony. It's wrong. I . . . can't . . ."

But he was too near. Harmony had never felt anything so physically powerful as her attraction to this man. She had never been so aware of every inch of her body, and the secret, private parts of her body. She had never wanted to kiss a man as badly as she wanted to kiss Anthony Allen. She surrendered to her longing.

The touch was searing. They came together not gently, but with all the pent-up passion that had built between them. Anthony's lips were crushed against hers, his palms pressed flat to her cheeks. Her body became a pillar of fire.

It was over before the fire could consume her. Anthony pulled away almost violently and held her at arm's length.

"We have to go," he said hoarsely. "Now."

In the next instant she was alone and trembling while Anthony saddled the horses. Her heart raced and she could scarcely catch her breath. Her body ached and tingled all at the same time. She felt as if she might faint.

But she did not. Somehow she managed to mount the gray mare, gather the reins, and follow Anthony out of the moonlit valley. As it had been at the inn, Harmony did not look back. She was afraid emotion would overwhelm her, but when they reached the meadow they broke at once into a gallop. She could only concentrate on the ride.

Anthony had told her they were not far from Agatha's house, and he had been correct. They reached the road, crossed it, and soon reached the dark, familiar silhouette of the forest surrounding Agatha's home. Harmony's muscles tensed.

The chestnut mare picked her way through the trees and all too soon they arrived in the clearing. Anthony turned in his saddle.

"This is as far as I go."

It took a moment for his comment to register. "But . . . but the money. Don't you have to go and . . . and pick it up someplace?"

"Oh, I don't think so." Anthony smiled and leaned forward, resting an arm on the mare's neck. "Let's just say . . . the pleasure of your company was enough. But don't let it get around!" He laughed as he straightened in the saddle and picked up his reins. "I wouldn't want to ruin my reputation."

Harmony did not return Anthony's smile, or respond to his casual good humor. "Why?" she demanded. "Tell me the truth." Suddenly, it seemed very important.

Anthony hesitated. His grin faded to a soft smile that barely touched the edges of his lips. "Why didn't you leave last night when you thought I was asleep?"

A wave of emotion moved through her, leaving warmth in its wake. It was a second before she could speak.

"You were awake, then."

"I wouldn't have stopped you if you *had* left, you know."

"You called my name."

"I never said I didn't *try* to stop you."

This time Harmony returned Anthony's smile, although teardrops quivered at the corners of her eyes.

"Then we're even," she said at length, softly.

But Anthony shook his head. "Not quite. I have something I've been meaning to return." He plucked a small object from his breast pocket and held out the sapphire ring. "I don't think I'll need this any longer to remind me of the lady with the sapphire eyes. I don't think I'll ever be able to forget her, as a matter of fact."

Harmony merely stared at the jewel in the palm of Anthony's hand. She looked up into his eyes.

"No. You keep it. Just to make *darn* sure you never forget."

She whirled the gray mare around before Anthony could see the tears spilling over, and set off on the now-visible path through the trees. Within moments she had disappeared into the shadows.

Chapter Ten

All too soon the house loomed into sight. She hardly would have realized it was there, standing darker than the night around it, but for a sliver of light coming from the parlor where the curtains had not been drawn together all the way. Harmony guided the mare to the stone lions and dismounted. She patted the animal's shoulder and fought back the lump in her throat.

The gray was the last remaining link to Anthony. She knew she had to sever it quickly. With numb fingers she tied the reins to the stirrups.

"Go back to the inn. Find Anthony." Harmony slapped the animal sharply on the rump. She did not look back as the mare cantered down the road. She took a deep breath, climbed the steps, and tried the door. Not surprised to find it locked, she rapped sharply.

Mrs. Rutledge opened the door. Her eyes widened in surprise. "Miss Simmons! Where—?"

"Never mind where I've been." Harmony brushed past the housekeeper. "Where's my sister?"

"In the par—" Harmony was already gone.

Agatha sat in her usual chair, a Bible open in her lap. When Harmony entered the room, she looked up with an expression remarkably similar to Mrs. Rutledge's.

"Harmony! It's about time you came home. Where have you been?"

Harmony stopped short. "What do you mean, where have I been? I was just released."

"Released? Released from what?"

"From . . . from the kidnapper!" Harmony was incredulous.

Agatha made a rude noise. "Kidnapper, my eye."

Harmony hardly knew what to say. "Well, where . . . where did you think I was?"

"Hussy!" Agatha spat. "Don't act innocent with me. I may not know exactly where you were, but I know who you were with!"

"You . . . you do?"

"You were with that . . . that . . . *criminal* . . . weren't you?"

In spite of herself, Harmony experienced a wave of guilt. "Yes, but . . . but he *kidnapped* me!"

"Don't you dare lie to me, you brazen thing! You had a romantic assignation!"

"Agatha!" Harmony was dumbfounded. "I was

kidnapped, I tell you. Didn't you get the note?"

"What note? I don't know anything about a note," Agatha said in clipped tones.

"The ransom note!"

"Hah!" Livid, Agatha pushed to her feet. Her Bible slipped to the floor, unnoticed. "Ransom note, indeed. You're nothing but a bitch in heat. I knew it the moment you stepped out of the coach and dared that devil to put his hands on you! You went away with him willingly, that's what you did! There is no note!"

Stunned, Harmony dropped her gaze. Was it possible there was, indeed, no note? Had Anthony abducted her for another reason altogether and covered it up with the kidnapping story? A curious thrill of hope surged through her veins. And then she noticed the Bible, spine broken, on the floor near Agatha's feet.

"Oh, no?" Harmony stooped and plucked something that protruded from the Bible's parchment pages. She scanned it briefly and held it out to her sister. "If there was no ransom note, what do you call this?"

An unbecoming flush crept up Agatha's neck. She recovered swiftly and straightened her already rigid spine. She snatched the paper from Harmony's grasp as a cunning smile touched her mouth.

"You expect me to believe that's a genuine ransom note? My, my, you do underestimate my intelligence, sister dear."

"What are you talking about?" Harmony breathed.

"I'm talking about your evil ways, Harmony. I know you. And I know that this was probably all your idea. A note to extort money from me so you could finance your elopement with your lover," she finished smugly.

"Agatha!"

"Don't 'Agatha' me, you little tramp!" the older woman hissed.

"Your notion is insane," Harmony flared. "I only arrived in England two days ago. Yesterday our coach was held up. I spent the afternoon here in the house with you and Mrs. Rutledge, then——"

"Yes, exactly, and *then*," Agatha interrupted in a high, shrill voice. "Then you took advantage of Mr. Henry's presence to sneak out of my house and rendezvous with your——"

"Stop it!" Appalled by her sister's insane accusations, Harmony stamped her foot angrily.

"How dare you raise your voice to me in my own house?" Agatha demanded. She pushed to her feet and stood nearly nose to nose with Harmony. With one forefinger extended, she poked her sharply in the shoulder.

"And don't think you'll ever get away with this kind of stunt again. Life is going to be a great deal different in this house! You're going to . . ."

Harmony didn't wait to hear exactly how her life was going to be different. She already knew. Hands covering her ears, she fled from the parlor to the dark, narrow stairs. She didn't stop running until she had reached her room and slammed the door behind her. Trembling, she waited for what she knew would come. She didn't have to wait long.

Angry footsteps trod along the hallway. A key turned in the lock. The prisoner was recaptured, the prison secure once again. Harmony sank to the ground, amid the billowing puddle of her skirts, and wept.

❧

Anemic daylight seeped into the bedroom. Harmony opened her eyes and found herself staring at the ceiling. Sometime during the night she must have picked herself up off the floor and found her way into the bed. She had not even bothered to undress. She closed her eyes again.

Was there a reason to do anything ever again? Harmony wondered. She had descended into hell. She knew she could not survive its fires for three whole years. Agatha was clearly insane, or as close as anyone could get to it without having to be removed from society. Harmony almost wished her time with Anthony *had* been a romantic rendezvous; that she *had* been able to extort money from Agatha; and that she *had* run away with Anthony. Anything, anything at all, was preferable to the life she was faced with now.

Tears tried to squeeze from beneath Harmony's eyelids. Anthony.

She tried to deny him, to ward off his memory. But it came back, stealing into her heart, constricting her throat. A great sob welled in her chest.

Try as she might, she could not forget their night together, or the following day by the water . . . and in the water. Despite the tears, a smile tried to pull at the corners of Harmony's mouth.

She couldn't deny it; she had never felt closer to anyone. They were so easy together. Conversation was so comfortable and effortless between them, and they seemed to have so much in common. The physical attraction between them was undeniable as well, almost overwhelmingly powerful. The only thing that was difficult to believe was that he was, truly, a criminal.

But he hadn't taken the ransom money, and he had tried to give back her ring. Did he really have a criminal's heart? And would she really never see him again? It didn't seem possible that the only light left in her life had gone out, never to be lit again. It was cruel, too cruel.

The memories, like her tears, were scalding. Harmony tried to banish them both. She couldn't let Anthony back into her head, into her heart. There was enough heartbreak in her life as it was. The years yawning ahead of her were grim and dismal as they were. She could not add weight to the already too-heavy burden on her shoulders.

And she could not lie in bed all day trying to fend off memories of Anthony.

Stiff and miserable, Harmony edged off the bed. She was opposite the mirror over her dressing table, and when she caught a glimpse of herself, she gasped.

The blue suit she had worn since the day of her arrival in London was torn, dirty, and rumpled. Her hair was snarled, matted, and lusterless. There were purplish bruises beneath her red-rimmed eyes. Arms braced on the dressing table, Harmony leaned closer to get a better look.

Was this what she was going to look like at the end of three years? Was she going to let her sister and her grim, dull life steal away her youth and beauty?

The spirit and determination that had always been the hallmarks of Harmony's personality struggled upward from wherever they had been in hiding. She threw back her shoulders and lifted her chin.

Agatha was not going to defeat her. Not now, not ever. It was simply not going to happen.

The blue suit almost ripped in Harmony's haste to tear it from her body. She didn't care. She kicked it aside, along with her soiled petticoats.

Agatha's house had not been updated with

modern bathing rooms. In the corner, however, was an antiquated copper tub that had been filled for her the night before last. The water was chilly, but Harmony didn't care about that either. She scrubbed until every inch of her skin was pink and tingling.

Wet hair clung to her shoulders and dripped down her back when she stepped from the tub at last. She donned clean underlinens and chose a morning gown of pink satin. Not only did the color compliment her hair color and skin tone, but Agatha would disapprove. It was perfect.

Harmony's hair was a damp mess, but at least it was clean. When she was finally able to run a comb through it unimpeded, she coiled it around the back of her head and secured it with pearl-studded combs.

Harmony smiled grimly at her reflection. She was herself again. Now all she had to do was wait for the knock on her door.

It was Mrs. Rutledge who arrived at length, and if she was surprised by the change in Harmony's appearance, she managed to conceal it.

"Miss Simmons requested me to inform you that breakfast is served immediately in the dining room," she announced without preamble.

Without reply, Harmony swept past her and down the hall. Posture erect and a smile on her face, she sailed into the dining room.

Agatha sat at the head of the long, formal table. There was a place set at her right hand. Harmony took it without hesitation.

"Good morning, Agatha. How are you?"

"Quite well," she responded tartly. "*I* sleep the sleep of the just. And you?"

Harmony did not rise to the bait. "Everything is wonderful, thank you very much. The bed was very comfortable, and the room is lovely."

Agatha snorted. "We'll see how 'wonderful' you think everything is when you've gotten into your routine and live life under *my* rules."

Still smiling, Harmony spread her napkin over her lap. "Would you pass the toast, please, Agatha? Thank you."

"You can wipe that smile off your face," Agatha persisted. "There'll be no more nights of sin spent with your lover."

"There never were any 'nights of sin' spent with my lover, Agatha," Harmony replied calmly. "The only . . . affair . . . exists in your own twisted imagination."

"Well, I never!" Agatha's blue-veined hands slammed down on the mahogany table. Her breakfast plate rattled. "How dare you speak to me like that?"

Fork poised, Harmony looked at her sister. "How dare *you* accuse me of something I never did?" The fork completed its journey.

Agatha's hands gripped the arms of her chair. "Go to your room!"

"I certainly will. When I've finished," Harmony said serenely.

"You'll do what I—"

"Excuse me, Miss Simmons." Mrs. Rutledge had appeared in the doorway from the foyer into the dining room. "I don't mean to interrupt, but—"

"Well, what is it?" Agatha snapped.

"There's . . . there's a coach coming up the drive."

"So?"

"It's a very elegant coach, Miss Simmons. I've never seen the likes of it before." The housekeeper's eyes were wide.

"Then I guess you'd best go and see who it is. Hadn't you?"

"Yes, ma'am." Mrs. Rutledge made a rapid departure.

"And you, Harmony, will go straight to your room. You will *not* backtalk me in my own home."

Harmony put her knife and fork neatly on her plate. "Since I've finished, I will happily go to my room." She pushed back in her chair in accompaniment to the knock on the door. As she walked to the exit that led straight to the corridor, she heard the sound of muffled voices.

"Miss Simmons!"

The excited tone of the housekeeper's voice caused

Harmony to hesitate.

"What is it now, Mrs. Rutledge?" Agatha inquired with irritation.

"I . . . I think you'd better come, Miss Simmons," Mrs. Rutledge said. "There's a gentleman at the door who insists on speaking to you. He says it's about your sister's sapphire ring."

"The *stolen* ring?"

Mrs. Rutledge nodded and Harmony's heart stopped in her chest.

"Go on to your room," Agatha ordered, and marched from the dining room.

Harmony couldn't have moved a single muscle had she wanted to. She stood frozen in place as voices droned on in the foyer.

What about her ring? What of Anthony? Terror had so tight a grip on her she could scarcely breathe. Had he been caught?

"Harmony!"

Agatha literally flew back into the dining room. Her features had been transformed.

"There's a gentleman here. He's found your ring! He wishes to return it to you!"

Her tongue felt as if it had cleaved to the roof of her mouth. "My . . . ring?" she said stupidly.

"Yes, you simpleton," Agatha said impatiently. "The sapphire ring that was stolen. This lovely gentleman's coachman apparently spotted it lying by the side of the road. Being the honest man that he is, the gentleman took it to the authorities at once. Mr. Henry directed him here!"

Harmony was baffled by her sister's excitement. The ring wasn't worth that much. In the next moment, however, she discovered the cause of the heightened color in Agatha's cheeks.

"Hurry up, Harmony," Agatha said crossly. "You mustn't keep Lord Allen waiting."

Lord Allen?

No, it wasn't possible. It was all a joke. A cruel and hideous joke.

Numb, Harmony let her sister pull her from the dining room into the foyer. What had happened to Anthony? As long as he lived, she knew, he would not give up possession of that ring. Nearly choking, she entered the foyer.

The elegantly dressed gentleman stood silhouetted in the front door, sunlight blazing around him, gazing outward. His body was long and lean, his dark hair pulled back into a tight ponytail. At the sound of Agatha clearing her throat, he turned.

Harmony saw the eyes first, impossibly dark. Then the crooked smile. As etiquette demanded, and as she had been taught, she offered her hand.

Anthony lifted it to his lips.

Chapter Eleven

*H*armony, have you lost your tongue?"

Agatha's prompting brought Harmony sharply back to reality. She looked up slowly and stared straight into Anthony's eyes, heart thudding madly. What was it he had just said? Her head ached trying to recall. Oh, yes. *Allow me to introduce myself. Anthony Allen, Lord Farmington.* Almost exactly the words he had used the night he had abducted her. Minus the Lord Farmington part.

"Harmony?" Agatha's graying brows nearly disappeared into her hairline.

"I . . . I'm sorry. I suppose I'm a bit overwhelmed. You see, I've never met a . . . *lord* . . . before."

"I shall take it as a compliment then, that my presence should so disturb a beautiful young woman of such obvious charm and poise. You do, however, look a trifle pale. Perhaps you'd like to sit down."

Anthony's act was unbelievable. Harmony could

only manage to shake her head. She was afraid to leave his presence, afraid he would vanish like smoke. It was almost incomprehensible that he had suddenly appeared at her door dressed as—and claiming to be—a lord.

"Ah, but I have a better idea," Anthony went on smoothly. He inclined his head deferentially in Agatha's direction. "If it's all right with you, of course, Miss Simmons, I should like to take your lovely sister for a short drive. She looks as if she might do with a bit of fresh air. Also, I would like to show her the spot on the road where my driver so fortuitously spied this ring."

Anthony extended his hand, palm up. Harmony made no move to take it.

"May I?"

Before she could respond, Anthony took her hand and slipped the ring on her finger. To her chagrin, his touch sent a shiver through her. Terrified her sister would notice, Harmony quickly withdrew her hand.

"Again," Anthony said to Agatha, "may I?"

Agatha tittered like a teenager. "If you mean, may you take my dear sister for a drive, why, I'm sure she'd be delighted. Wouldn't you, Harmony?

"I hardly see how she could refuse, since you've been so kind," Agatha verbally prodded when Harmony remained silent and unmoving.

Harmony glanced from Anthony to Agatha. If she only knew, Harmony thought. If she only knew that the "lord" her sister was so eager to have her step out with was a kidnapper and a thief. The irony of it made her smile.

"I shall take that as acquiescence," Anthony said swiftly, and crooked his arm.

The shock had begun to wear off. Against all odds, he had found a way to come back to her. And the irony was truly delicious, the taste of it ambrosia to her soul. Harmony took Anthony's arm.

The coach was resplendent. Its black sides glistened as if they were wet. The trim appeared to be gold, as did the metal appointments on the harness. The horses themselves were magnificent: four perfectly matched blood bays with white diamonds on their foreheads and almost perfectly matched white stockings all around. Harmony caught her breath. In the doorway behind her, Agatha *oohed* and *aahed*.

"I don't think I've ever seen such a glorious vehicle, Lord Farmington, or such magnificent horses," she gushed.

"This coach's greatest asset is its coachman, whose vision is uncannily sharp."

Harmony glanced at the coachman, who held the door for her. His features, which were pulled downward and resembled melting wax, remained impassive. He was obviously in on Anthony's little charade. Maybe even a compatriot, a fellow bandit. She winked at him as she climbed into the carriage.

Harmony felt she had fallen down a hole and into another dream world. The coach tilted slightly and the sunlight was momentarily blotted out as Anthony climbed inside and sat down beside her. It tilted to the opposite side when the coachman climbed up to his bench. She heard the crack of the driving whip and felt the crunch of the gravel beneath the carriage wheels. They were on their way. She turned to Anthony.

"How long before we're arrested for driving a stolen coach?"

Anthony threw back his head and laughed.

"It wasn't all *that* funny."

"Oh, Harmony . . . Harmony." He paused to wipe a tear from his eye. "There's really no one like you. Everything I've done is worth it to have found you, gotten to know you, and come back for you."

"I do hope you mean that, Anthony. I hope it's worth it to you. How long is the sentence, do you suppose, for stealing a carriage? Not to mention a fine suit of clothes like that." She glanced pointedly at Anthony's attire: the beautifully cut dove gray jacket and ruffled shirt; skintight, dust-colored breeches; a diamond pin in his maroon silk cravat.

"Do you like them?" He brushed an imaginary speck of dust from his knee. "I shall pass the compliment on to my tailor."

Harmony had had enough. "Stop it, Anthony. Stop pretending. It isn't funny anymore. It's serious. You're going to get caught being this brazen! If my sister gets even a whiff of your deception, she'll . . . she'll . . ."

"She'll what? Have me skinned?"

"Knowing her, yes. She probably will, as a matter of fact."

"Does this mean you care what happens to me?"

"Oh, Anthony." The shock of seeing him when she had never thought to lay eyes on him again, the strain of knowing the risk he was taking to see her, all took its toll. Tears welled in Harmony's eyes.

"Harmony . . ."

"No, don't touch me." She turned away when Anthony tried to brush away her tears. "Just take me back, Anthony. Please. I'm so frightened for you!"

"Harmony." This time he didn't allow her to turn from him. He grasped her shoulders with gentle firmness. "Look at me. Please."

Slowly, reluctantly, Harmony raised her eyes.

"Nothing's going to happen to me. I promise. No one's going to arrest me for theft because these really are my clothes and this really is my coach. I traveled all over England to find four Hackney horses that matched this well and I trained them myself. I really am a lord, Harmony. I really am."

Harmony shook her head, hardly able to even think straight anymore. "No," she whispered. "You . . . you're the man who kidnapped me. For ransom. I saw the note. You robbed our coach. You took my ring."

Anthony took Harmony's hand in his and turned the sapphire ring on her finger. "Now I've brought it back. Whoever would have thought such a small gem could bring a man such great good fortune?"

Harmony continued to shake her head, although she was scarcely aware she was doing so. Her thoughts were very far away. Back at an inn with a cut-crystal decanter of first-class brandy. Crystal stemware and fine wine. A bandit with manicured hands. A bandit who knew a great deal about horses. Hackney horses, no less. She'd read about them. They were a popular and quite refined English breed. And Anthony also apparently knew a great deal about cattle.

"Where . . . where do you live?" Harmony asked at length, a thoughtful furrow on her brow.

"Far to the north of here."

"On a farm?"

"Well, yes. Sort of."

"That has cattle?"

Anthony visibly brightened. "Excellent guess, yes. I'm doing experimental breeding with a cross of High-land cattle, as a matter of fact."

Either he was a very, very good liar. Or he was

telling the truth. At last.

Anthony had no warning of the danger to come. One moment he was looking into the loveliest blue eyes on the face of the planet. In the next moment they had narrowed and he saw her hand coming at his face.

"Ow!"

"I hope that *did* hurt, Anthony Allen . . . or whatever your name is!"

"Harmony, why—?"

"Don't you dare ask me any questions!" Harmony flared. "It's *you* who should be giving answers. And they'd better be good!"

"All right." Anthony held up his hands in surrender. "I apologize. I do. You're absolutely right. What do you want to know?"

"You can start with why you robbed our coach and stole my ring. I think I'll find it extremely fascinating to learn why *Lord* Farmington was reduced to holding up two women alone in a coach."

"All right . . . all right." Anthony tentatively lowered his hands. "I'm sorry. I really am, Harmony."

"Just start talking."

"I will, I . . . I know it was ridiculous. But it was the only thing I could think of at the time. I had to stop the coach. I had to see if you were real."

"So, in order to see if I was real, you shot off your

gun and robbed the coach."

"Yes, well . . . let me start at the beginning."

"Please, be my guest."

Anthony took a deep breath. "I had business down on the docks and saw you get off the ship. I thought you were the most beautiful woman I'd ever laid eyes on. Despite how forward it would have been, I wanted to introduce myself to you immediately. But you were carried away in the disembarking crowd. I lost sight of you." Anthony's dark eyes seemed to lose focus as his thoughts went back in time.

"I finally spotted you and your sister leaving in a coach and followed it to your hotel."

"Why didn't you come and introduce yourself then?"

"You'll recall the way I was dressed."

"Yes. Which is another good question. Why would a lord dress like that at all?"

"I enjoy the ride when I have to come to London. I like to ride alone and I don't like to look conspicuous."

"So you dress like a . . . 'man of the people.'"

"Exactly."

"And you stay in cozy little inns along the way where they call you Tony and have no idea who you really are."

Anthony had the good grace to flush. "Right again. It's just easier that way. I pay them well to supply the things I like. They're friendly and I like that, too. It wouldn't be the same if they knew who I really was."

"That still doesn't explain why you robbed our coach."

"Well, I didn't. Not actually. You see, I . . . I couldn't go into your hotel, so I decided I'd come back the next morning, early, and wait for you to come out. But I didn't get there early enough, I guess. You'd already left."

"So you rode after us."

"Yes. And rode hard, too. I had the devil of a time catching up to you. When I finally saw your coach, I . . . well, I got this wild idea."

"To rob us."

"Foolishness, I admit. But then I am often foolish, I'm afraid, and inclined to believe I can get away with things that aren't actually possible. I decided to play a little game. I never intended to steal anything, you understand. I only hoped to make a rather impressive introduction. But you . . . you didn't react at all as I had expected."

"You mean I *spoiled* your little game."

"Just the opposite. You enhanced it, rather. Made it more intriguing."

"To the point that you decided to kidnap me?"

Anthony sighed heavily. He looked out the window for a moment, thoughtful, then returned his attention to Harmony. "The first time I saw you I thought you were the most beautiful woman I'd ever seen. As I said, I had to see you again, see if you were real. Posing as a bandit was a game, a lark. I never intended to be . . . bowled over by you. I didn't think you'd turn out to be not only the loveliest woman in the world, but the most fascinating. I knew then I'd have to see you again. But after what I'd done, I thought you would never want to see *me*. I feared I'd never get the chance to know you better. Or to have you get to know me better, and know I wasn't such a bad sort after all. I knew you'd never willingly agree to see me again, and that's when I came up with the idea to see you, well . . . *unwillingly*."

"Kidnap."

"Yes. It wasn't such a stretch since I'd already masqueraded as a bandit."

"What about the note? Why didn't you simply take me?"

"What would your sister have thought if you disappeared for the night?"

"Exactly the same thing she thought even though you left the note."

"You don't mean . . . ?" Anthony's expression grew more sober still. His black, finely drawn brows knit together. "She accused you of—?"

"Running off with the bandit who robbed us," Harmony finished for him. "Leaving the note not for ransom, but extortion. She said we planned to use the money to finance our elopement."

Anthony shook his head. "That . . . that's almost unbelievable."

"True, nonetheless."

"I . . . I'm sorry, Harmony. I didn't mean to cause trouble for you."

"What about the trouble you could have caused for yourself? What if she *had* alerted the authorities?"

"I didn't worry, to tell you the truth. Because I . . . well, I am who I am."

"So the only person who was worried throughout all of this was me." Harmony felt her emotions begin to swing. She had been so glad to see Anthony, so relieved. Now her temper was taking over. "The only person who was genuinely frightened was me."

"Harmony—"

"Once you had me, why didn't you tell me who you were?" she demanded, voice rising. "Why did you have to keep playing your stupid little game?"

Anthony hung his head. He stared at his hands, then looked up again at Harmony. "You're a remarkable woman. When I realized how remarkable, I knew you were far better than I, no matter what my lineage. I realized I should simply enjoy the time I had with you and let you go. I'd never be good enough for you. There was no point in telling you the truth because I never thought I'd see you again."

"But if you had just been honest with me . . ." It was all too much suddenly. Furious with herself for doing so, Harmony started to cry.

"I'm being honest now," Anthony replied quietly.

"Well, it's too late!" Harmony had already twisted the door handle before she realized the coach was moving at a brisk clip. Sobbing with frustration and anger, she pounded on the door. "Stop the coach . . . stop!"

"No, *you* stop, Harmony."

Anthony's arms were muscular and his hands strong. He held her as gently as he could while she struggled against him. Finally he managed to turn her back to face him.

"Listen to me. Please. The greatest mistake of all was in coming back today to reveal my true identity. I know that now. I should have left it as I did, with you thinking of me as a criminal. At least you liked that man. It's quite evident that you loathe this one."

Harmony couldn't seem to stop crying. It was no use even trying. Surrendering to the flood of emotion that threatened to drown her, she buried her face in her hands and sobbed brokenly.

"Oh, my God," Anthony groaned. "I'm so sorry . . . so sorry."

She was unresisting when he took her in his arms again. He held her and rocked her while she wept, and hated himself. He would have given anything to undo what he had done, to have made different choices, different decisions. But it was too late.

"Harmony," Anthony whispered when her wild weeping had subsided. "I have to tell you one more thing." When she didn't respond, he continued. "I shouldn't have come back, I know that. But I had to because I . . . I've fallen in love with you, Harmony. I love you. I had to see you again and tell you."

She had thought all emotion had drained from her with her tears. But it had not. She sat up, rigidly erect, and looked Anthony directly in the eye.

"How can you possibly expect me to believe you?"

If she had stabbed him in the heart with a dagger, it would not have been nearly as painful.

"I guess you can't," Anthony replied at length.

"There is something you can do for me, though."

"Anything, Harmony. Anything. Just tell me what you want."

"Take me home, Anthony. Please just take me home."

Chapter Twelve

Harmony pulled the lamp closer to the sheet of paper on which she wrote. It was a gray day and only the dimmest light filtered through the ivy-covered window. It was difficult to see the letter, the words she scribed on the page. But at least it kept her busy. It was something to do to fill her long, dull, colorless days. It also kept her in touch with her few friends in America. When her time with Agatha was up, she fully intended to take her inheritance, leave this cursed country, return to her beloved ranch, and stay as far away as possible from her dreadful sister.

Harmony bent to her task, only to be interrupted by a loud and angry rumble. Was that thunder she heard? A storm could hardly make this depressing place worse. It might even be a welcome distraction. She rose and crossed to the window.

Sure enough, purplish clouds roiled in the sky against a backdrop of gray. Another boom of thunder rolled across the woodlands. Harmony didn't hear her door open.

"Busy as usual, I see," came the sound of her sister's voice behind her. Harmony turned on her heel.

It had actually been better when Agatha had locked her in her room. The turn of the key had been a warning. Now, since Harmony rarely left her room and there was no reason to lock her in, Agatha simply walked in unannounced. It was not pleasant.

"As a matter of fact, I was writing a letter," Harmony replied evenly. "I got up to look at the weather."

"It is quickly turning foul," Agatha agreed. "Which makes Lord Farmington's visit here again today even more impressive."

"Please, don't start." Harmony turned her back on her sister and gripped the windowsill to keep her hands steady.

"Three days in a row, Harmony," Agatha persisted, voice rising. "Three days that young man . . . a *lord*, no less . . . has come to call on you, and you won't even give him the time of day. What's wrong with you?"

"Nothing's wrong with me." Harmony's temper rose along with the timber of her sister's voice. She faced her. "He found my ring, and I'm grateful. He earned the right to my appreciation, which he received. He's entitled to nothing else. Besides, I don't know anything about him."

"And you never will unless you march yourself down those stairs and take the time to *get* to know him."

"If you're so eager to get to know him better, why don't *you* go talk to him?"

Agatha's nostrils flared with indignation. "I've a mind to do just that!"

"Well, please . . . do it, then."

With a huff, Agatha spun and left the room. Harmony stared after her for a long moment. She had to fight to control her emotions.

Every day, for three long days, Anthony had come to see her, although she had made it very clear she never wanted to see him again. The fabric of the lies he had woven was too dense to penetrate. How could she ever possibly trust him again?

Furthermore, his games had been childish, not to mention dangerous. What kind of a man would practice such trickery? Certainly not someone she would like to spend more time with.

At least he had been right about one thing, Harmony mused bitterly. She *had* preferred the bandit to the lord.

None of her unhappy musings, however, could erase the feel of his lips on hers, or the memory of the heat that had seared through her veins.

And whatever in the world would he and Agatha find to talk about?

Overwhelmed at last by her curiosity, Harmony cautiously opened the door. When she saw the corridor was deserted, she ran for the stairs.

⤜⤛⤜

"I'm so sorry to hear your sister is . . . under the weather . . . again." Anthony smiled to cover the sting of disappointment. He was not fooled in the least by the excuse. "Please tell her I hope she recovers soon."

"Oh, I will. I certainly will, Lord Allen. But won't you sit down and have a cup of tea with me before you leave?"

Anthony eyed the uncomfortable-looking parlor furniture. "I haven't the time for tea, thank you. I'm leaving on the morrow and have to ride to London to finish up some business before I go. But I'll stay for a few minutes," he finished politely.

Harmony, concealed behind the door in Mrs. Rutledge's usual listening post, pressed a hand to her mouth. Anthony was leaving tomorrow? Something unpleasant stirred in the pit of her stomach.

"When you leave tomorrow, you'll be going north, I understand," Harmony heard her sister say.

"Yes, indeed. I'll be leaving London early. It's quite a distance."

Early? Then he wouldn't call again. Harmony

closed her eyes and pressed against the wall to keep from rushing into the parlor.

"Where, exactly, is your home?" Agatha queried.

"Almost on the Scottish border."

"Near which town, I mean," Agatha persisted.

"Near a lake, actually," Anthony replied smoothly. "The prettiest lake in the north of England."

"How nice for you." Agatha smiled and folded her hands in her lap. "Might I inquire if you have family?"

"Of course you may. And I'll tell that I do. My father passed on, but my mother lives in a cottage on the estate." Anthony chuckled. "She says she prefers it to the drafty old house she had to live in with my father all those years."

"She sounds like a very practical woman," Agatha said approvingly. "Have you any brothers or sisters?"

Anthony shook his head. "I'm an only child."

"Cousins?"

"Distant ones, spread about the country. We're not a particularly cozy family."

I see. Well, neither was ours, actually. As you may know, my sister and our parents lived in the United States."

"Yes, I did know. It's an interesting country. I hope to visit one day."

Agatha sniffed. "I'm sure you'll find, as I did, you're far better suited to the British Isles. You're aristocracy, after all. Although . . ." Agatha tilted her head to one side coquettishly and smiled demurely. "I've never heard of the name 'Farmington' before. Not that I know all the lords of the realm, of course."

"It would be quite impossible to know them all, I'm sure." Anthony rose swiftly to his feet. "I don't mean to be rude, or abrupt, but I really must be on my way."

"Oh, Lord Allen . . . I hope I haven't put you off with all my questions!"

"Not at all, dear lady. I simply must be on about my business."

"Of course. Such an important man . . ."

Harmony lost the shape of the words when Anthony and Agatha left the parlor.

Tomorrow. He was leaving in the morning. She would never see him again. The unpleasantness rumbled once more in her stomach.

This time, however, it was of her own choosing. He'd been deceitful. She didn't *want* to see him again.

Good riddance to him.

As if to punctuate her last thought, thunder boomed directly overhead, followed by a blindingly bright flash of lightning. Harmony wondered if his coach horses had been frightened and run off with him. At the very least, he'd probably get a good soaking.

Harmony smiled.

Harmony was unable to see the front drive from her bedroom window. She could hear nothing either. But he had to be gone by now. His coach would be well up the drive. He was gone and she would never see Anthony again.

Whatever it was that rose in her chest was painful and made Harmony restless. It was no longer possible to stay confined in her room.

Once in the corridor, Harmony realized she had never even been in the opposite direction. She started up the long, dim hallway.

How many rooms did the horrible old house have? Harmony wondered. Why had Agatha bought such a place when there was only herself, Mrs. Rutledge, and a coachman who lived in a room over the stable? Surely she didn't have many houseguests. Who would want to come? Were all the rooms even furnished?

Curious, Harmony stopped and turned a door handle. It was locked and she moved on. She didn't try any others. It was just like Agatha to keep everything locked up tight like a prison.

At the end of the corridor, however, just before a second set of stairs, Harmony spotted a door that was slightly ajar. She approached it cautiously and tried to see through the crack.

Another sudden crash of thunder startled her, and Harmony stepped down onto the first riser. Then lightning crackled, visible to her around the edge of the door. It almost seemed to make her skin tingle. She edged forward again and put her eye to the crack.

The room was obviously a bedchamber. It was as gloomy as her own, though a little larger. The furnishings were also a bit more ornate, and there were various bric-a-brac scattered about tabletops. Harmony was about to move on when she heard someone humming.

The sound was tuneless, but it was humming nevertheless. Could it possibly be her sister? Harmony couldn't resist. She pushed the door and it swung inward.

With a gasp, Agatha spun around. She jammed what appeared to be a key into her pocket, and was obviously holding something else behind her back.

"What are you doing in my room?" she demanded.

"Noth . . . nothing, I—"

"Out! Get out!" Agatha shrilled. She made a shooing motion with her right hand and, when she did, Harmony saw she held a fistful of money.

Ignoring Agatha's order, Harmony advanced into the room. She leaned to one side to see around her sister and noticed an open safe built inside a commode.

"So that's where you keep all your ill-gotten gains," Harmony said dryly, amused by her sister's reaction. Anyone would think she had walked in on Agatha in her "altogether."

"It's not ill-gotten!" Agatha retorted. "It's mine!"

Harmony's amusement was fleeting. Agatha's re-action was almost scary. Her eyes bulged, red-veined where they should have been white, and her hands clenched into fists. Veins throbbed in her neck and at her temples.

"I'm sorry, Agatha. I didn't mean—"

"It's mine, I tell you," Agatha spat. "And it's going to stay mine. All of it. If you were smart, you'd let that Lord Farmington court you. You'd do everything you could to get him to propose and marry you, because your husband's money is all you're ever going to see!"

As was becoming usual whenever Harmony had an encounter with her sister, her anger ended up being the dominant emotion. It erupted and spilled over when the meaning of Agatha's words finally registered.

"You can't do that!" Harmony spit back. "You have to give me my inheritance when I turn twenty-one!"

"Oh, do I?" A sly look slipped over Agatha's features.

"Yes, you do, Agatha. You were only given the money to hold in trust until my majority."

"Well, that's not the opinion of my solicitor."

"What . . . what do you mean?" A sinking feeling held Harmony rooted to the spot, though she longed to flee and not hear what her sister was going to say.

"You always thought Daddy was so smart, didn't

you?" Agatha's fists planted themselves on her narrow hips. "And you always thought you were Daddy's girl. But Daddy's dead now. And Mummy. They aren't here to spoil you and coddle you and tell you you're the best and the prettiest. They're both gone, and neither one was as smart as they thought they were. Do you know why?"

Harmony, stunned, could only shake her head.

"Because they underestimated me, that's why," Agatha continued in a vicious, spiteful tone. "They never thought I was good enough, or smart enough—"

"Agatha, that's simply not—"

"Oh, yes it is. Just look how they named us! You were their 'little precious' right from the start. They gave the beautiful name to the beautiful child, the redhead. Nothing special for the homely little brunette. I never had a chance. Until now."

Agatha held up her fistful of money and shook it in Harmony's face. "According to my solicitor, the terms of our father's will are ambiguous. To make a long story short, the money is in my care . . . until I see fit to give it to you. Until I determine you are mature enough, and of sound and appropriate moral character, to responsibly handle your inheritance." An ugly crackle of laughter issued from Agatha's thin, pale, lips.

Harmony felt a chill run down her spine.

"It will be a cold day in hell before I think you have

any moral character at all!" Agatha shrieked. "Do you understand, Harmony?"

Harmony understood all too well. Her future was in the hands of a madwoman. She turned from her sister and started to run.

"That's it!" Agatha screeched in her wake. "Run, sister dear . . . run! Run to your lord and beg him to take you. It's the only way you'll ever escape . . .!"

Chapter Thirteen

Lingering clouds from the previous day's rain hung low in the sky. They pinked with the dawn, and by the time the sun had climbed above the horizon they began to tatter and fray. Rays of sunlight found their way down and glinted off the carriage's polished black sides.   .

The four matched bays trotted smartly along the road. When they reached the turnoff into the wooded parkland, their driver slowed them. He looked askance at the well-dressed man beside him.

"You're sure you want to do this?"

"I have to give it one more try, Sneed."

The coachman eyed the gentleman a moment longer, long face and sagging features seeming to pull farther downward. He shrugged. "Have it your way."

"Thanks. I guess I will." Anthony chuckled.

"You've spent too much time here already."

Anthony's smile faded. "I know."

"Someone's going to get suspicious if you're not careful."

"I know that, too." Anthony sighed. "But I still have to take this chance."

"Please tell me that if she turns you down one more time, we're going home."

"If she turns me down one more time, we're going home."

The coachman grunted and slapped the reins on the horses' backs. They quickened their pace and minutes later the gloomy house with its sentry lions loomed into view. Sneed hauled on the reins and the horses halted. Anthony climbed to the ground.

"Wish me luck, old friend."

"You'll be lucky only if she turns you down again."

"Maybe you're right," Anthony admitted. "Maybe you're right." He mounted the steps and knocked on the door.

Harmony sat in the parlor near her sister, heart pounding so hard it was almost painful. She had heard the knock on the door, and her sense of relief was nearly overwhelming.

Anthony had come back one last time. She knew it. It had to be him. Anthony had come back.

"You are lucky beyond what you deserve if that is, indeed, Lord Farmington," Agatha said tartly.

Harmony ignored her. She could hardly look at her sister after the confrontation they had had. Agatha's jealousy and greed had become monstrous, twisting and shriveling her soul. The situation was not to be borne.

Mrs. Rutledge's familiar footsteps clicked across the foyer. The front door creaked open.

"Good morning, Lord Farmington," the housekeeper purred. "How nice to see you again."

Harmony didn't realize she had been holding her breath until she heard the housekeeper's words. She was unable to hear Anthony's reply, however.

"You'll be polite, if you know what's good for you," Agatha snipped. "Remember what I told you yesterday."

"Believe me," Harmony said steadily, looking at her sister at last. "I'll never forget." She heard Agatha sniff huffily as she rose and left the parlor.

"I think Miss Simmons is in the parlor," Mrs. Rutledge said. "Let me tell her you're here and see if—"

"Thank you, Mrs. Rutledge," Harmony said, and moved past the housekeeper to the front door. She prayed the cool expression on her face belied her inner turmoil. "Good morning, Lord Farmington."

Taking his cue from Harmony, Anthony inclined his head briefly and politely. "Good morning, Miss

Simmons. I hope you're . . . well."

"I am very well, thank you. I seem to have recovered from my indisposition of the past few days."

"I can't tell you how pleased I am to hear it. Does that mean you would come out for a drive with me this morning?"

"I should be delighted . . . Lord Farmington."

Anthony crooked his arm and Harmony took it. She wondered if he could feel her trembling. She bit her lip, angry with herself for her reaction.

Anthony had lied to her. He had behaved in an unspeakable way. His trickery and deceit were beyond imagination. She should be furious, still, with him, not herself. So why did the mere touch of his arm make her tremble?

It didn't matter. All that mattered was that he had returned one more time.

The driver stood by the carriage door. Harmony remembered how she had winked at him, thinking him a criminal and a coconspirator of Anthony's. She hesitated at the small step that led up into the coach.

"I . . . I'm sorry," Harmony stammered. "When I . . . when I . . . winked . . . the other day, it was because I . . . well, I thought you were someone else."

Sneed looked down his long nose. "I quite understand, ma'am."

She had never heard him speak before. His accent

was not that of a lowborn or uneducated man. Harmony blushed as she climbed into the coach. Anthony settled beside her.

"Have you a destination in mind?" he inquired lightly. "Or would you simply like to drive a bit?"

"Would you mind if we . . . if we went back to that stream, by the willow?"

It was an effort to control his surprise and delight. "Of course I wouldn't mind." Anthony leaned out the window to call instructions to Sneed. A moment later the coach rolled forward.

"You realize," Anthony said, "that we'll have to walk down the hill? The coach can't get down there as there's not a road."

"I don't mind."

They rode in silence for a time. It was Anthony who finally broke it.

"I'm almost afraid to ask, but I have to. Does this mean you've forgiven me?"

Harmony continued to look straight ahead. "I'm not sure I can."

"Then why—?"

"Can this wait until we stop?" Harmony interrupted. "I want to talk to you. But it's not easy."

"Whatever you wish, Harmony."

It wasn't long before they reached the point on the road where the coach could go no farther. Anthony didn't wait for Sneed but opened the door and handed Harmony down himself.

"Just wait for us, please, Sneed. I'm not sure how long we'll be."

"Of course, Lord . . . Farmington."

Harmony had dressed carefully that morning, in a gown of yellow muslin sprigged with pink rose-buds that grew from green-leafed stems. Her slippers matched and made it difficult to walk down a hill slick with summer grass. Anthony noticed.

"May I help you?"

She feared his touch. It made it so much harder to think straight. But neither did she wish to land on her bottom and go sliding down the hill.

"Thank you."

He put one arm around her waist and curled his free hand around her fingers. He was entirely too close. At the bottom of the hill, near the willow, she promptly extricated herself from his grasp.

"We have to talk."

"So you said."

The rushing of the little river was musical. A breeze puffed, rustling the hanging boughs of the willow and blowing a long strand of dark hair across Anthony's forehead. He pushed it behind his ear and smiled patiently.

Harmony had thought it would help her to return

to this magical spot. She had felt so comfortable, and she was sure of their privacy. So why did she find it so difficult to speak? Irritated with herself, she cleared her throat.

"I want to be honest with you about why I came out with you today," Harmony began eventually.

"I respect your honesty," Anthony replied simply.

"Do you?" When Anthony remained silent, Harmony experienced a twinge of guilt. She reminded herself she had every right to question his honesty and forged on. "I feel betrayed by you, Anthony. But I have also been betrayed by my sister. Since she is my only living relative, and you and I are scarcely acquainted, I feel her betrayal is the greater. I am entirely alone in England but for you and Agatha. Therefore, I must now turn to you."

Anthony's expression remained perfectly sober and composed. "I told you before that I loved you. Whether you believe it or not, it is the truth. I would do anything for you, Harmony. You only need to tell me what you wish."

How she wished she could believe him. Perhaps just one little test.

"Yesterday you told my sister you had to leave because you had to travel to London so you could leave from there early in the morning to travel somewhere else on business. I had thought that meant I would not see you today. Yet, here you are. Did you lie to my sister yesterday?"

"To get away, yes. Certainly. I certainly did tell a lie."

Once again, Harmony cleared her throat, both to stall and gather her thoughts, and to hide the smile tugging at the corners of her lips. "You'll recall," she continued at last, "I told you my parents left my inheritance in my sister's care until I attained majority. Their wills also dictated I live with her until that time."

Anthony nodded.

"Well, I . . . I've discovered that Agatha has discretion over my inheritance. She need not give it to me at all. At least, so she told me. According to her solicitor the terms of the will were broad enough to leave room for interpretation."

Anthony knitted his brow. "Did the two of you have an argument?"

"How did you know?"

"You told me she hadn't believed you were kidnapped, that you concocted the event to extort money from her. That doesn't sound like something a loving sister would say. I imagine, in fact, that she's quite hard on you."

"You're so right." Harmony had to swallow back a sudden lump in her throat. "She's told me that she will never exercise her discretion to give me my money.

She says I haven't the judgment or moral character to handle it."

Seeing the tears well in her eyes, Anthony longed to reach for her, crush her to his chest, and make all the evils in her world go away. He also knew how tentative the moment was, how fragile. Beyond all reason, all hope, he had been given a second chance. He wasn't going to destroy it.

"We can fight her, Harmony," Anthony replied calmly. "I know people who can help."

"In the meantime, how and where would I live? I wouldn't be able to live with my sister if I brought the fight with her out into the open. And I have no money to live anywhere else."

"Harmony—"

"No." She shook her head. "It's only Agatha who thinks I'm lacking morally. If I were to accept *anything* from you . . . anything at all . . . what would the rest of the world think?"

Anthony dropped his gaze. "You're right. I'm sorry." He lifted his eyes once again. "But I think you have something in mind. Please tell me what it is."

Harmony curled her fingers and pressed her fingernails into her palms. "I told you I was going to be honest with you. Totally honest."

"And I told you I respect your honesty."

"I hope you still do when I'm finished." Harmony

looked away for a moment at the silvery water rushing between the sloping, grassy banks. She took a deep breath. "My sister told me the only way I could escape my dilemma would be to marry. As much as I am loath to admit it, she's absolutely right."

"Harmony, I—!"

"No." She pulled away when Anthony tried to take her hands. "Please don't say anything you might regret."

Anthony had to clasp his hands behind his back to keep from reaching for her again. He made a concerted effort to keep his voice as calm as possible.

"I haven't regretted a single thing I've said so far," Anthony said quietly. "I know, I understand, why you can't trust what I say. But it's true nonetheless. I love you. I'll marry you if—"

"Please, Anthony, don't say it!" Harmony put her hands to her ears. "Please," she begged. The uncomfortable lump had returned to her throat. She bit her lip until she tasted blood.

"I . . . I have feelings for you," she went on finally. "I won't deny it. But I can't trust those feelings any more than I can trust you. I . . . I want . . . I need . . . time. Do you understand?"

"Time," Anthony repeated slowly. "You mean . . . time with me?"

Harmony nodded hesitantly. "I won't lie to you.

If Agatha hadn't told me what she did, I would never have wanted to have anything to do with you again. But . . . here we are. You're my only way out of an impossible situation. The way my sister lives, I know I'll not be able to meet many other people. I have to rely on you."

Anthony felt as if he might snap, the tension was strung in him so tightly. "You want to go out with me to . . . meet other people?"

"Yes," Harmony replied. "I know of no other way. My sister said I should pursue you and get you to marry me because you are a lord, wealthy and socially desirable. I could never use someone like that. I could never be so dishonest."

Anthony winced as if he had been stung. It gave Harmony no pleasure.

"If you were my escort, however, with the entrée you have into society as a lord, I might—"

"Meet someone suitable," Anthony finished for her. It was difficult keeping the bitterness from his voice. "Someone who doesn't play . . . games."

"That's right." Harmony felt her heart might break in two. But she had to say it. What he had done was outrageous. And now she could say what else she had to say.

"Or," Harmony said softly, a tremor in her voice, "I might find that I am able to trust you . . . and my feelings for you."

Anthony didn't move a muscle. He wasn't sure he could. He wanted to savor the moment, make it last forever. Because every step he took from now on was going to be a treacherous one. The present, this moment, now, might be the only moment of happiness he would ever know with Harmony again.

Why was he looking at her like that? Had she said the wrong thing after all? Had she been wrong to believe, even a little, that he had told the truth when he had told her he loved her? Had she made a fool of herself?

Anthony had spent many hours hunting. He knew the look of a frightened deer that was poised to flee. He knew the exact second to loose his weapon.

Harmony had no time to react. One minute he was standing before her; in the next he had taken her face in his hands, gently, ever so gently. His eyes closed as he lowered his lips to hers.

It was as it had been before. She was burning. The instant his mouth closed on hers she became a pillar of fire. Quite against her own will, her own determination, she melted into the embrace, let her body sink against his, longed to feel the hard, masculine length of him.

It was over as quickly as a flame might consume a sheet of dry, brittle paper. Anthony held her at arm's length.

"I won't press you, now or ever," he said, voice husky. "I'll do exactly as you ask. I would do anything, risk anything, to bring you happiness." Although he knew the difficulty, and the danger, of what he pledged with all his heart and soul, he was powerless to do otherwise.

She could hardly catch her breath. She didn't even think about the meaning of his words.

"I . . . I think we should go back," Harmony mumbled. She turned before Anthony could reply and started back up the hill.

Chapter Fourteen

Like a very large dog, Maggie wiggled all over with delight when she greeted her favorite customers.

"Tony! What're ye doin' back here s'soon, me luv?"

"Hello, Maggie."

"An' all dressed up, y'are. Look at yerself!"

"Look at *yourself*, Maggie. Beautiful as ever." Anthony leaned over the bar and kissed the blushing woman on the cheek. She giggled.

"Are ye stayin'? Or did ye just come by t'give ol' Maggie a kiss?"

"It appears my business is going to take a little longer than I thought, Maggie. Can you put us up again?"

"You'll be wantin' yer same room, I expect." Without waiting for a reply, Maggie reached under the bar for a key. "You, too, Mr. Sneed?"

The man nodded, expression dour.

"Here y'go then."

Sneed caught the key Maggie tossed in his

direction and followed Anthony up the narrow flight of stairs. Once in the second floor corridor, he put a hand on Anthony's shoulder.

"Don't say anything, old friend," Anthony said quickly.

"Just tell my why. The world is full of women."

"Not like this one." Anthony opened the door to his rooms and stepped inside, Sneed on his heels. "I'm certain this one will prove to be the one I've been searching for."

"You're taking a very big risk," Sneed said when Anthony had closed and locked the door. "This is the longest time you've ever spent in this area."

"It's going to become longer still."

"Someone is bound to recognize you sooner or later. It will change everything."

Anthony sighed. "Maybe things are meant to change. Maybe the way I've been living my life isn't such a good idea after all."

"Might I say it's been highly effective?"

"You may." Anthony smiled ruefully. "I've been successful, I'll admit. I've gotten almost everything I want. Everything except for what I want most."

"I daresay you think you've found it now, however. Haven't you?"

Anthony nodded slowly. "She's worth the risk, Sneed. I've never met anyone like her."

Sneed lowered his gaze, then looked up from

under his ponderous brow. "The biggest risk you're taking is with the young woman herself, you know. How is she going to react when she finds out you've continued to deceive her?"

"I'll deal with that when the time comes, Sneed. In the meanwhile, I've got to make plans to accommodate the young lady's . . . wishes."

"For you to be her escort into society, you mean?" This time Sneed lifted his brows.

"Exactly." Anthony turned and gazed out the window for a long moment. "Contact Applegate, Hall, and Turner. I can trust them. Have them arrange a . . . an evening."

"Very well. And then?"

Anthony clapped the man on the back. "Then you can fetch our things upstairs, and I'll buy you a drink."

"A dinner party?"

Agatha smiled unctuously. "I thought I would give you the opportunity to be the first."

Lady Margaret Donnelly fingered the long ropes of pearls that lay across her ample bosom and gazed about at the opulent splendor of her parlor. With a feeling of immense satisfaction she smiled tightly at Agatha in return.

"His name is . . . Lord Farmington . . . you say?"

"Anthony Allen, Lord Farmington. Surely you've heard of him."

"I can't actually say that I have. Ah, here's our tea." Lady Margaret indicated a gallery table to the right of her plush, gold-brocaded armchair. "Set it there, please. I'll pour."

The maid did as she was bid and withdrew from the sumptuously appointed room, footsteps silent on the pale green and gold Aubusson carpet. When she withdrew from the salon she pulled the doors closed behind her.

Lady Margaret gave a single brief nod, touching one of her chins to her silk-clad bosom, and with a practiced hand, served tea from the elegant silver service. She held up a Limoges cup.

"One lump or two?"

"Two please.

Dainty silver tongs nearly disappeared in her meaty hand, but she handled the instrument skillfully and deposited the lumps in Agatha's cup.

"Cream or lemon?"

"Lemon. Thank you, Lady Margaret." Agatha held her pinkie out daintily to sip her tea. "Excellent," she pronounced. "No one makes it like you, Lady Margaret, I must say."

Lady Margaret made a satisfied noise that came

from somewhere deep in her overly generous bosom. "You're too kind. But tell me more of this . . . Lord Farmington."

Agatha set her cup on a small, gilt table and folded her hands in her lap. "Well, you're simply not going to believe how we met him," Agatha began. With undisguised relish, she described the holdup of the coach on the journey back from London.

"How horrible!" Lady Margaret exclaimed. "And a sapphire ring was stolen, you say?"

"From my poor, dear sister. Yes, indeed." Crocodile tears filled Agatha's eyes. They disappeared as she related Lord Farmington's fortuitous discovery of the purloined item. "Can you imagine?"

"Amazing. Absolutely amazing. Not to mention the luck involved. The scoundrel who stole it was not only base but clumsy to have dropped the ring. And how clever of Lord Farmington to go at once to the authorities upon its discovery."

"Yes. They directed him to me. I recognized the ring immediately, of course, and was overjoyed for my dear sister."

Lady Margaret had leaned forward in her chair, listening avidly. Her tea, unnoticed, had grown cold. "What happened then?"

"Why, I called Harmony to come and thank Lord Farmington personally."

"Very smart."

Agatha flushed with the compliment. "Thank you, Lady Margaret. It did seem the thing to do. My sister is . . . rather lovely. And Lord Farmington, well . . ." She rolled her eyes upward.

"Do tell me what he looks like, Agatha dear," Lady Margaret urged.

Agatha snickered. "*So* very well dressed. And *such* a fine figure in those close-fitting trousers. I could tell dear Harmony was taken with him at first glance."

"How romantic!"

"Quite. And Lord Farmington seemed taken as well."

"So he's asked to call, has he?"

Agatha gave a deep nod. "He has even, I understand, extended his business trip to this area in order to call."

"He's not from London, then?"

"Oh, no." Agatha shook her head.

"I thought not. As I said, I'm not familiar with the name."

"Nor am I. However, as Lord Farmington told me himself, he's from the north. A rather secluded area, as he describes it."

"I see. Well, that explains it, I suppose." Lady Margaret sat back. "Despite my husband's many lofty connections and wide social circle, one cannot be familiar with each and every noble of the realm."

"My exact words, Lady Margaret." The two women exchanged knowing smiles.

"A dinner party is just the thing then, I agree," Lady Margaret pronounced. She poured the cold tea into a dregs container and prepared herself a new cup from which she sipped with an exaggerated moue. "I'm grateful to you, Agatha, for letting me be the first to féte our visiting lord."

"The pleasure is mine, Lady Margaret, believe me." Smiling with heartfelt gratitude and contentment, Agatha touched the pearls decorating her barren, black bodice. Her jewels could in no way compete with Lady Margaret's, but things were beginning to look up in her world. Someday . . .

"I shall set a date at once and send over a guest list for your approval. Is that acceptable?"

"You're too kind."

"Nonsense. I shall look forward to it."

"So will I," Agatha readily agreed.

"And if all goes well . . ."

Lady Margaret left her sentence to dangle intentionally. If Agatha had been a cat, she would have purred. For the first time since her sister's arrival, a ray of sunshiny hope pierced the bleak, gray fog that had become her existence.

"Exactly, Lady Margaret. As you very well know, it's quite nice to have a nobleman in the family. And thank you so much for your help."

"Not at all, Agatha dear. Not at all."

Following polite farewells, Agatha took her leave. She had to force herself to walk slowly and sedately down the flower-bordered flagstone path to her coach. Charles, the coachman, climbed stiffly to the ground when he saw his mistress approach.

"Home, ma'am?" he asked when he opened the door and lowered the steps for her.

"No, I think not, Charles." Agatha paused, pale, narrow brow knitted in thought. "No," she repeated. "Take me into Millswich, to the library. I have to do a little research."

"Yes, ma'am."

Agatha settled into her seat with a satisfied smirk. Lady Margaret had been all too willing to entertain a lord, just as she had supposed. It was a shame, however, she hadn't heard of the Farmington title. From the looks of Anthony Allen, Lord Farmington, his dress, his coach, his manner, he was very highly placed and wealthy indeed. A little research would prove her out. Lady Margaret would be pleased to know the exact position of the aristocrat she entertained.

It would also be nice to know more about the man she hoped would soon become her brother-in-law.

Yes, it was absolutely the thing. She would find out exactly who Lord Farmington was, where he came from, what peerage rank he held, and how his title had come by its obvious wealth.

Chapter Fifteen

Harmony stared at the gowns strewn over her bed, their jewel-like colors brightening the otherwise dim and gloomy chamber. She reached out to stroke a velvet ribbon on an amethyst-hued bodice, and felt tears spring to her eyes.

Her parents had always been so very, very generous with her. She had been given everything she could ever want. Agatha was wrong to think that anyone had to suffer deprivation if they lived on a cattle ranch in the West. They had been members of a lovely and lively community with many a social gathering. There were trips to New York as well, and St. Louis. Harmony had led a gay and happy life and had never lacked for anything. Her trunks had been full of beautiful clothes when she had arrived in England, and her heart full of wonderful memories. It was a good thing. There would be no more of either now.

Harmony moved from the amethyst silk to a gown

of midnight blue. Her tears dried and a faint smile touched the corners of her mouth.

Lady Blue. The girl with the sapphire eyes. That's what the bandit had called her. The bandit who turned out to be Lord Farmington. Lord Farmington, who was going to take her in to London tonight for an intimate dinner with some of his friends. Whoever would have believed such a thing could be true, that it could actually happen? A dime novel come to life. A handsome bandit who turned out to be a lord. And she, little Harmony Simmons, on his arm attending an intimate dinner party in London.

A quiver of excitement tingled to the very tips of Harmony's fingers. She couldn't help it. Just the thought of being alone with Anthony on the carriage ride to and from London, on a warm and moonlit summer night, made butterflies swarm in her stomach. As much as she would like to, she couldn't deny that her feelings for Anthony were strong. She had told him she wasn't certain she could ever trust him again, but that didn't erase the physical attraction between them. Was it strong enough to overcome her lingering doubts?

Harmony didn't know. She did know, however, that she looked forward to meeting his friends. The type and character of a man's friends spoke a great deal about the man himself. The slightly wicked side of her also continued to enjoy the irony of the situation.

Harmony held the blue gown up to her breast and looked into the mirror. It was perfect. Her smile broadened.

Agatha had probably been absolutely right when she had said there seemed to be an instant attraction between her sister and the man who robbed their coach. The same man, the same physical attraction, that had so scandalized her, was now the most important and exciting thing in Harmony's life. Simply change the bandit into a lord and everything was all right, desirable even. If Agatha only knew!

Harmony chuckled bitterly to herself. Maybe she would tell Agatha the truth one day, merely to see her reaction. Although it might not matter at all. As long as Agatha kept Harmony's portion of the inheritance, she undoubtedly didn't care who Harmony married. To have a lord as a brother-in-law, even if he had momentarily masqueraded as a bandit, would purely be icing on an already rich cake.

But Harmony didn't want to think about that anymore. She glanced back into the mirror and ran her fingers from the low-cut bodice down to the pinched waist and flare of the skirt. She had small, diamond pendant earrings her mother had given her for her eighteenth birthday that would look elegant with the dress. Her hair would be worn up, of course, but styled into ringlets that would frame her face and lightly touch the tops of her bare shoulders. A touch of rouge to her lips and cheeks would complete the picture. A portrait of Lady Blue. She knew Anthony would approve.

And it was really all that mattered.

⌘

Anthony stood before the tall, oval cheval glass and gave his cravat a final adjustment. His eyes slid to the left and found Sneed's reflection behind him.

"If you have dressed to impress," the tall man commented dryly, "then you've succeeded admirably."

"Why, thank you, Sneed."

"Shall I bring the coach 'round?"

"Do you think it's time to go?"

"You know exactly what I think."

"Fetch the carriage anyway."

"I live to serve."

Anthony wasn't able to suppress his smile, but managed to contain his chuckle. He didn't want to give Sneed any more encouragement than was necessary. He watched the dark-clad man leave the room and returned to his reflection in the mirror.

Sneed was right. At least he hoped he was. Anthony regarded the tight black trousers of the finest material, perfectly fitted linen shirt, maroon and black cravat, and slate gray jacket. He adjusted the cravat one more time and ran his fingers through his shining hair. It was unfashionably long, he knew, and he should probably pull it back. But Harmony seemed to like it down, to brush off his shoulders with that sweet, small smile on her lips. Anthony smiled himself, in anticipation of it.

He wanted everything to be just right. He couldn't lose her, not again. There was not another woman like her. There was no one else who could lead this life. His life. Although, he had to admit, there were women who had thought they would enjoy his lifestyle. It did seem glamorous at first. But the glamour inevitably faded. It was the long periods of virtual seclusion, the "hiding out," he supposed. The endless charade.

He loved it; he lived it. It suited him. But women found it was not all they had thought it would be. Besides, Anthony mused, it was the lifestyle that attracted them in the first place, not necessarily the man.

With Harmony it was different; he knew it. He had known from the first moment. Although he was sorry that what he had done had damaged his potential relationship with her, he wasn't sorry he had spent the time and gotten to know her so well. He wouldn't have discovered how special she was, how incredibly spirited and individualistic. She was perfect for him. Perfect. Furthermore, he simply didn't think he could ever live without her.

He would have to move swiftly, however. Time was of the essence.

With a last glance in the mirror, Anthony strode from his room.

Harmony had considered sitting in the parlor while she waited for Anthony to arrive. She would have relished Agatha's disapproving glances at her neckline, knowing all the while her sister dared say nothing about it. Almost anything at all was permissible in order to snag a wealthy and aristocratic husband.

On second thought, however, she hadn't wanted to ruin her good mood. She looked forward to seeing Anthony. Despite all that had come between them so far, she wondered if she had, indeed, met the man she was destined to marry. Was this the man who, in spite of everything, she was going to fall in love with?

It was possible; Harmony couldn't deny it. The mere thought of seeing him again sent a shiver through her. When Mrs. Rutledge announced he had arrived, Harmony doubted she could stand and walk because her knees suddenly felt so weak. Short of breath although she maintained a sedate pace, she walked to the foyer.

"You look lovely. Absolutely lovely."

"Thank you," Harmony breathed. He looked absolutely lovely himself. She had to bite her tongue to keep from saying so. At her side, she heard Agatha clear her throat.

"You'll be home at a respectable hour, I trust?"

"Of course," Anthony replied smoothly. He had barely glanced Agatha's way. He could hardly tear his gaze from Harmony's face. "My friends are very important and highly placed people. They have busy lives and are not inclined to spend an entire night indulging in an entertainment."

If Agatha had caught the subtle rebuke, she seemed not to notice. Quite the opposite, in fact.

"Oh, yes, certainly," she tittered. "Don't worry about time. Don't worry about anything at all. Enjoy your evening."

Without further ado, Anthony crooked his arm and Harmony glided to his side. She walked on air all the way to the coach.

The days had lengthened. Light lingered and the perfumed dusk of England's summer evening fell softly. The world glowed with pink radiance as the sun finally set below the distant horizon. The interior of the coach became a rose-tinted, secluded island of magic.

"You smell wonderful." Anthony took a deep breath. "What is that perfume?"

"Gardenia."

"My favorite flower."

"Mine as well."

"Really?"

Harmony nodded. Why did she feel so shy? "Our ranch was too far north to grow flowers like that. But once, when we visited New York, my father bought some gardenias from a flower shop and gave them to my mother and me. I loved them."

"Too far north," Anthony mused aloud, still heady from the scent of Harmony's perfume. "Where exactly *was* your parents' ranch?"

Harmony forgot her shyness. She came alive as she described her former home and her family. The warmth and love of her parents; the great, wide plains of tall grass and the grazing herds, overlooked by the sentinel peaks of the distant mountains. Anthony listened with rapt attention and interrupted only to ask an occasional question. Like their day spent by the river, the time together was comfortable, easy. The rosy daylight faded and darkness fell. The countryside was left behind as well and they entered London's outer sprawl.

"We'll be there in just a few more minutes," Anthony announced.

Harmony returned abruptly to reality and experienced a tingle of nerves. "I . . . I hadn't realized the time had gone by so fast."

"Are you nervous?"

"A little." Harmony clasped her hands in her lap. "But I'm truly looking forward to meeting your friends."

Anthony was glad for the darkness that embraced them in the coach. He feared she might otherwise see the guilt etched into his features.

"They look forward to meeting you as well," he said at length. Anthony cleared his throat. "Although I'm a bit concerned about my friend, Edward Applegate. His health hasn't been all that good recently."

"Isn't that whose home we're going to?"

Anthony nodded, afraid to say too much. "He and his wife were kind enough to arrange this small dinner party so you could meet a few of my closest friends."

"How very thoughtful and generous," Harmony murmured.

Anthony remained silent. He was about to deceive her again and, while it had seemed a good idea at the time, he was currently having second thoughts. She valued honesty highly, as she should. And almost all of his relationship with her so far was based on a series of lies. He hadn't meant for it to happen, but he had made a bad beginning and then had had to run with it. One thing had led to another, and now here he was.

It had occurred to Anthony, more than once, that

he took a greater risk with deception than with the truth. But now he was afraid—afraid of losing her. Everything was working at the moment; she was coming around. She might, indeed, even love him, he dared to hope. He simply couldn't take the chance of overwhelming her with the entire truth.

One thing was absolutely true, however. He loved her. He would do whatever he must, whatever he had to do, to win her. And he had to do it soon, before his house of cards came tumbling down. He would go through with the plans for the evening, which had been oh-so carefully and painstakingly arranged.

"What a beautiful area," Harmony commented.

"It's known as Mayfair," Anthony replied. "And yes, you're right. It's beautiful. One of the nicest parts of London, as a matter of fact."

Harmony leaned forward in her seat for a better view out of the window. It was certainly different from the sights she had seen when she had first arrived in London. Even the area where their hotel had been located was not nearly as nice as this. She stared admiringly at the rows of stately homes, with their elegant front doors and pretty front walks. Gaslights flickered over well-dressed couples strolling through the summer evening, and smartly appointed coaches pulled by high-stepping teams passed by briskly.

Was this Anthony's world? Harmony wondered.

Was it something she might someday become a part of? The thought was oddly thrilling.

"Here we are," Anthony said as the coach pulled to a halt. While they waited for Sneed to climb from his box, he gazed at the lovely profile of the woman beside him. Before he could stop himself, Anthony reached out to caress Harmony's cheek.

The touch took her by surprise. She turned her head sharply, and Anthony withdrew his hand. But she did not want the physical communication between them to end. She captured his fingers and placed the palm of his hand once more to her cheek. She closed her eyes.

"Thank you," she whispered. "Thank you for bringing me out tonight, to meet your friends."

"Harmony, I . . ."

The coach door opened and Sneed was there. The moment had passed.

Hating himself, Anthony stepped to the ground.

Chapter Sixteen

The parlor of the Applegate townhome was similar to the sitting room in a luxury hotel her parents had once taken her to in New York. The furnishings were tastefully understated; paintings hung between the tall, narrow windows were obviously true works of art. Harmony was impressed.

"Your home is lovely," she told Mrs. Applegate when introductions had been completed. Like the room Harmony had entered, Nora Applegate was the quintessence of elegance. A tall, slender, and graceful woman with snow white hair, she appeared the embodiment of "class."

"How kind of you to say, my dear," Nora Applegate said in reply to Harmony's compliment. She took Harmony's hand. "I'm so pleased Anthony has brought you here to meet us. He said you are special. It appears he was correct."

Harmony felt herself blush.

"I'm just so sorry," Mrs. Applegate continued, "that Edward is unwell and cannot join us."

"Oh? What's wrong?" Anthony asked quickly.

"I'm not sure." Nora's perfectly smooth brow creased slightly. "He believes it's similar to an indisposition he suffered once while in India."

"Nothing serious, I hope," Anthony remarked with concern.

"Not at all. Although it has caused a change in our plans for the evening. But please . . . where are my manners? Let me introduce you to the rest of my guests."

Harmony was immediately charmed by the couple introduced as Mr. and Mrs. Jeremiah Turner, with whom she exchanged brief pleasantries. She was a bit surprised they were not titled, although unsure whether her surprise was because she assumed Anthony's friends would all be lords and ladies of some sort, or whether she simply assumed everyone in England was titled. Regardless, she was delighted to meet Anthony's friends. Jeremiah seemed so jovial and jolly with his impressive muttonchop whiskers and round, rosy cheeks. His wife was his opposite, as thin as he was ample, her complexion porcelain and her demeanor serene.

The second couple, Mr. and Mrs. Randall Hall, were well-dressed and well-spoken, if less outgoing than the Turners. Introductions complete, Anthony at her side, Harmony returned her attention to her hostess.

The alert and socially correct mistress of the house stepped right back into her role.

"As I said, due to my husband's indisposition, there's been a slight change in plans. Please sit down and make yourselves comfortable while I explain."

Harmony let Anthony guide her, with a gentle hand on her elbow, to a velvet covered settee. He sat beside her, while the other two couples and Mrs. Applegate sat to their left and across from them. A maid appeared with a laden silver tray and set it in front of Mrs. Applegate.

"I have sherry and a nice champagne," she said. "Harmony?"

Harmony chose a glass of champagne, as did Anthony. He caught her gaze and lifted a silent toast to her as drinks were passed out all around.

"Once again, let me apologize for my husband's absence," Nora began. "He asked me to apologize to all of you, but you in particular, Harmony. He was so looking forward to meeting you tonight."

"As was I to meet him," Harmony replied politely. "Please convey my wishes for a speedy recovery."

"Mine as well," Anthony added.

"Most certainly." Nora Applegate sipped her sherry. "Thank you."

"In light of Edward's illness, we've taken the liberty of changing your plans for the evening," said

Jeremiah Turner. His gray muttonchops quivered with the apparent effort to restrain his broad smile.

"My husband owns a restaurant," his wife continued. Her pride was apparent and she laid a pale, slender hand on his forearm.

"The finest restaurant in London, I might add," Randall Hall commented.

"Thank you, Randall." Jeremiah Turner beamed at the other man. "I hope you will think so as well, Miss Simmons, at the end of your evening. I've arranged one of the private dining rooms for you and Anthony."

"That's very kind of you," Anthony said. "But absolutely not necessary. We—"

"Now, you know I won't take no for an answer, Anthony, my boy. Go ahead, take your beautiful young lady, and enjoy yourselves."

Harmony didn't know what to say, and was glad Anthony did the talking for both of them. His friends had turned out to be nicer even than she had imagined they might be. They were warm and generous, obviously prosperous and genteel. She glanced at Anthony from the corner of her eye.

The caliber of his friends spoke volumes. Perhaps she shouldn't have been so hard on him. Perhaps he was exactly what he said he was . . . an impetuous gamesman who had seen no harm in his little charade as a bandit. He had not, after all, hurt or compromised her in any way. Harmony relaxed in the glow of the softly lit room, and in the warmth of Anthony's friends. Before she knew it, her champagne glass was empty and it was time to leave.

Amidst the farewells, Harmony found the courage to ask, "Will you all be joining us? It would make for such a merry evening."

Were there meaningful, if enigmatic, glances exchanged between the room's occupants? Jeremiah Turner even cleared his throat, fisted hand pressed to his lips. Harmony looked sideways and up at Anthony.

His face was expressionless, although she had thought he might echo her inquiry, or assure her either they were all, indeed, dining together, or had made other arrangements. It was Mr. Turner, instead, who replied.

"You are most considerate, Miss Simmons, but please rest assured that as soon as I learned of Mr. Applegate's indisposition, I made arrangements to have dinners delivered to our residences. All will be provided for. And again, thank you for your thoughtfulness."

"Thank you so much for coming," Nora Applegate said as the group moved as one into the foyer. "It was a pleasure to meet you. And let me add that I also commend your polite consideration. Perhaps some other time we may all get together to dine. Tonight, however, do enjoy your private evening at Mr. Turner's most excellent establishment."

"Yes, do enjoy the food," Jeremiah chimed in. "And make sure you eat plenty of it!"

Something was going on. Harmony just knew it. But even as she sensed it, she chided herself. Everyone had been so pleasant and genuine, and she was, after all, getting to spend the evening alone with Anthony. She should relax and enjoy it.

"I hope you don't mind this change in plans," he said, guiding Harmony down the front path, arm linked through hers.

"Of course I don't," Harmony replied promptly. "I'm merely sorry for Mr. Applegate's illness. I do hope it's truly not serious."

Anthony looked away for a moment and cleared his throat. "I'm sure he'll be just fine. Nora wouldn't have had us over at all if her husband was in any real trouble."

"What about you?" Harmony paused on the carriage step. "You don't mind, do you?"

"Mind? Mind having a romantic dinner alone with the most beautiful and charming woman in the world?"

"Oh, Anthony . . ."

"Go on. Get in. Let me take you to dinner and I'll show you how much I mind."

Aglow from the company and the glass of champagne, Harmony allowed herself to appreciate her surroundings. The parts of London she was currently seeing were beautiful. Romantic as well, bathed in the light from the streetlamps, sidewalks lined with trees fully leafed in their summer foliage. Romantic—or so she imagined—couples strolling side by side. She did not mind when Anthony reached across the space between them and took her hand.

"May I ask what you're thinking?" he queried softly.

Harmony hesitated. She wanted to say something nice to him. She had begun to feel guilty about some of the things she had said to him the day by the river.

"I . . . I want you to know that when I told you I wanted to meet someone suitable, I . . . I mean . . . well, I guess I already have."

She couldn't look at him, although she could feel the heat of his gaze on the side of her face. The grip on her hand tightened.

When she didn't turn his way, Anthony allowed his eyes to close for an instant. Was his plan working? Would it continue to go as smoothly as it had so far? He could only pray. He had no time to lose, and could not bear to lose Harmony.

The edifice of London's finest restaurant was

modest. It appeared as nothing more than an elite town house such as they had just visited in Mayfair. When the door opened, however, Harmony stepped into another world.

The main room was paneled in gleaming wood of a cherry hue. A crystal, teardrop chandelier flickered with the light of dozens of candles, and silver candle-sticks graced each white-clad tabletop, along with a single rose in a crystal vase. A low murmur of voices rose above the clink of flatware against porcelain. It momentarily hushed when the couple, escorted by the restaurant host, walked through the room.

All eyes were upon them. Anthony hung his head and coughed discreetly into his hand. Despite his pre-caution, however, he watched a pair of eyebrows rise on a familiar face. He raised his hand to his nose to scratch a nonexistent itch.

"This way, sir."

The host gestured to a door leading out of the room and Anthony hurried through it, shepherding Harmony in front of him.

"Mr. Turner reserved our best private dining area for you, sir. I hope it meets with your approval."

Anthony surveyed the chamber they had entered. It was similar to the main dining area, though much smaller, having only a single table. Rich red velvet ma-terial covered the banquette seat that curved around half the diameter of the table, which was set with a variety of cut-crystal goblets and glasses, sterling flatware, and silver-rimmed Limoges dinnerware. A bowl full of creamy roses sat in the center of the table, with a silver candelabrum on either side. A bottle of champagne reclined in an iced bucket, and the perfume of an English summer garden wafted through an open casement window.

"Very nice," Anthony pronounced.

"I'm glad it's to your liking, sir. May I?"

Anthony nodded and the host pulled the table a little to one side. Harmony took her cue and sat on the banquette. The host pulled the table to the other side, and Anthony slid into his seat. The *maitre d' hote* glanced at the champagne, and Anthony nodded once again.

Harmony watched with interest as the host poured a small quantity of a fragrant red liqueur into the bottom of the two champagne glasses, then filled them with champagne. He placed a raspberry in each and served them.

"To you." Anthony raised his glass to Harmony's while the host discreetly withdrew, closing the door behind him. "And to our evening."

It was magical. Everything was magical. Harmony sipped the raspberry-flavored aperitif and inhaled the summer scents drifting in the window. Gauzy curtains lifted in a passing night breeze. Was this really happening? Was she really here? Or was she caught once more in the stuff of a dream?

"I . . . I think you should pinch me."

Anthony set his glass down. "Pinch you? Why?"

"It's all so lovely, Anthony. Everything. Your friends are so nice. Now all . . . all this."

"You're happy, then?"

"Oh . . . oh, yes."

"Good. It's what I wanted. All I care about." Anthony took Harmony's hand in both of his and raised it to his lips. His eyelids closed as he pressed a kiss into the palm of her hand, and Harmony noticed how long and black his lashes were against his cheeks. Her heart seemed to swell within her breast.

There was a light tap on the door. Anthony called permission to enter.

A liveried waiter appeared with a laden silver tray. He set it on the table before them, and Harmony was not able to suppress her gasp of delight.

There was seafood of every description: a pair of lobsters, shrimp and crayfish, grilled scallops, paper-thin slices of cured salmon with a garnish of finely chopped onions, clams, raw oysters, and whelk.

"Please tell me I'm not expected to eat all this!"

"Just eat what you like. As little or as much as you like." Anthony plucked a shrimp from the platter and fed it to her. "Bear in mind it's only the first course."

Harmony groaned. The waiter whisked away the champagne glasses and filled another set of glasses with a pale white wine. An instant later he was gone.

Anthony tasted the wine. "I think you'll like this. It's a Sancerre and goes well with the seafood. Particularly with the little purple sea snails I love so much, although none were available tonight. I apologize, my love."

The side of his mouth that made his smile so adorably crooked was twitching the tiniest bit. He was up to something. *All right*, Harmony said to herself, trying not to react to Anthony's incipient smile, *I'll go along with it.*

"Purple sea snails? I've never even heard of such a thing. Where did you ever eat a purple sea snail?"

The smile broke through. "A coastal town in northern France, Honfleur. I sat at a little outdoor table right by the docks and watched the fishermen on their boats empty their nets onto the wharf. Piles and piles of tiny purple snail shells. Chefs from the seafood restaurants around the water bought what they wanted on the spot. They simply couldn't be any more fresh."

Harmony's delighted giggle erupted unexpectedly. "But . . . but how does one *eat* a tiny purple sea snail?"

"Ah, I'm glad you asked." Anthony took time out to extract the succulent white meat from a cracked lobster claw. "With a tiny little pick."

Harmony didn't have to ask another question.

Her expression said it all.

"You hold the shell like this." Anthony demon-strated with the thumb and forefinger of his left hand. "Then you take the tiny little pick and quickly—before the snail can pull his little door shut—you stab him, pull him out, and pop him in your mouth."

Harmony felt her jaw drop. There was nothing she could do about it. Anthony laughed out loud.

"The little door," he explained, "is called an oper-culum, and it's what the snail uses to lock his house up tight to keep out the predators. Like me."

"Oh, Anthony!"

He watched the shining curls touching the tops of her shoulders quiver with the effort to suppress her mirth. Enchanted, he kissed the exposed flesh at the juncture of shoulder and neck.

The touch sent a shiver through Harmony's entire body. Now she was not only trembling with laughter but with goose bumps and prickly skin. In an effort to regain control, she took a sip of wine.

"So, do you like it? The wine, I mean?"

Harmony nodded, took a bite of lobster tail, and another sip of wine. Anthony was right. The wine and seafood were a perfect pairing, but she ate and drank sparingly, having no idea how many courses there might be. Furthermore, Anthony's nearness and the intensity of his gaze was intoxicating enough, and doing something peculiar to her stomach. She watched him pick up a raw oyster, tilt his head back, and let it slide into his mouth. She licked her lips.

"Have you ever had one?" Anthony asked.

Harmony could only shake her head.

"Would you like to try?"

"I . . . I'm not sure. If I do, are you going to make me . . . um . . . make me stab and eat a live sea snail, too, someday?"

"I would never make you kill your own food. These oysters, however, are merely raw, not alive." Chuckling, Anthony picked up a half shell. His brow quirked. Harmony nodded almost imperceptibly.

"Now remember, simply swallow, don't chew. Are you ready?"

Another nod.

Anthony smiled encouragingly. Harmony tilted her head, opened her mouth, and closed her eyes.

The sensation was amazing and surprisingly sensual. Harmony's eyes popped wide open. Anthony laughed.

"Another?"

"I think one was enough, thank you."

The platter of seafood was diminished but not done when the waiter reappeared. He took away every item that had been used and within moments a second waiter arrived and set down cunning little crystal cups in the shape of flower blossoms. Each held a small scoop of what appeared to be shaved ice, a rarity in winter, much less summer.

"To cleanse the palette," Anthony explained. "Champagne-flavored, I believe."

His culinary knowledge was as impressive as the dinner being served. Anthony continued to surprise and delight her. It no longer seemed so strange to her that he had masqueraded as he had, or done the things he had done to get to know her. He was a multilayered and complex man.

Harmony gazed over at him, at the angular lines of his face softened in the candlelight, the straight, shining hair brushing the tops of his shoulders, and knew in her heart that she had forgiven him entirely.

"You're looking thoughtful again," Anthony said as the interim course was removed by the silent waiter.

"I have a lot to think about, I suppose," Harmony murmured.

"Good things, I hope."

"Yes. I hope so, too."

The second waiter entered with a large tray covered by a silver dome, as the first uncorked and decanted a bottle of red wine. He poured a measure in still another of Anthony's glasses, one with a larger bowl than the white wine glasses, and waited for a nod of approval. When it came, he filled both glasses.

"A Saint-Julien," Anthony informed her. "To go

with our Chateaubriand."

Harmony caught her breath as the waiter lifted the dome from the tray, but not because of the beauty of the dish's presentation.

"You remember, don't you?" Anthony whispered.

Harmony felt inexplicable tears sting her eyelids, and she nodded.

"Even then," Anthony continued, "barely knowing you, I knew you should have the best. Now I can give it to you."

"Shall I carve, sir?" the waiter asked politely. Anthony shook his head and the man departed.

Anthony got up from the banquette and poised a carving knife over the tenderloin. "And how do you like your steak, my love?"

Harmony smiled up at him. "I'm a cattleman's daughter."

"Rare it is, then." With an adroit stroke, Anthony severed the meat at its center and quickly prepared three thin slices. He arranged them on a plate with a selection of vegetables that had accompanied the meat and set it in front of Harmony.

"I had no idea you were so multitalented," she said.

"You simply bring out the best in me. I'm a changed man since I've met you."

They ate for a few minutes in silence. The wine Anthony had selected complemented the meal superbly and everything was cooked to perfection. The curtains billowed in another fitful stirring of the night wind, and the faint, faraway sound of someone playing classical piano came to their ears. Harmony arranged her knife and fork on her plate and sighed.

"Are you quite content, my love?"

Harmony paused a moment, surprisingly unsure what to say. Mere words didn't seem to be enough. How did one thank someone for . . .? Harmony cocked her head to one side.

What Anthony had given her was more, far more, than an introduction to his friends and an incredibly excellent and delicious dinner. He had given her warmth, and light, and . . . *hope*. With a shudder, Harmony recalled Agatha's dark and dank manor house. The memory made her cold, so cold. She swiftly forced her thoughts back to the present, and her body warmed at once.

"Harmony?" Anthony prompted. "Are you all right? Is *every*thing all right?"

"Oh, yes. Very." Words would have to do after all. "I merely find myself quite unable to thank you for all of this. Anthony, it's been . . . incredible. Every bit of it. The food, the wine, the room . . ."

Anthony stopped her with a finger to her lips. "The best is yet to come."

"Oh, no. Oh, Anthony, I couldn't. *I can't!*"

"Just wait and see."

As if on cue, the duo of waiters appeared. The dinner remains were removed, the table freshened, champagne poured from a new bottle, and something in a covered dish was placed before them. The waiters retreated.

In spite of herself, Harmony's curiosity was aroused. "What is it?"

Anthony removed the top from the dish and spooned something into a crystal bowl. It had the appearance of chocolate satin.

"Mousse," Anthony said. "Have you had it before?"

"I've never even heard of it."

Anthony captured some on a spoon and offered it to her.

Harmony hugged her stomach. "I can't . . . I'm sorry . . . I'm so full!"

Anthony popped the spoon into his own mouth and sucked it clean. "Mmmmm. You don't know what you're missing."

It did look good. "Well, maybe just a taste."

Anthony abandoned the spoon and dipped his finger into the chocolate. He offered it to her.

Nothing in Harmony's experience had prepared her for a night like this. Nothing in her experience had ever prepared her for a man like Anthony. It seemed perfectly right and natural to simply part her lips and accept his gift.

The chocolate was as smooth as silk. The sensation of her lips wrapped around Anthony's finger was delicious. Slowly, slowly, he withdrew it.

"Do you like it?" he murmured.

"It's sinful."

"Exactly." Anthony smiled his crooked smile. "Would you like another taste?"

Harmony could barely manage to nod. Something hot and liquid seemed to be moving downward from her belly to her groin.

Anthony dipped his finger back into the chocolate and then brought it to her mouth. This time, however, he merely dabbed the chocolate on her lower lip.

"Oops," he whispered. His tongue flicked out and licked at her lip.

The molten liquid continued downward into Harmony's legs. She could scarcely breathe. She was totally unable to take her eyes from Anthony's mouth. She watched him slowly, languorously, run his tongue over his lips.

"Another?" he breathed.

Harmony didn't respond. She didn't need to. Anthony placed another spot of chocolate on her lip. His face drew near. Long, dark, silky hair caressed his cheeks and framed the angular planes of his face.

She waited for the warm caress of his tongue. Her

eyes closed of their own accord. Anthony's lips fastened on her mouth.

All restraint left her in an instant. With a small cry of passion that issued from somewhere deep within her breast, Harmony threw her arms around Anthony's neck and drew him against her. Her breasts throbbed and ached where they were pressed to his chest, and the liquid fire continued to course through her limbs. At last, unable to breathe, she pulled away.

"Are you ready to leave?" Anthony asked in a hoarse voice.

"I want to be alone with you," Harmony whispered. She couldn't believe she had said it. She couldn't believe how passionately she meant it.

"Your wish is my command, my love." Anthony rose from the table and held out his hand to her. "Our carriage awaits."

Chapter Eighteen

Anthony escorted Harmony from the restaurant as swiftly as he was able, glad of the excuse to hurry through the main dining salon. He kept his head down and his hand on Harmony's waist. Sneed, parked a distance down on the curb, moved the carriage forward as soon as he saw them emerge from the building. Anthony motioned for him to stay up in the box and handed Harmony into the coach himself. They had barely begun to move when he turned to her on the seat beside him.

"Harmony," he breathed. "Harmony, my love." Her hair, pinned at the crown of her head to fall in cascading copper spirals to her shoulders, was bathed in the lambent moonlight. Her cheeks were flushed with the heat of her need for him, and her eyes glinted, gemlike. Her breasts heaved with her rapid breathing and strained against the material of her midnight blue gown. He touched the rising swell of them and felt the heat rise to his own face.

It had all seemed so impossible. Yet here it was, the future, the best thing that would ever happen to him, right within his grasp. Harmony wanted him. But did she trust him? Could she love him? He had so little time to win her, before she eventually discovered the truth. He *had* to make her love him so she would not ever want to leave him, no matter what.

But how? What was the right thing to do? Harmony wanted him and he wanted her more than anything he had ever wanted in his life. He might throw caution to the wind and give her what she wanted, what they both wanted. But was it too soon? Would it destroy the foundation he had built so carefully, so painstakingly?

Anthony managed to tear his gaze from the bodice of Harmony's gown and pull her against him protectively when the coach bounced through a pothole in the street. He continued to hold her tightly and rested his chin on the top of her shining head. Her perfume caressed his senses. He closed his eyes.

Nothing had ever felt so wonderful as to be held like this in Anthony's arms. Harmony never could have imagined it was possible to feel this way. She felt so safe, so protected. Nothing outside the circle of Anthony's arms existed. She tried to remember how they had met, how he had tricked her, lied to her. But it didn't seem to matter any longer. All that mattered was that this delightful dream go on forever.

The carriage moved inexorably forward, however. In too short a time she would be back at her sister's home. The warm and rosy glow that surrounded and embraced her would be leeched away by the cold and stony atmosphere of Agatha's prison. Harmony didn't want it to happen. Not now. Not yet. Not when she was only beginning to know what it was like to allow Anthony to love her.

Anthony didn't want the moment to end, didn't want to release Harmony from his arms . . . ever. So it was with misgiving that he felt her stir in his arms. In response he held her tighter.

"Anthony," Harmony whispered.

He bent his head to her, lips nearly brushing her cheek. "What is it, my love?"

My love. Something churned in Harmony's stomach. She turned her face into his neck and inhaled the clean, masculine fragrance of him. Unbidden came the memory of his tongue licking the chocolate from her lip, and she quivered.

"Anthony, I . . . I don't want this to end," Harmony murmured at last, surprised she had been able to find her tongue at all. The instant the words were out, however, she feared she had been too bold, too forward. What must Anthony think of her? In the next heartbeat she found out.

"You have only to say the word," Anthony sighed, "and it will go on forever."

What did he mean? Harmony's heart skipped a beat. No, it couldn't be. It was too soon, too soon for both of them. He only meant the magic of the evening.

"I don't want to go back to Agatha's house. Not yet. Please."

"Where would you like to go, my love?"

"Oh, Anthony, I don't know!" Harmony pushed away from him slightly to look up into his face. His eyes glittered darkly in the reflected moonlight. A suggestion of his crooked smile lifted one corner of his handsome mouth. Lightning coursed, white-hot, from the center of her breast to the secret, sacred spot between her legs.

"I think I know just the place," Anthony replied finally. He leaned forward and called a brief instruction to Sneed. When he sat back, Harmony melted against him again, and he wondered at the chance he was taking.

She wanted him. He knew, certainly, that he wanted her more than he had ever wanted anything. But what would happen if he gave in to her? Would he lose what he had gained? The question, and the need, tortured him.

In a short while the carriage slowed and Anthony

knew he must make his decision. With every ounce of willpower he was able to muster, he straightened and held Harmony away from him as Sneed opened the door.

"Would you like to take a little walk with me?"

Harmony could only nod. She extended her hand to Anthony and let him assist her from the coach. Dazed as she was by his nearness, and her nearly over-powering desire for him, it took a moment for her to register her surroundings. She gasped with surprise and delight when she at last allowed the moonlit scene to fill her senses.

"Anthony! Oh, Anthony . . . where are we?"

"The gardens of the estate of a . . . a friend . . . of mine." Lying yet again. Oh, God, when would it end? When *could* it end?

"And they won't mind that we're here?"

"Not at all, I assure you." Anthony crooked his elbow and Harmony took it. Her eyes were wide and glittered with the inner fires of the gem they so closely resembled.

"This must be the most beautiful place I've ever seen!"

"I'm so glad you approve. Walk with me a way?"

"Oh, yes," Harmony breathed.

The path they followed was of carefully laid flag-stone, cunningly fitted together. It meandered and branched over what had to be acres and acres of gently rolling green hills. Copses of alder and ash studded the distant hilltops, cow parsley growing in their shade. Yew trees, branches streaming upward like smoke, lined the pathways here and there. Ivy crept along the ground and twined up the trunk of an oak tree. Silver and downy birch marched up the slopes like a silent and stately army. In the minivalleys between the hills were gardens of varied description: snapdragons and daisies; petunia and periwinkle; bluebells and violets. There was a rose garden, in the center of which stood a gazebo, covered with wild, climbing roses. Fragrant tuberoses lined the walkway to the gazebo. Swans and ducks, now still and peaceful for the night, slept beside small, scattered lakes and ponds. Weeping willows trailed their branches in the moonlit surface of the dark waters.

Side by side, arms linked, Harmony and Anthony walked for several minutes. It was as if they walked in a wonderland. At length, Anthony led Harmony to the rose-covered gazebo. They sat together on a stone bench in the perfumed shadows.

"Thank you for bringing me here, Anthony," Harmony whispered. "It's the perfect ending to the perfect evening."

"Was it really? Perfect, I mean?"

"The most perfect night of my life," Harmony replied honestly.

"Does this mean that you . . .?" Anthony swallowed. "That you forgive me for our . . . our bad beginning?"

It was almost as if he had read her mind. Over and over again Harmony had tried to summon the anger and betrayal she had once felt. It was gone, however, vanished as if it had never been. When she recalled their initial time together she did not experience dismay, but excitement. She would never be able to forget how he had looked in his tight buckskins, large, dark, expressive eyes shining above his kerchief. And when she remembered the night they had spent together, side by side . . .

"Are you cold?" Anthony asked with concern when Harmony shivered.

She shook her head. She was not cold at all. She was, in fact, burning.

"Anthony . . ."

He could almost feel the heat rising from her. He had known many women. He had never known one so completely sensual . . . and so completely unaware of it. He felt the stirring in his groin and knew he must do something soon, or lose control.

With a groan, Anthony stood and offered his hand to Harmony. She took it, but he did not miss the flick of her gaze over the crotch of his trousers. He watched her cheeks redden, and waited for his own flush of embarrassment.

But it didn't come. Instead he felt the full and awesome power of his manhood. Still holding Harmony's hand, Anthony pulled her against him.

She thought she might faint. Never had she experienced anything as overpowering as the desire she felt for the man who had pulled her into the hard, strong circle of his arms. She placed her hands against his chest. Not to push him away, however, but to feel the rhythm of his heart pulsing into her palms and fingers. Then his grip on her tightened and she raised her lips to meet his.

The electricity of their passion sizzled through both of them simultaneously. One arm around her shoulders, the other around her waist, Anthony unconsciously bent Harmony backward as his mouth, in his hunger, devoured her. Harmony became aware of the hardness of him pressing against her, igniting a flame that spread from her belly to her throat. Her hands slid away from his chest to slip around his neck, the better to pull him to her that she might be consumed.

For it was all Harmony wanted now. To be drawn into Anthony, into his body, his soul. To meld with him and become one with him, never to be separated again. Like molten metal, her body flowed against his.

The enormity of what Anthony felt lent an unaccustomed weakness to his knees. Trembling now himself, he straightened, Harmony still held to his chest, and he pulled his lips from hers. He couldn't let it go any further. He couldn't.

"Harmony, no . . . we . . . we can't do this. It's too dangerous."

Dangerous. The word echoed with surprising clarity in her head. Yes, Anthony was right. It was dangerous. Dangerous to feel this way about someone she wasn't even sure she could trust. Worse, she didn't care if she could trust him or not. She cared about nothing except the way she felt in his arms, in his very presence. Without fully realizing what she was doing, Harmony leaned into Anthony and raised her face to his, eyes heavy-lidded.

"I don't care," she murmured.

But Anthony did. He cared far too much to make a mistake at this juncture. It seemed she might love him. He couldn't risk losing that love, or the promise of it. He dared not exchange a moment for a lifetime.

"Come," Anthony said hoarsely. "Walk a little farther with me."

Unprotesting, Harmony allowed Anthony to lead her on down the path. Arms entwined, leaning against one another, they strolled beneath the moonlight. Despite the beauty of the gardens, they were aware of nothing but each other. Yet when the moon reached its zenith and began the downward half of its arc, Anthony forced himself to take stock of the situation.

"We should start back, my love," he said at length. "I don't want to return you too late."

"I never want to go back."

Anthony sighed. "I know. But you have to. I want to see you again, so I don't wish to incur your sister's . . . displeasure." He stopped abruptly and faced Harmony. "You do want to see *me* again, don't you?"

She wanted to tell him she never wanted to be separated from him. Instead, Harmony merely nodded. "Please," she whispered.

Breathing seemed suddenly easier. "I'll come tomorrow morning to take you for a drive. Harmony, we . . . we have to talk."

Harmony experienced a faint prick of alarm and her eyes widened. Anthony spoke again before she could form a question.

"I'm going to have to leave soon," Anthony said in a rush.

"No . . ."

"I've been here too long already. I have to go . . . go home for awhile."

"Anthony, why?"

"There are many things I have to take care of," Anthony replied carefully.

"But you'll come back?"

The lopsided grin was barely visible in the fading

moonlight. "Of course I'll come back."

She didn't want him to go. And she wanted to ask him a thousand questions. But they could wait, everything could wait, until she had kissed him again. Before he could react, Harmony captured Anthony's face in her hands and pressed her lips to his.

He was not going to be able to resist her any longer. He was not going to be able to stop himself. The mere fragrance of her stirred his manhood. Her touch, her nearness, was overwhelming. It was with a regretful kind of relief, therefore, that Anthony heard Sneed's familiar footsteps. He pulled away from Harmony an instant before he heard Sneed clear his throat.

"I'm sorry to disturb you, sir. But it's quite late."

Anthony did not miss the subtle warning in Sneed's tone. It had been a gamble to come here. Just as every moment he remained in one place was a gamble. He couldn't afford to overplay his hand.

"We're coming," Anthony replied. "We'll be right behind you."

Sneed departed at once. Anthony lifted Harmony's chin with a forefinger.

"Tomorrow?"

"Tomorrow."

Hands clasped, they followed Sneed to the waiting coach.

Chapter Nineteen

$\mathcal{I}$t had been difficult, the next morning, to pry her eyes from sleep. Harmony had vowed to rise early, however. She wanted to be ready the moment Anthony arrived.

From the armoire, Harmony chose a morning gown of pale blue. Anthony loved her in blue. And she liked it when he called her "Lady Blue." Perhaps she could persuade him to do so again. She secured her hair with a simple ribbon at the nape of her neck, applied a touch of color to her lips, and hurried down to join her sister at the breakfast table.

Agatha did not greet her. "You were out very late last night," she said without looking up from her plate when Harmony seated herself.

"I had a wonderful time, thank you for asking." Harmony unfolded her napkin across her lap.

"Don't be impertinent." Agatha looked at her sister at last, pale eyes flashing. "Tell me about the friends he took you to meet."

Harmony met her sister's gaze coolly. "They were very nice."

"Do they have names?"

"Of course they have names." Something prickled uncomfortably on the surface of Harmony's skin. "Why do you ask?"

"You're my sister," Agatha retorted sharply. "I'm responsible for you. Furthermore, you live in my house and I have a right to know where you go and who you see."

"I was with *Lord* Farmington. That's all you really care about, Agatha." Harmony watched her sister's expression register shock. She didn't care.

"How *dare* you?!"

"How dare *you* steal my inheritance?" Harmony let a grim smile touch her mouth as she watched a now-familiar and unbecoming flush rise to Agatha's face. "You've made it perfectly clear that you want me out of your house and safely away from my claims on my own money. You want me well married and gone. And it will be a feather in your cap to have your sister married to a lord. So, why the charade, Agatha?"

"I *never*!"

"No, you never did," Harmony continued calmly. "Which probably accounts for you being the way you are."

Agatha sputtered, but Harmony felt no remorse.

Merely pity. Perhaps it was because of what was growing between her and Anthony, the confidence he gave her in herself, but Agatha no longer intimidated her. Her sister was greedy, mean, spiteful. And pitiable. That was all.

"I ought to order you out of my house!" Agatha spit.

"It would be a pleasure, Agatha. I have nowhere to go, however, since I have no money. Nowhere to go except with Anthony, that is. And I'm sure you would prefer I was married to a man before I went away with him. Imagine the scandal."

"Yes, imagine it!" Agatha slammed her napkin down on the table. "And imagine the scandal if your *Lord* Farmington proves to be an impostor!"

Harmony felt herself grow cold all over. She watched her sister's eyes narrow. "What . . . what are you talking about?"

Agatha smiled thinly and, with her right forefinger, tapped a letter lying to the left of her plate. "This came only this morning, hand delivered from the Millswich library."

Harmony's gaze slid to the piece of paper, gleaming bright white against the dark mahogany of the tabletop.

"You haven't asked, but I'm sure you'll be interested to know what the letter says." Agatha picked it up and scanned the lines. "'In response to your request for information on Anthony Allen, Lord Farmington,'" she read, "'we find no such name listed in our archives.'"

A chill seeped into the very marrow of Harmony's bones. And with it a cold, hard anger. She leaned across the table and snatched the letter from Agatha's fingers. Quickly she ran her eyes over the page and began to breathe again.

"'Our information is only local, however, primarily for this county,'" Harmony continued to read out loud. "'Should you wish to pursue your investigation you would be advised to apply to the county of origin.'" Harmony laid the paper down carefully, and slid it back across the table to her sister. "I suggest you do as the letter advises," she went on, "before you refer to someone as an . . . 'imposter.'"

Agatha remained silent, eyes glittering.

"Why did you do this?" Harmony asked quietly.

The smug smile returned. "I've already told you. You're my ward, my responsibility. I have every right to know Lord Farmington's background if he wishes, as it seems, to court you. Furthermore," Agatha said casually as she pushed her chair back from the table, "it would serve Lady Margaret to know something of the gentleman who will be escorting you to the party she is giving in his honor."

Harmony's jaw dropped. "What?"

"You heard me." Agatha plucked an imaginary

piece of lint from the bodice of her high-necked, pale gray dress. "Because she values my friendship, Lady Margaret has kindly and generously offered to host an evening in order to introduce you . . . and Lord Farmington . . . to our neighbors and friends."

Harmony managed to stifle the retort that came immediately to her lips. If Lady Margaret was indeed a friend of Agatha's, no doubt the sole motivation for the party was to parade Anthony in front of the locals. She had half a mind to tell her sister they had no interest in attending such a gathering. But on second thought, the idea appealed to her.

Smiling to herself, Harmony imagined how handsome Anthony would look dressed for such an evening. She saw herself at his side, arm linked through his. She envisioned a sea of smiling faces, admiring the handsome couple. The dream was irresistible.

"When is this . . . event . . . to take place, Agatha?"

"Friday next."

Harmony did a swift calculation. The date wasn't far off, but Anthony had told her he had to leave soon. Would he return in time?

"I'll have to speak to Anthony," she replied at last.

"Is there a difficulty?"

"I . . . I'm not sure. Anthony told me he had to go away for awhile."

"Oh?" Agatha question-marked her brows.

"He's a very important man, Agatha. He has a great many affairs to attend to," Harmony said defensively.

"One does not say no to Lady Margaret," Agatha responded archly.

"I'm going to see Anthony soon. I'll talk to him about it." Harmony did not look again at her sister, but applied herself to her breakfast. In a matter of moments, she heard the sharp rap of her sister's footsteps exiting the room.

"Lady Margaret?"

"Yes. Lady Margaret Donnelly. A friend of my sister's, apparently." Harmony pulled her feet from the chill water of the little river, bent her knees, and tucked her toes under her skirt. She wrapped her arms around her knees. "Agatha told me only this morning."

"And what is the date?"

"Next Friday."

Anthony lowered his head and pressed a finger to his lips in a thoughtful expression. He knew he appeared calm to Harmony, but inwardly he quailed. "I told you last night I have to go away for awhile."

"I know. I remember." Harmony patted the grassy bank beside her and Anthony sat down. She laid a hand on his arm and looked into his eyes. "You also said you were coming back."

"I simply don't know if I'll be back in time, Harmony." He would have to make sure he was away. He couldn't take the chance of being recognized.

Yet when she heard his response, and he saw the expression on her face, the look in her eyes, something inside him softened to the point of melting. His life, this lie, was so unfair to her. He laid a hand on top of Harmony's.

"Is this very important to you?" Anthony asked.

"Well, it's not that it's important, really. I'm certainly not socially inclined."

"But . . .?"

Harmony withdrew her hand and wrapped her arms around her knees again. She stared into the water and wondered how much she should say to Anthony, how much of her longing to be with him she should reveal. Then she remembered how she had behaved in his arms last night and chuckled.

"What's so funny?"

Harmony turned her smile on the man beside her. "I was just thinking about how much I want to be with you," she admitted honestly. "I wanted to tell you that. Also that I would be so proud to meet Agatha's friends with you at my side. But I thought it might be too forward a thing for me to say. Then I thought about last night."

"Yes? And?" A smile tugged at the corners of Anthony's mouth.

"And how . . . 'forward' . . . I was."

"Is that what you were? Forward?"

"Yes," Harmony replied soberly, entering into Anthony's game. "Until you bent me over backward."

Anthony guffawed. He slapped his thighs, then turned on his side and stretched out. He motioned with a forefinger and Harmony lay back as well, facing him. His grin softened to a smile.

"I hope you know I would do anything to make you happy, my Lady Blue," he said quietly.

Something about the way he said that name made her insides seem all quivery, like aspic. To make matters worse, the sentiment he expressed brought a lump to her throat. She didn't think she could respond.

"You really want me to attend this party, don't you?" Anthony asked finally.

"Not if you don't want to, Anthony. Or simply can't be here." Harmony kept her voice low in hopes it would remain steady. "It is my wish also, you know, to make *you* happy."

So simple, so honest, so forthright. Yet it affected him like a blow to the chest. In some ways it was more powerful even than the way she had surrendered to him last night.

"You really do care about me, don't you?" Anthony

asked with wonder, his heart beating a peculiar rhythm he had never experienced before. He smoothed a strand of bright red hair from her temple. "You care about *me*."

So much so she couldn't tell him. But she could show him.

It was rare, in Anthony's experience, that a woman initiated a kiss. And when it did happen, it was almost always for reasons less than pure. This kiss, however, in the purity and gift of its innocence, rocked him. When the soft touch of her lips withdrew, he trembled, much like it seemed his heart was doing.

"Harmony," Anthony murmured, and stroked her cheek with the back of his hand. "My God, Harmony . . . I love you so much."

She closed her eyes. Did she love him in return? Was it true?

"I . . ."

"Ssshh." Anthony laid a finger to her lips. "Don't say anything. Not yet. I want you to be absolutely certain."

In her heart she was certain. It was her mind that was the problem. Could she truly trust him yet? Could she?

The answer to the question would have to wait a little longer. It was time to leave. Anthony had told her he had to take her home by midday to be on his way by early afternoon. They stood and brushed bits of grass from their clothing. Their timing was perfect, as Sneed appeared moments later.

"I'm sorry to intrude, sir," he said in his lazy, gentlemanly drawl. "But we must be off if you're to remain on schedule."

"You should have been born a dog, Sneed," Anthony remarked lightly. "You would have been so good at herding sheep."

Harmony laughed and took Anthony's arm as they left the fragrant shade of the willow and walked back up the hill to the waiting coach.

The return journey to Agatha's house was passed largely in silence. There seemed little to say after what had already been said between them. Harmony was glad of the opportunity to collect her thoughts.

The question of the party was still undecided. Anthony had not given her an answer one way or the other. In truth, she didn't mind at all whatever his decision might be. She had been honest with him when she had told him she was not socially inclined. She had been raised in wealth. She knew how to behave, how to act, if she needed to. She was grateful for the luxuries wealth afforded. But it was not, as she had observed in so many others, a thing that made her feel better about herself, or more important. She was who she was and she was comfortable with that person. She did not need the trappings of a social event to amuse her. She didn't need to be the center of attention.

It would have been nice, of course, as she had imagined, to be seen on Anthony's arm. She was proud of him, proud that he took an interest in her. But she had also been truthful with Anthony when she told him she wished for his happiness. If he did not want to go, or was unable, she would abide by his decision without the slightest regret or word of rebuke.

With those thoughts in mind, Harmony descended from the coach and climbed the steps to Agatha's front door. Anthony accompanied her, as usual, and Harmony expected Mrs. Rutledge, as usual, to open the front door. She was surprised, therefore, to see her sister.

"Agatha!"

"Yes, of course, Agatha," her sister replied with an edge to her tone. A heartbeat later she smiled ingratiatingly at Anthony. "Lord Farmington, how nice to see you again."

"My pleasure entirely."

"Won't you come in for awhile? Have a cup of tea, perhaps?"

"Thank you, but I must be on my way. I have to go

. . . home . . . to take care of some business."

"Harmony told me you would be away for awhile. Which is what I wanted to talk to you about."

In response, Anthony merely raised his brows.

"Did Harmony inform you of Lady Margaret's little get-together?" Agatha continued.

"Yes, she did, as a matter of fact. I'm simply not sure I'll be able to attend."

"Oh, but you must. You must!" Agatha tittered. "Lady Margaret is a scion of our community. It's so important that you meet her. Especially since you are . . . friendly . . . with my sister. Lady Margaret is a great friend to me, you know. As well as many others who will attend."

"Just out of curiosity," Anthony said, and tapped a finger to his chin. "Have you put together a guest list yet?"

"Why . . . why, yes. Would you like to see it?"

"I *would* actually. Yes. Just out of curiosity, as I said. I'd like to see if I recognize any names. Perhaps we have friends in common. It would be interesting to find out."

"Well, then, by all means, come in. Come in."

Bewildered, Harmony followed Anthony and Agatha into the morning room, where Agatha generally sat and answered her correspondence. It was the most cheerful room in the house. Most of the climbing ivy had been cleared from the mullioned window, the flowered drapes had been pulled aside to let in the sun, and the furniture was lighter. The seat of the chair in front of Agatha's escritoire was even covered in a cheerful, floral petit-point.

"Here you are." Agatha opened a drawer in her delicate, French-made desk and withdrew a sheet of paper that she handed to Anthony. He scanned it and began a silent debate with himself.

To attend the soirée, even though he was personally unknown to any of the names on the guest list, would be the biggest risk he had ever taken. His true identity might very well be unmasked. Was it worth it? To escort the most beautiful, charming, intelligent woman in the world? Spend more time with her? Have others regard them as a "couple"? Was there really any doubt?

"Very impressive," Anthony said at last with a slight nod. "There are, indeed, many important and prominent names on this list. None, alas, with whom I am personally friendly." Agatha's face fell, but Anthony smiled. "It will be a delight, therefore, to make their acquaintance."

"You . . . you mean . . . ?"

"I will be honored to attend Lady Margaret's party. I shall make certain to return in ample time."

"Oh, Lord Farmington!"

"But I really must take my leave now. Good day, Miss Simmons."

Still slightly puzzled, Harmony walked Anthony back to the door. At the threshold he took her hands and squeezed them.

"I'll count the hours I'm away, and think of you every moment," Anthony said in a lowered voice. "Don't forget me."

"How could I?" Harmony replied simply.

Anthony squeezed her fingers one last time, turned, and was gone.

Chapter Twenty

Anthony climbed into the carriage without assistance from Sneed and they started off immediately. Sneed kept the horses to a sedate pace until they were well away from the house. Then, at the flick of his carriage whip over their backs, the team moved into a brisk trot. It was the moment Anthony had waited for.

He tugged at his cravat, removed it, and threw it on the seat beside him. The morning coat followed, and Anthony loosened the top buttons of his shirt. Then he pulled up the window on the door of the coach.

He was a slim man, lean and hard, with narrow hips. It served him well. Anthony turned his back to the window, leaned his upper body outside, and reached up to grab the luggage rails on the top of the coach. Once he had a firm grip he flexed his arms and, like a practiced acrobat, pulled himself up and through the window. He swung his legs and hooked one over the rail. A moment later he was on top of the carriage. He ran forward and jumped down onto the bench seat beside Sneed.

"What took you so long?" Sneed asked.

"What's the matter? Did you miss me?"

"Every moment we're not together," he commented dryly.

Anthony laughed. "That's almost what I just said to Harmony."

"Why am I not surprised?"

Anthony did not reply, but reached for the reins. Sneed relinquished them willingly.

Disdaining the use of the whip, Anthony manipulated the reins to coax more speed from the horses. Soon they were moving at an even faster pace. Fingers deft and nimble, he guided the horses expertly through the twists and turns of the narrow country road, branches from encroaching trees slapping at the sides of the coach. At last they came to a fork in the road and Anthony hauled on the lines. The carriage came to a halt.

"This is where I leave you, old friend," Anthony said as he climbed from the bench seat.

"For how long this time?"

"I'll be back by next Friday."

"So soon?"

"I have a party to attend." Anthony watched

Sneed's jaw drop and ducked his head into the coach door before the man could say a word. He pulled a leather bag out from under the seat and extracted its contents. Then he stripped out of his clothing. Behind him, Sneed climbed down from the coachman's box.

"You have a 'what' to attend?"

"You heard me," Anthony replied without turning. He pulled on his tight buckskins. "I'm going to come back in time for a party."

"I see." Sneed watched Anthony fold the clothes he had just removed, tuck them into the leather bag, and push it back under the seat. "And we have considered the risks involved, have we?"

"We have." Anthony exchanged his highly polished and fancy black boots for a more comfortable pair of brown doeskin. "I've also seen the guest list. I know no one."

"Well, isn't that comforting?"

Anthony chuckled. "I know some of the names, certainly. Local landed gentry, by in large. Nothing to worry about."

"You hope."

Anthony straightened, looked Sneed in the eye, and widened his smile. "Yes, I hope. If not, well, as I've said before, she's worth every risk I take."

Sneed's reply was the barest arch of his bushy brows and an unusual, not particularly polite, noise that seemed to come from somewhere in the nasal area.

"I'd tell you to go on home for awhile," Anthony continued. "But by the time you get up there, it'll be time to come back."

"The accommodations at Maggie's are adequate."

"So glad you approve." Anthony took a few steps into the wood until he came to the chestnut mare Sneed had earlier tied to a tree. He patted her shoulder, untied her, and led her from the shelter of the wood. "I'll see you some time next Friday, Sneed."

"Shall I meet you at Bluefield? Or will you go to Maggie's?"

"I'll go to the manor first. I'll need the proper clothes, you know."

"God forbid you should reveal the real you."

"Yes, God forbid," Anthony repeated with a grin. "Thanks for everything, old friend. I'll see you next week." He whirled his mare, putting his heels to her sides, and in moments disappeared around the bend in the road.

Lady Margaret fingered the pince-nez that hung from a golden chain around her neck. With her other hand she tapped a Sevres porcelain plate, rimmed in gilt.

"I thought I'd use this set," she said. "And this set

of crystal." Lady Margaret waved a languid hand over the china and crystal that had been set out for display on the long, mahogany table.

"Beautiful. Absolutely beautiful," Agatha oozed. "Your taste is impeccable, Lady Margaret."

The ghost of a smile touched the older woman's mouth. She picked up a cut-crystal goblet and put it down again.

"Your guest list is most impressive as well," Agatha pattered on. "I showed it to Lord Farmington, and he agreed."

"Did you, now?"

"Oh, yes. He was interested in looking at the list to see if he might know any of your guests. He said that although he recognized several names, he knew none of them personally."

"Odd you should mention that. All the people I've talked to say the same about Lord Farmington. They seem to be familiar with the name, but can't quite place the gentleman."

"I'm having a bit of trouble pinning him down myself," Agatha admitted.

"What do you mean?"

Agatha told Lady Margaret of her inquiry at the Millswich library and their response to her.

"Did you write to the county of origin, as they suggested?" Lady Margaret asked.

"Yes, I did. At least . . . I think I did."

"What on earth do you mean, Agatha?" Lady Margaret demanded impatiently. Suddenly restless, she walked to the windows and began arranging the folds of the lavishly fringed gold damask drapes framing the tall, narrow windows.

"I mean, I wrote to three counties, actually. Lord Farmington never exactly told me where he lives."

"How mysterious."

"Well, yes, it is. Somewhat." Agatha smiled with sudden brightness. "I'm sure it will all be explained to our satisfaction very soon. And your party will be a brilliant success."

"Mmmmm. I hope so." Thoughtful, Lady Margaret strolled from the ornate and formal dining room into the adjacent salon. "The season is over in London and many of the people I would have liked to invite have gone from the area to their summer homes in the country." She stopped and looked around her, as if realizing where she was. "I'll have the staff rearrange the furniture so there will be a bit more room. What do you think?"

Agatha's face fell, but she quickly concealed it. "We aren't going to use the ballroom?"

"I hardly think so," Lady Margaret replied disparagingly. "The group is far too small, for one thing. For another, we still don't know precisely who Lord Farmington is. Or how important. Do we?"

"No, we don't," Agatha agreed under her breath. "But, believe you me, I am *going* to find out."

❧

Mr. Henry, the constable, looked up from his cluttered desk. "What?" he asked tiredly.

"There's been another one," the man in uniform replied.

"Another what, Jones?"

"Another robbery, sir."

Henry ran his hand over his bald head, as if rearranging something that had once been there. "Where?" he inquired at length.

"The McGowans, sir."

"The who?"

"The McGowans," the man repeated. "They're the new folks on the other side of the village."

"Oh, yes. Yes. Now I remember. An older couple, rather set in their ways, as I recall."

The officer stared down at his feet for a moment. "You could put it that way. Yes, sir."

"Well?"

"Well 'what,' sir?"

"The robbery, Jones!"

"Oh. Yes, sir. Mrs. McGowan apparently kept her heirloom family pearls in a cookie jar in the pantry.

They're gone."

This time Henry ran both hands over his head. "Might they have been misplaced?" he asked slowly.

"Definitely not, sir," the man replied confidently. "Mrs. McGowan, well, let me put it this way, sir. The queen herself is not more proud of, nor fond of, the crown jewels of England. Or more likely to know where they are at any given moment."

"I see." Henry rubbed his eyes. "Did the thief leave any clues?"

"Not really, sir. There were hoofprints up to the house and away, and the McGowans don't ride. They only use their horse with a cart or buggy. But there's no telling whose horse made the prints."

"Of course not," Henry responded irritably. He pushed back from his desk and stood up. He crossed the room and stood before a map that had been pinned to the wall beside the single window. With a pen, he made a mark near the north end of the village. "Here, Jones?"

"Yes, sir. Right about there."

Henry stepped back and surveyed the map. There were at least half a dozen other marks.

"He's making fools of us, Jones."

"We're not the only ones, sir," Jones replied. "There have been incidents in villages all around us."

Henry ignored him. "It started with Miss Simmons and her sapphire ring."

"But that was a simple bandit, sir, who struck right out in the open. You don't think—"

"I don't know what to think!" Henry snapped. "I only know that the residents of the village we're supposed to protect are having their valuables stolen right out from beneath our noses."

"Yes, sir."

"'Yes, sir' *what*, Jones?!"

"Yes, sir, they are, sir. Being robbed right under our noses, I mean. But we'll catch 'im." Jones grinned sheepishly. "It's just a matter of time."

"A very short time, I hope," Henry growled. "Because I haven't got much time, Jones. The citizens are demanding a warm body behind bars, and I had better produce one. Soon. Or else."

"Or else what, sir?"

"Oh, shut up, you idiot, and come with me."

Chapter Twenty-one

*H*armony leaned over and clipped a dead blossom with her pruning shears. She straightened, a hand to the small of her back, and looked around her with a glow of pride. Slowly but surely, Agatha's neglected garden was being transformed.

As soon as Anthony left, Harmony had sunk into a pit of despair. She did not realize how much she was going to miss him until he had actually gone. Then the full weight of his absence fell upon her. Anthony was gone. The light, happiness, and . . . yes . . . the love he brought into her life was gone. She had not realized how large, how important, his presence had become in her world.

Now she was virtually alone in the cold, forbidding house. She avoided Agatha whenever possible. Her sister's resentment of her was almost overwhelming. Indeed, it seemed Agatha openly hated her. And Mrs. Rutledge was an echo and a mirror of her mistress.

Bored and lonely, Harmony had found her way to the kitchen one day, and discovered an elderly, white-haired woman who evidently cooked all their meals. Harmony had tried to strike up a conversation, but the woman was both taciturn and hard of hearing. All she had been able to learn was that her name was Sophie, she was originally from Sweden, her husband had once been the gardener, but he had passed on some years earlier.

Agatha had apparently been too parsimonious to hire another groundskeeper. Harmony would have thought her sister would take pride in her home, her surroundings. But it was obviously not one of her sister's priorities. It became, however, a distraction for Harmony.

In the somewhat rundown stables, Harmony had found a number of gardening implements. She set to work at once on the brambly and overgrown mess that had once been a formal garden. Less than a week later, the results of her labor were dramatic.

Almost all the weeds had been pulled and the overgrowth trimmed back. The garden still had a wild appearance, but all the beds were neat and blossoms had begun to appear. Harmony had even uncovered the remnants of an old lily pond. She had cleaned it out and rearranged the decorative rocks around its perimeter. Two days of a drenching rain had taken care of the rest. Though the lilies were long gone, a small family of tadpoles now darted about in the shallow water. Wood pigeons, a greenfinch, and a pair of thrushes had found the oasis and came to bathe and drink. It was a pleasant area at the far end of the garden, out of view of the house, and it had become Harmony's refuge.

She sat down on a stone bench near the little pool, closed her eyes, and lifted her face to the sun. Agatha would scold her if she saw her. A lady's skin, her sister liked to preach, should never so much as be touched by the sun. The slightest coloring, even a flush to the cheeks, was unbecoming and bespoke of a lower class of person. Harmony smiled to herself.

She had once been nearly as brown as an Indian, and her deeply red hair—almost auburn, in fact—had acquired some blond streaks. She had worn a hat, of course, when she rode out on her horse through the vast pastures and into the mountains, but she was in the open all day, every day. On the yearly round-up when everyone—her mother, father, and all the hands—spread out to bring in all the cows and their calves, she had sometimes stayed out for days. She had barely used a comb, much less bathed or paid any special attention to her complexion. She had had only her bedroll, her guns, a knife, some coffee, bacon, hardtack, matches, a skillet, and a coffeepot. How different her life was now!

Harmony opened her eyes and stared in the

direction of the house, glad she could not see it. Her only moments of peace and relative happiness were found here, in the garden. Her stomach churned at the mere thought of returning to Agatha's house and encountering either her sister or Mrs. Rutledge. Back home, on the ranch, she had scarce known a moment's sadness or unease. What had become of her?

Harmony forced back the lump that tried to rise in her throat. Thinking this way, dwelling on the past, would do her absolutely no good at all. She had to think about the future. And not the three endless years until her sister's wardship came to an end. The immediate future. Anthony.

A quiver of pleasure ran all the way from the top of Harmony's head to the tips of her toes. She couldn't deny that she longed to see him again. She no longer *wanted* to deny it. Having never been in love before, she wasn't sure if she knew what it was. But if it meant wanting him as much, if not more, when they were away from each other as when she was in his arms, then perhaps she would have to admit she returned what Anthony professed to feel for her. Maybe, just maybe, she was really and truly in love.

The funny feeling returned to Harmony's stomach, but not this time because of dread. It was instead anticipation.

Only a few more hours and she would see him

again. Only a few more hours and—

"Harmony!"

Agatha's shrill and piercing voice dashed away Harmony's reverie and left her as cold as if a bucket of icy water had been thrown on her. She rose slowly, reluctantly, from her bench.

"Harmony! Where are you?"

"Here, Agatha. I'm here. I'm coming."

Agatha stood on the back terrace, arms folded across her thin and shriveled breast. She was clearly agitated. "What have you been doing?" she demanded sharply. "Idling away your time again sitting in the sun?"

"I've been working on the garden," Harmony replied quietly.

"Without a hat, I see." Agatha harrumphed. "And today of all days."

"Why is today special?"

"Don't be ignorant," Agatha snapped. "Tonight you will be a guest in Lady Margaret's home. Do you want to look like a common peasant who's been laboring in the field all day?"

Harmony refrained from comment. She ducked her head and moved past Agatha toward the terrace doors.

"Now where are you going?"

"I'm getting out of the sun, Agatha. Isn't that what you want me to do?"

"I want you to stand still and listen to me. I came

out here to talk to you for a reason."

"Which is?"

"Don't be impertinent!"

Harmony sighed. "I'm sorry if I gave that impression, Agatha. What is it you want?"

Agatha's arms came away from her breast and she planted her hands on her narrow hips. "I want you to get a message to Lord Farmington. At once."

"A . . . a message?"

"Yes, a message. That good-for-nothing driver, Charles, packed up his belongings and left. He didn't even have the courtesy to *tell* me he was leaving!"

Harmony refrained from comment.

"I want you to contact Lord Farmington," Agatha went on, "and let him know I will be accompanying the two of you in his coach this evening."

Harmony managed to keep her features expressionless while, at the same time, trying not to choke. "I'm sure that won't be a problem, Agatha," she replied evenly.

"Nevertheless, I want you to advise him of my situation. It is simply not to be borne!"

Harmony didn't move.

"Well? What are you waiting for?"

A peculiar uneasiness spread through Harmony's midsection. "I . . . I'm not sure where to send the message," she answered at last.

"What do you mean you're not sure where to send it?"

"Just as I said, Agatha," Harmony repeated, uneasiness growing. "I don't know where to send him a message."

"You mean you don't know where he stays when he's here?"

"That is exactly what I mean."

"That's preposterous. Surely he has a townhome in London, at least."

"If he does, I know nothing of it. Besides, for all I know, he might reside in a hotel when he's in London."

"Well, what *do* you know?" Agatha flashed. "Has he even told you where his home is in the north?"

Harmony slowly shook her head.

Agatha's eyes narrowed. "I find that very odd, Harmony," she said in a strange tone.

"Why?" Harmony replied abruptly, her defensive hackles bristling. "Anthony and I have many things to talk about when we're together. The precise location of his home, its official address, has simply never been one of them."

"Perhaps it should be."

"Why? Just to satisfy your curiosity? Why don't you ask him yourself when you see him tonight?"

"Well!"

Harmony whirled away from her sister and stormed through the terrace doors before Agatha could say another word. She didn't want to hear any more. In truth, Agatha had struck a chord.

Where did Anthony live, exactly? He had talked about his home in the north, his mother living in a cottage on the grounds, cattle and horses. She had imagined the rest: a handsome manor with sprawling, rolling farmlands. But it had all been created by her imagination, not by fact. Then she remembered Maggie at the inn.

Anthony's suite of rooms was quite comfortably decorated, much more so than she imagined would be the case in an average country inn. He even had what seemed to be personal items there, like the crystal decanter and glasses . . .

Was that where Anthony lived? No, it couldn't be. Anthony was obviously a well-educated gentleman; his clothes were expensive and well-tailored; his coach was the most elegant and well-appointed she had ever seen, and his team impressively matched and trained. Anyone who could afford any of those things surely would not live in temporary rooms at an inn.

Unless he was not who he appeared to be. Harmony exhaled a deep breath and felt her shoulders slump. She thought she had long ago banished any doubts about Anthony. She had believed his story of the charade as a bandit. The inn rooms could have many explanations. But how many explanations could there be for the clothes, the coach and horses? Even his friends. Surely Nora Applegate would never entertain anyone whose background she wasn't thoroughly familiar with. Nevertheless, doubt began to eat at her again.

Arriving at her bedroom, Harmony closed the door behind her and leaned against it.

Harmony brought to mind the night Anthony had taken her to the inn and tried to recall every little detail. The proprietress appeared quite familiar with him. They were on a first name basis. She hadn't treated him at all like a lord. She certainly hadn't seemed surprised to see him dressed in boots and buckskins. Nor had she seemed surprised that he was taking a girl to his rooms.

And why wouldn't he tell her where he lived? Wasn't that something people normally shared?

Harmony pushed away from the door and paced to her window, something peculiar gnawing away at her belly.

Many mysteries surrounded Anthony. She had tried to ignore them. Did she do so at her peril? Who was Anthony Allen after all?

Elegant, charming lord?

Or handsome, carefree bandit?

Thief masquerading as an aristocrat, or aristocrat posing as thief?

Harmony pressed her fingers to her temples and squeezed her eyes tightly shut. She could ignore the questions no longer, could no longer keep them at bay.

He had masqueraded as a bandit in order to meet her, get to know her. Or so Anthony said. But was he telling the truth? Having gotten to know her, did he now masquerade as a lord in order to pursue her? Had he taken on this persona to woo and win her with the approval of her sister?

Which was it, bandit or lord? Who was the real Anthony Allen? And when would she find out for sure?

Harmony pressed a hand to her heart, suddenly aware of its pounding. In only a few hours, perhaps. In a few more hours, as previously arranged, Anthony would arrive to escort her to the party. She silently cursed the driver whose departure put Agatha into the coach with them tonight and reawakened all her doubts. When would she have an opportunity to speak with him alone?

Alone. Alone with Anthony.

The pounding of Harmony's heart escalated. There was a familiar weakness in her knees, a melting sensation in her abdomen.

Did it really matter who he was, what he was?

That was the central question, the most important question, Harmony realized.

She would have her answers soon. Only a few more hours.

Harmony hurried to bathe, arrange her hair, and dress. She had decided to wear the pink satin, a somewhat modest gown with delicately scooped neck-line and fashionably puffy sleeves. It made her feel somewhat prim and virginal, although her thoughts when she was around Anthony were anything *but*. To-night she, too, would masquerade.

Chapter Twenty-two

Agatha sat at her dressing table, peered into the mirror, and primped. Her hair, as usual, was pulled into a tight chignon at the back of her head. She loosened a strand at her temple and twirled it around her finger, curling it. Liking the result, she repeated the process on the opposite side. She smiled at her reflection.

It did no harm to indulge in the smallest of vanities, she told herself. A wisp of curl at her cheeks, a faint touch of pink on her lips. She was, after all, attending a festive event given in honor of her sister and her sister's suitor. Her hostess was a pillar of the community. Other notables would be attending. She did want to look her best. If, for nothing else, Lord Farmington himself.

A girlish giggle rose in Agatha's throat, although she swiftly suppressed it. As much as she would like to, she could not deny the man was overpoweringly good-looking. And the way he looked in those tight-cut trousers . . .

A flush rose to Agatha's cheeks and she scowled at her reflection. She had to stop thinking such thoughts. Not only was it entirely unladylike and immoral, she wasn't even certain exactly who Lord Farmington was. There had not been time enough yet to hear from the other counties she had written to, and she would undoubtedly learn much more to her satisfaction. But in the meantime, it did no harm to continue to harbor some healthy suspicion. It would be just like Harmony to have attracted some no-account ne'er-do-well looking for a wealthy bride.

Lips pursed, Agatha remembered the way her sister had openly flirted with that horrible robber who had held them at gunpoint. That was obviously the kind of man she was drawn to and the kind who would most probably be drawn to her.

No, it wouldn't hurt to maintain her distance from Lord Farmington and nurse her most reasonable suspicions. It wouldn't hurt at all.

Nor would it hurt to indulge just a little bit more and put on one of her finer pieces of jewelry, one of the lovely pieces her grandmother had left to her. Dear, dear Grandmama Grace. So generous, so kind. Unlike her daughter.

Agatha's scowl returned as she thought about her

mother. She had most certainly left all of her jewels to the little princess, Harmony. Well, she hoped she enjoyed them. They would be *all* Harmony was ever going to get.

Agatha flounced out of her seat and crossed to the opposite side of the room, black silk skirt swishing and rustling. She glanced over her shoulder then pulled open her armoire. Another backward glance, and she knelt.

The key was always in her pocket, no matter what she was wearing, no matter where she was going. Agatha extracted it and shoved it quickly into the lock. It turned smoothly and the door swung wide. She removed the key and put it back in her pocket.

There was a modest array of velvet-lined jewel cases stacked neatly on the floor of the safe. On top of the boxes were neat piles of paper money. Agatha picked up a thick bundle of notes from the box she wished to open.

"Excuse me, Agatha, but I—"

"Harmony!" Startled, Agatha's fingers slipped and the money spilled onto the floor. "What are you doing here?"

Despite how used she had become to Agatha's venom, Harmony was still taken aback by the vehemence of Agatha's tone and expression. She took an involuntary step backward.

"I . . . I just came to . . ."

"Get out!" Agatha spat, furious. "Get out of my room!"

Harmony took another step back. She couldn't help but see the open safe, the money. Agatha followed her gaze and rounded on Harmony once again.

"Get out of here!"

So violent was Agatha's reaction, she lost her balance. In an attempt to rise, she fell sideways. The key slipped from her pocket onto the floor.

It was the last thing Harmony saw before she backed all the way into the corridor. She looked up to see Mrs. Rutledge coming in her direction.

"My sister's . . . upset. I didn't have a chance to tell her Lord Farmington's coach has arrived. Would you let her know, please?"

With a curt nod, Mrs. Rutledge sailed past her through the open bedroom door.

Shaken, Harmony hurried through the dark corridors to return to the foyer where Anthony awaited. Agatha's attitude toward her, the depth of her anger, her hatred, definitely seemed more than mere sibling jealousy or rivalry. Something was wrong with Agatha, something deep and disturbing. It frightened her.

Anthony was where she had left him, just inside the front door. Their greeting had been brief and unsatisfying after so many days apart. Nor would they have any time alone together now that Agatha was accompanying them in Anthony's coach. The prospect of a party no longer pleased her. She wanted to be alone with him. She wanted to be comforted by him. Even the questions and the doubt that had preyed so on her mind no longer seemed quite as important.

"Harmony, what's wrong?" Anthony held out his hands to her as she hastily entered the foyer.

"Nothing. Not really." Harmony allowed the warmth and strength of Anthony's grasp close around her fingers. "My sister is . . . well . . . difficult . . ."

"I know. I'm sorry."

"No, I'm sorry. Her coachman departed abruptly and she'll be riding with us tonight. We won't even have a chance to be alone together."

Harmony looked up into Anthony's eyes, deep into his eyes. She could almost feel herself flow into him, into his very soul. The intensity of the gaze he returned was like a welcome, an invitation, a promise of the love he had vowed he felt for her. She could scarcely believe how much she had missed him, how right, how perfect it felt to be with him again. Nothing, nothing at all, was as important as being with him. Her doubts and questions no longer mattered. She only wanted to be with him.

Anthony felt Harmony lean into him. The look

in her eyes told him what he needed and longed to know. Thank God he had been able to return to her. And thank God she appeared ready to accept what he had to propose. Time was running out. Tonight was a huge risk.

The desire to take her into his arms, crush her against him, was nearly overwhelming. Only the sound of approaching footsteps prevented him. Gently, reluctantly, he pushed her away.

"Anthony . . ." Harmony whispered and clung to his upper arms, feeling the smooth bulge of his muscles. "Will we have any time tonight to be alone together? I . . ."

"Yes, I promise," he swiftly replied, glancing over her head toward the corridor. "I have to talk to you."

"And I you."

Anthony laid a finger to her lips. "Promise," he murmured. He drew away as Agatha marched into the foyer.

Harmony did not miss the angry glitter in her sister's narrowed eyes. She returned Agatha's glare, not at all surprised when her sister turned her attention to Anthony and a wide smile of greeting bloomed on her lips.

"Lord Farmington, how lovely to see you again," she gushed.

"You're looking well, Miss Simmons," Anthony replied smoothly and raised her proffered hand to his lips.

"Thank you. Thank you, as well, for escorting me to Lady Margaret's little gala. I can't *imagine* what possessed my coachman."

Harmony resisted the urge to roll her eyes. Anthony was not as circumspect.

"Perhaps he is still unnerved by the unfortunate incident with the bandit," he said as he offered Agatha his arm. "The event must have been traumatic indeed."

Harmony could hardly believe Anthony had said what he did. She avoided his gaze when he turned to walk Agatha through the front door. She had difficulty controlling the tug at the corners of her mouth. If only Agatha knew.

Followed swiftly on that thought came another, the one that had plagued her all day. What did she herself really know? And did it matter? Was it *going* to matter? She didn't think so. Not now, not having seen him again. She allowed the smile to form as she followed Anthony and her sister to the coach.

Agatha chattered endlessly all the way to Lady Margaret's country manor. Bemused, Harmony simply took it all in. She was happy merely to be in Anthony's presence, to be within the circle of the glow that seemed to emanate from him. She fingered the diamond pendant at her throat, a legacy from her mother, and absently smoothed the folds of her satin gown. The spiral curls she favored bounced against her bare shoulders when the carriage jolted through an occasional rut. She hardly heard what Agatha was saying. Until the subject of Anthony's home came up once again.

"Really, Lord Farmington," she heard Agatha say. "You must stop being so mysterious. You've told us so much about your home, your cattle, and horses. But we still have absolutely no idea where exactly your home is!"

Harmony's eyes widened and she sat a little straighter.

"It's no mystery, I guarantee. It's a manor, much like the others in my area."

"But what area?" Agatha persisted. "Are you in the Lakes District?"

"A bit farther north, actually," Anthony responded promptly.

"Are you near Yor—?"

"Ahh, look. It appears we've arrived."

Harmony turned obediently to the window and saw the myriad of lights shining from the windows of the Donnellys' country home. A circular drive led to a *porte-cochere*, where another carriage stood to allow its passengers to exit. Several other coaches were lined up to one side of the brick-faced manor.

"It appears to be a somewhat modest turnout," Agatha said. "Lady Margaret feared that would be the case. So many of her friends have gone to their country estates for the season."

"Just what one would expect at this time of year," Anthony responded politely. "Nevertheless, it was most kind of her to make the effort on my behalf. I'm most appreciative, believe me."

Harmony watched her sister blush and fan herself with a lace handkerchief she pulled from the reticule attached to her wrist.

"As we are appreciative of your presence in our little community, Lord Farmington," Agatha replied.

Thankfully, Sneed appeared to assist Agatha and Harmony from the coach. Anthony joined them, offered each an arm, and proceeded toward the house. Wisely, Harmony avoided catching his gaze.

Anthony tried not to hold his breath as the three of them entered the Donnelly House foyer, but failed miserably. He glanced about hastily, noting the Lady's tastes ran to the baroque, a style he abhorred, and took a slow, deep breath in order to make the appropriate and exceedingly polite responses to his hostess's gushing greeting.

"How good of you to come, Lord Farmington," Lady Margaret purred when introductions had been made.

"The pleasure is all mine." Anthony turned his brilliant, crooked grin on Lady Margaret, who appeared to blush as easily, and unbecomingly, as Agatha, and on her husband, who cared not at all and whose own flush appeared to be entirely alcohol related. He blinked uncertainly, mumbled something unintelligible, and moved away. In search of another drink, Anthony was fairly certain.

With a single, disapproving glance in her husband's direction, Lady Margaret returned her attention to Anthony. She fingered the ropes of pearls draped over her generous bosom.

"You must allow me to introduce you to our friends, Lord Farmington, Miss Simmons. You, as well, Agatha. I believe there are some people here you've not yet met."

"You're too kind, Lady Margaret," Agatha murmured.

"Indeed, far too kind," Anthony echoed. "I do not wish to distract you from your duties as hostess of this lavish and lovely evening."

Harmony was amused to see Lady Margaret's cheeks flush an even deeper shade of pink. She was gratified as well to see so many feminine gazes turned in Anthony's direction. Interested and appraising gazes. She licked her lips like the cat whose owner ran the dairy and tightened the arm hooked through

Anthony's elbow.

Distractedly, Anthony patted Harmony's hand where it lay lightly on his forearm. He had scanned the guest list, it was true, but one could never be completely sure of anything. Sneed was right. He was taking the biggest risk of all tonight. This single evening could change everything. And he didn't care. Anthony glanced down at the crown of Harmony's shining head.

She was worth it. If he harbored the slightest, lingering doubt, it had vanished as if it had never existed. She was the one. He would tell her everything. Soon. He had to. But not before he was absolutely certain of her, sure she was his for all time. He was almost there.

In the meantime, he simply needed to exercise care. He wanted to be the one to tell her. He wanted no unpleasant surprise to mar the beauty of what was being created between them. Anthony's eyes swept his surroundings.

Not a single familiar face. There were names he recognized, of course, as Lady Margaret introduced them around the room. But it was as he had reassured Sneed; he had been very, very careful so far. There was no compelling reason to fear that anyone at all would recognize him. For awhile longer, at least, the charade could continue.

Close to Anthony's side, Harmony sensed him

begin to relax as they moved about, meeting and greeting Lady Margaret's guests. She was glad of the attention everyone paid to Anthony. It minimized their curiosity about her, and she had to answer very few personal questions of her own. It was obvious most people knew who she was, where she had come from, and why. She was scrutinized, of course. But Anthony, Lord Farmington, drew most of the attention. And she found his answers to all the polite, but clearly curious inquiries, fascinating. He avoided giving out any concrete information as smoothly as he had evaded all Agatha's questions.

"So your interest lies in cattle, Lord Farmington?"

"And horses."

"Any breed in particular?"

"My eye is not for any one breed, but for the particular qualities of the breed I happen to be looking at, at that moment."

Or: "Farmington . . . Farmington . . . so familiar, eh? But I can't quite place it."

"The queen's realm is vast, her subjects many, and I am but one."

A little later: "Northumberland, did I hear someone say? You're from that northern district?"

"No, but not far, not far at all."

"Then you're—"

"—in the perfect place to graze cattle, I assure you.

They grow fat and happy on my lands."

It was almost a game to him, Harmony mused, as they moved on from group to group, chatting amiably, never stopping too long in one place. His life was like a disassembled puzzle, with never enough pieces to put the whole together. She wondered how he would respond if she, herself, asked him a direct question.

"Anthony . . ."

"Yes, my love. What would you like? Are you hungry?"

"Well, yes . . ."

She couldn't deny it, the sumptuous buffet looked inviting. Guests had lined up to sample the various dishes, and Harmony's stomach rumbled. She let Anthony guide her toward the long table.

"Anthony, what would you answer if *I* asked you—?"

"Plate, my love?"

"Thank you. What would you say if I . . ." Harmony paused to smile at the woman next to her, who seemed to have taken a sudden interest in their conversation. She turned back to Anthony and lowered her voice as he spooned a small mound of black caviar onto her plate.

"What would I say if you asked me what, my beautiful lady?"

"If I asked you where you live. Exactly."

Anthony leaned down so his lips were very close to Harmony's ear. "I'd tell you," he whispered, "that it would be paradise on earth should you ever consent to live with me there as my love."

Her heart leapt within her breast. The laden plate trembled in her hand and her cheeks warmed. "Anthony, what . . . what do you . . .?"

"Later, my love. Later. As I promised."

❧

"Well, well, well." Brows arched, Lady Margaret turned from the handsome couple, heads bent together as they whispered intimately. "It seems to me, at least, Agatha, that you are well on your way to having a nobleman in your family. No matter how vague he may be about his background, there is nothing vague about his attraction to your lovely young sister."

"No, there isn't, is there?" Agatha sniffed, lips pursed. "And the attention he pays her in public is unseemly."

"They do seem quite . . . familiar."

"I do apologize for my sister's behavior, Lady Margaret, I . . ."

"Pish tosh." Lady Margaret waved a hand dismissively. "The important thing is that we pin down precisely who the gentleman is. Although the fact that he is, indeed, a gentleman, is without question. His clothes and his manners are impeccable. His education is obvious. Nevertheless, there are certain things we absolutely *must* know."

"Yes! Yes, of—"

"Ancestry, for instance," Lady Margaret forged on. "The source of his wealth, not to mention its approximate size."

"Oh, yes . . . yes."

"What are the results of your inquiries so far?"

"I've only heard from Cumbria to date. Nothing. I'm awaiting two other responses."

"Curious," Lady Margaret said. "Curious that neither you nor your sister even know where he lives. Does it not concern you?"

"Absolutely, Lady Margaret!"

"Still, some eligible and quite wealthy men are very closemouthed about their personal details, their histories. You understand."

"Of course I do."

"It is the price the wealthy aristocracy must sometimes pay."

"I understand perfectly, Lady Margaret."

"Still and all, we must persist in our efforts. Especially in light of the obvious interest the two young people appear to have in one another."

Agatha resorted to a vigorous nod, bobbing the curls at her temples.

"It would be scandalous, absolutely scandalous to discover, for instance, his was an impoverished title.

That he is a bounder, a rogue, preying on an innocent young woman with wealth of her own."

"Insupportable!" The very idea made her quake.

"Indeed. So we shall persist in our efforts, shall we not?"

"Oh, yes, Lady Margaret. Yes. Certainly!"

With a condescending smile, the lady moved on. Agatha glanced back over her shoulder at Harmony and her suitor.

Yes, without a doubt she would learn all there was to know about Lord Farmington. She would find out if he was suitable. Or not. And if not, well . . .

Agatha smiled thinly. She would either be well rid of her sister, with a titled brother-in-law as icing on the cake. Or Harmony could languish with a broken heart. She didn't really care which.

The hour was late. Harmony had had more than enough of polite, idle conversation. She was eager to be alone with Anthony, as he had promised. And to learn the answer to her question. As he had promised.

In anticipation of their imminent departure, she had visited Lady Margaret's overdecorated powder room. Re-entering the parlor, she looked about for Anthony.

He was nowhere to be seen. She watched two or

three couples head toward the grand foyer, where the Donnellys stood to bid a good-evening to their departing guests. She spied her sister standing by the buffet table stuffing a petit four furtively into her mouth, and then gazed out the open double doors to the terrace. Anthony was not in sight and Harmony turned around to look elsewhere.

The bloodcurdling scream froze her in her tracks.

Chapter Twenty-three

Pandemonium reigned. Secondary cries and gasps followed the scream. Women grabbed their escorts. A servant dropped a tray of glasses and an elderly woman fainted. Harmony picked up her skirts, as if prepared to flee, and cast about desperately for a sign of Anthony. At last she caught sight of him.

He was entering the salon through a second set of doors at the far end of the room that led to a terrace at the side of the house. His expression was sober, his pace rapid. Harmony started in his direction.

At that moment, Anthony looked up and saw her. He slowed his pace perceptibly and smiled. Harmony could easily tell it was forced. She hesitated, nearly stumbling, and almost fell into his arms.

"What's happened, Anthony? What's happened?"

"I have no idea. Stay here and I'll find out."

Before Anthony could take another step, however, a middle-aged matron flew from the foyer into the salon, hands pressed to her cheeks. Lord and Lady Donnelly followed on her heels.

"My bracelet! My diamond bracelet," the woman sobbed. "It's gone!"

Harmony couldn't help it. As icy fingers clutched at her heart, she raised her eyes to Anthony's. He did not meet her gaze. She knew, however, that he was well aware of her glance. His hand tightened briefly on her elbow. Then he left her and walked straight to Angus Donnelly's side.

"I'd like to help," he said quietly.

Donnelly blinked at him stupidly. Lady Margaret put her hand comfortingly on the shoulder of the distraught woman.

"I'd be grateful for your aid, Lord Farmington. But what can you do?" Lady Margaret asked. Her voice was unsteady.

He turned to the weeping woman. "When did you last know for certain you were wearing your bracelet?"

"I . . . I'm not sure, really. Sometime during the evening I . . . I glanced down at it. But I didn't notice it was gone until I went to bid Lady Margaret good night." A fresh spate of sobs ensued.

"At least we know it's here, somewhere in this house. Don't we?"

The woman pressed a handkerchief to her eyes and nodded dolefully.

"Have you been anywhere else besides this room?"

"The . . . the powder room."

"Would you be so kind?" Anthony said over his shoulder to another woman who stood nearby.

Without a word, she hurried to do his bidding. Anthony looked around the room, his glance taking in every remaining guest.

"I'm sure that what happened is simple mischance with a faulty clasp," Anthony said. "If everyone would be good enough to look around them, we'll find the bracelet in no time."

Harmony remained standing stock-still. A diamond bracelet. Missing.

Yet Anthony had hurried to help.

Or was it that he had not expected the woman to notice her jewelry was missing until much later? Later, when he would have been safely away?

Harmony's dinner turned to lead in her stomach. Almost as if in a dream, she watched the people around her walk slowly about the room, eyes downcast, searching for the missing bracelet. Was it an exercise in futility? Was there a thief among them who was merely trying to throw them off the scent? She raised her eyes with difficulty when Anthony moved to her side.

"I know what you're thinking," he murmured.

"Do you?" Harmony surprised even herself by the steel in her voice. A heartbeat later, watching

Anthony's expression, she regretted her tone. It was too late. He turned on his heel and walked away from her. Conspicuously, it seemed to her, he started to search the floor. Harmony turned away.

And found herself face-to-face with her sister.

"How traumatic for poor Mrs. Darrow," Agatha said at once. She fingered the cameo at her throat. "I can't imagine the distress she must feel, losing something so valuable."

Harmony glared at her sister, unblinking. "No, Agatha. You're right," she said in a level, icy voice. "You cannot."

"Well! There's no call to be rude!"

"To the woman who has stolen my inheritance? No, of course not. How silly of me." With grim satisfaction, Harmony watched her sister flounce off. She'd had enough of Agatha, her greed, her mean-spiritedness, and poisonous temper. And she was very, very afraid for Anthony.

The hunt continued, although with noticeably less enthusiasm. Many of the remaining guests were finally departing. Harmony wondered what Anthony would do now. Then she heard him.

"I've found it!"

Everyone left in the room turned in his direction. Mrs. Darrow gave a small cry of delight when she saw the bracelet dangling from Anthony's fingers.

"Oh, Lord Farmington . . . thank you! Thank you!"

"You're welcome. But the pleasure is all mine, Mrs. Darrow," he replied gallantly.

"I feel as if I should give you some reward."

"Finding the bracelet, and returning it to you, is reward enough. Believe me." His words were for Mrs. Darrow. But as he spoke, he looked past her. Right into Harmony's eyes.

Assailed with guilt, she had to look away. How could she have thought it of him?

Or had he merely produced the stolen bracelet to make her feel this way? Had her suspicions spoiled his plans?

Harmony moved through the next several minutes in a daze. She knew she said the appropriate words of farewell to her host and hostess, but could not remember a thing she said. With Anthony at her side, she moved in the thinning queue toward the waiting coaches. She did not even notice that Agatha had lagged behind.

❦

Agatha watched the couple walk away from her, down the front steps, and along the pathway to the curving drive. Resentment seethed within her like a churning, angry ocean. Her heart beat erratically.

It wasn't fair. It never had been. From the moment Harmony was born, her world had changed. She was no longer the center of her parents' universe. With her mousy hair and plain looks she could never compete with the golden child, Harmony, who had the perfect features, shining red hair, and sunny disposition. No matter how hard she tried, how hard she studied, how rigidly she controlled her behavior, she could never seem to win her way back into the center of her parents' attention. There was always the laughing, adventurous, tomboyish Harmony to steal the moment, the scene, the entire play.

Worse, she could not get away from her. Even now. Her parents' final curse was to give her Harmony's guardianship. But was Harmony grateful for the roof over her head? Was she mindful of the extra responsibility her older sister had to shoulder? No! Just look at the spiteful, evil way Harmony treated her, the way she talked to her. How could she be that way when she had it all? Looks, personality. And, now, a charming, handsome suitor. It wasn't fair.

But things were going to get better. Oh, yes, they would. She already had firm, legal control of Harmony's inheritance. There was absolutely nothing Harmony could do about it. She would be dependent on her older sister forever. Unless, and ideally, she found a husband. Which it seemed she had. But it wasn't fair.

Anthony Allen, Lord Farmington, was like Harmony: golden, blessed. He, too, had it all: charm, looks, money. He and Harmony appeared to be perfect for one another. They would wed, live happily ever after. Have shining, golden children.

It wasn't fair.

Harmony couldn't have it all. She wouldn't allow it.

"Agatha." Lady Margaret cleared her throat. The foyer was empty. Even her husband, Angus, had shuffled unsteadily off to bed. "Agatha, your sister and Lord Farmington are waiting for you. Isn't that your carriage?"

"Oh . . . oh, yes. But I . . . I must have a quick word with you."

Lady Margaret's only reply was a lift of her eloquent brow. It was all the encouragement Agatha needed.

"Earlier this evening you advised me, quite rightly, to exercise caution where my sister was concerned."

"Yes, yes . . ."

"You pointed out how scandalous it would be to discover that Lord Farmington's title was impoverished, for instance. But what . . . what if it turned out to be something even worse?"

"Like what?" Lady Margaret prodded impatiently. "Whatever do you mean, Agatha?"

"I mean, what if he turns out to be something

worse than a bounder? What if we were to discover he's a . . . a thief?"

"Oh, Agatha. It's late. I—"

"No, listen, please. Especially in light of what happened here tonight."

"You don't mean Alicia Darrow's—"

"That's exactly what I mean!" Agatha said excitedly.

"But he's the one who found it."

"Yes, yes! But perhaps merely to deflect suspicion from himself. Think about it, Lady Margaret. Remember I told you how he made his introduction to us by returning Harmony's sapphire ring?"

Lady Margaret nodded.

"Don't you find it a bit odd that he, or his coachman as he claims, was able to spot such a trifling bauble from a carriage seat?" Agatha had to pause to catch her breath. Her excitement was growing exponentially as she warmed to her tale. "What if *he's* the one who stole it? What if *he's* the one who held up our coach? And what about all the jewel thefts that have occurred since? Ever since Lord Farmington started coming 'round to court my sister!"

Lady Margaret was suddenly a bit wider awake. "Agatha, you don't really think . . ."

"You yourself have never heard of a Lord Farmington. Neither has anyone else. Why not? Perhaps because no one by that name actually exists! Why else is he so mysterious about his background and where he lives?"

Lady Margaret exhaled noisily. "You just may have a point, Agatha dear," she murmured in a conspiratorial tone. "You just might have a point."

Agatha's fervor had produced beads of perspiration on her brow. She dabbed them away with her handkerchief. "I'm so very glad you agree, Lady Margaret."

"Oh, I do. I do. We can't let you, or your ward, be taken in by a common thief! We must expose him! Discredit the impostor!"

My sentiments exactly." Agatha pressed a hand demurely to her furiously pounding heart. "But how, Lady Margaret? I fear I haven't your resources."

"You do now," the older woman pronounced with finality. "Angus has connections. We'll use them. If there is, indeed, a Lord Farmington, we'll find out. And if there isn't, well . . ."

The two women shared a long, slow smile.

"Thank you so much, Lady Margaret," Agatha said as she backed toward the open door. "Thank you . . ."

"What in the world is keeping Agatha so long?" Harmony was uncomfortable. She and Anthony had scarcely exchanged two words since they climbed into the coach.

Anthony leaned forward slightly to look out the window. "Here she comes now." He sat back and took Harmony's hand and tightened his grip when she tried to withdraw her fingers.

"I have to talk to you, Harmony," Anthony said. His voice was low, his tone urgent.

"Anthony . . ."

"Tonight. As I promised."

His words took her back to the start of the evening. She remembered how glad she had been to see him, how much she had looked forward to being with him. More importantly, she recalled her realization that the answers to her questions were not nearly as significant as her feelings for Anthony. Hadn't she told herself it didn't matter who, or what, he was, as long as she could be with him?

The warmth of Anthony's grasp sent a sensation up her arm she knew would soon spread through her entire body. She knew how helpless, how vulnerable she would become.

Helpless and vulnerable because she did love him. No matter what. Even if he had taken that woman's bracelet, or was responsible for any of the other jewel thefts in the area. She loved him, and the emotion was overpowering. It was bigger than any other fact, any other reality.

"All . . . all right, Anthony," Harmony whispered as Agatha approached the coach.

"Thank you, my love." Anthony squeezed her hand. "Wait an hour after you arrive home. Then meet me . . . your sister's coachman left, didn't he?"

Harmony nodded.

"Then meet me in the stable."

A meadowful of butterflies took flight in Harmony's stomach.

Anthony released her hand when Agatha climbed into the coach. She sat down opposite them with a smug, satisfied smile.

Her expression sickened Harmony. But she wasn't going to let it ruin her moment. Or the moments to come. As the coach rolled forward, she closed her eyes.

Soon, very soon, she would be in Anthony's arms.

Chapter Twenty-four

Harmony stood by her bedroom window and buttoned her shirt slowly. Lights shining from the parlor windows illuminated the hedge below her. They would be extinguished soon, she knew, when Mrs. Rutledge made her final rounds. She waited until they went out, then unlatched her window and pushed against the restraining vines. The gap she created was only inches wide, but it let in the scent of the summer night: the surrounding woodland, the decaying debris on its floor, the sweet green of new growth. She listened hard, but heard only the faintest of sounds: a night bird, the stirring of leaves in a breeze.

Anthony was out there. Perhaps he already awaited her in the stable. It had been nearly an hour. Her stomach tightened.

Harmony backed away from the window and cinched the belt at the waist of her cotton skirt. She pulled the pins from her hair and let it fall down her back. She brushed it until the curls softened into waves.

Almost an hour, but not quite. She didn't want to take any chances. Harmony sat on the edge of her bed.

What was he going to say to her? How was he going to answer her questions? Did she truly mean it in her heart of hearts when she told herself it didn't matter?

She only knew one thing for sure at the moment. Every nerve in her body tingled. Her blood seemed to hum through her veins. She didn't think she had ever felt more alive.

In only a few more minutes she would be with Anthony. She would be in her lover's arms. No matter what he had to say, no matter who he turned out to be, nothing could dim the anticipation she felt.

The minutes ticked away. The house was silent. Harmony rose and extinguished her lamp. She looked out her windows, but saw no other light shining from the house out into the soft, summer darkness.

Fortunately, Agatha apparently no longer thought it necessary to lock Harmony into her room at night. She opened her door and peered into the corridor, but saw absolute blackness. Not a single sconce remained lit. Yet she now knew the way by heart.

The front door creaked and was too familiar a sound in the house. Harmony chose the terrace doors.

Once out into the night, she breathed a small sigh of relief. A half moon cast a silvery light on the garden and its path around the side of the house. Harmony picked up her skirt and hurried around the corner.

The gravel drive crunched beneath her feet. Although she knew it sounded loud to her ears alone, her heart pounded wildly in her breast. She cast a look over her shoulder at the dark, silent house. Not so much as the flicker of a candle or the creak of a shutter in the night wind. She headed for the stable.

Was it fate that had sent Agatha's coachman on his way? Harmony could not help but think so. She felt, in fact, as if fate guided her every footstep this night. One way or another she was walking into the future, regardless of what it held, by walking into Anthony's arms.

She could see the stable doors now. Was one of them ajar?

It felt as if her heart might pound right out of her throat. Her footsteps faltered with the sudden weakness in her legs.

"Anthony?" Harmony called softly.

There was no sound from within the stable. She took a cautious step forward and pushed the partially open door. It groaned.

"Anthony?"

Had he not come after all? Her heart pumped frantically with a new emotion and she moved hastily into the stable.

One of the carriage horses stamped a foot and nickered. She heard another shake its head, heard the rustle of straw. The fragrance of horsehide, hay, and dust filled her nostrils.

And then the scent of Anthony as he took her in his arms.

"My love . . . my Lady Blue . . ."

Harmony's surrender was instant and total. She had no control over her body, her mind, her emotions. She belonged to him, completely, and sagged into his arms.

Anthony knew he must restrain himself. But it was hard, so hard. She was in his arms, where she belonged. And he knew from her response what her answer would be. Yet he couldn't resist. Only a few kisses. A few . . .

Harmony felt his lips at her neck, nibbling. He inhaled the perfume at the hollow of her throat, and his tongue tickled the oh-so sensitive flesh there. Her head fell back. His kisses ranged upward, finally reaching her mouth. Her lips parted to receive him.

Their passion for one another was total. Each body yearned for the other, strained against the other. Harmony was dazed by emotion and sensation. She would have died, happily, in his arms, and gave a little moan of protest when she felt him push her away.

"Anthony . . ."

"Sssshhh, my love." He ran a finger over her lips,

savoring the wetness of them, and smoothed a strand of hair from her forehead. "I must talk to you . . . I must. I have something to ask you."

Harmony merely looked at him, breast heaving, as she struggled to control her breathing. He held her at arms' length and she gripped his forearms. She felt the strength there, the tension. Finally, she nodded.

"Come. Come sit next to me."

Harmony let him take her hand and lead her to a bale of straw. She sat obediently beside him, still clutching his hand.

"I think you know what I want to ask, Harmony," Anthony said softly.

Did she? Yes. In her heart she knew. She nodded, slowly.

"Tell me first," Anthony said. "Tell me first what you are certain of."

"I am certain that you love me," Harmony replied in a barely audible voice.

"And?"

Harmony's thoughts flew back to the time he had urged her to say nothing until she was sure. She allowed the shadow of a smile to touch her lips.

"And . . . I love you in return."

Anthony expelled a long sigh. He believed her. More, he believed that she loved him enough.

"I loved you almost from the first moment I saw

you," he said at length.

"I know," Harmony whispered.

"I have made mistakes. Great mistakes."

"You made them because you love me."

Anthony's heart swelled. Tears threatened to unman him. "I would die for you, Harmony."

"I know that, too," she murmured. "As I would die for you."

"Then . . . then you'll . . . marry me?"

He seemed so boyish suddenly, so unsure. She loved him so much.

"Of course I'll marry you, Anthony. Of course." She reached up to stroke his cheek.

Anthony captured her hand and pressed her palm to his lips. He closed his eyes. He was the luckiest man on earth. He didn't want the moment to end. But there was more. He wasn't finished yet.

Though she smiled, a tear slipped down Harmony's cheek. She felt his love, the intensity of it. She had absolutely no doubt of it. She was incomparably blessed. Regardless of what else he might have to tell her.

"Harmony, I . . ." Anthony swallowed, his mouth dry. "I have to ask something of you. It's a request, a very great one. I want you to consider carefully before you answer me."

Harmony's brow furrowed slightly. This was not exactly what she had expected. Again, however, she nodded. "Go ahead, Anthony. Tell me what it is."

He braced himself. There was nothing for it but to forge ahead.

"I know it's every girl's dream . . . indeed, her right . . . to have a beautiful wedding. A gown, flowers, champagne. But I . . . I have to ask you to forego all that."

"Those things aren't important, Anthony," Harmony replied truthfully. "What matters is our love for each other. What *causes* us to wish to marry. The trimmings of the wedding itself are not the cause."

"Then you wouldn't mind a . . . a quiet, private ceremony?"

"Not at all."

Anthony drew a long, deep breath. "I have one more request." When Harmony remained silent, he continued. "I'd like for us to wed . . . as soon as possible."

In spite of the hour, the location, and the strangeness of Anthony's proposal, Harmony felt very calm. Nothing seemed to surprise or disturb her. Was it because of the depth of her love for him? It didn't matter. It simply was.

"How soon do you think that will be?" Harmony asked quietly.

"How soon can you be ready?"

Harmony thought for a moment. "I'll need a day or two to tell my sister and pack my things."

"How about three days? That will give me time to make arrangements on my end."

Harmony smiled gently. "Three days it is."

Anthony took her face in his hands. "I love you."

"I love you, too," she replied simply.

Anthony took another deep breath. "In spite of the fact that you don't . . . you don't really know who I am?"

"You mean you're not really Anthony Allen, Lord Farmington?"

"Oh, I'm most certainly Anthony Allen," he replied swiftly.

"But are you, or are you not, properly addressed as 'Lord'?"

"I am titled. That is the truth."

Harmony felt as if her brain was reeling within her skull. Was he telling her the absolute truth? She had no doubt of it. She simply didn't know if he was telling her all of the truth. He could very well be a lord and . . . something else. The title could be an impoverished one and he'd had to resort to . . . Harmony banished the thought.

"And your home, Anthony. Are you able to tell me now, at last, where you live?"

Anthony gripped her hands tightly. "This is a night of truth. Simply not all the truths of my life. Suffice it to say I do, indeed, have a home."

There it was, right out in the open. Truth, but not all of it. Yet Harmony had already confronted it in her heart.

"No matter who you are, or what you are . . . I love you."

Anthony's eyes closed briefly. "You are the most remarkable woman I have ever known," he breathed. "I knew from the first you were the only one who could ever be for me. It has been my constant prayer that you would return my love. And now . . ."

"Now?"

"Now my prayer has been answered. And I must ask you the most difficult thing of all."

Her sense of calm flowed into serenity. She was loved and in love. It was all that mattered. Nothing could disturb the peace of her soul.

"Go ahead, Anthony. Say, ask, what you must."

Coming into the evening, he hadn't thought he could love her more. He had been wrong.

"I . . . I am not Lord Farmington, although I may be correctly addressed as 'Lord,'" he said quickly. When Harmony started to speak, he put his hand gently over her mouth. "I know you already guessed that. But neither am I . . . whatever else you might think. Will you trust me? Please?"

Harmony considered her response for a long moment. Then: "I trust you, or I wouldn't consent to marry you. I know you are keeping secrets from me. I also know that you love me and would never do anything intentionally to harm me. It's . . . difficult, I admit, to understand why you would keep your true identity from me. But it doesn't alter who you are essentially. So, yes. Yes, I trust you."

Anthony raised her hand to his lips and kissed it. "Just until we're married. Then I'll tell you everything. I swear."

"Three days." It was almost impossible to imagine. In three days she would be Mrs. . . . who? Despite the solemnity of the moment, Harmony giggled.

"What is it? What's funny?"

Harmony shook her head. "I don't know. I'm just . . . happy, I guess."

The weight of the world seemed to have lifted from Anthony's shoulders. He felt his own smile begin to spread.

She loved his crooked grin. She loved everything about him. The circumstances of their meeting, their brief courtship, were impossible. Anthony's proposal, his conditions, were crazy. Yet here she was. And she had never been happier. The laughter bubbled up inside her and escaped.

Anthony winced. Harmony clapped a hand over her mouth. Then they were holding each other, shaking with silent laughter. And then they were simply holding one another.

"Harmony . . ."

Anthony's breath was warm against her neck. The way he said her name sent a shiver of pleasure through her. She turned her head and kissed the hard, square line of his jaw. The stubble of his beard was rough, and pleasing, against the softness of her lips. She felt his fingers tangle in the mass of her hair. He pulled her head back gently.

"Harmony . . ."

His mouth closed over hers. His tongue sought to part her lips and she surrendered willingly, drawing him inside of her. She tasted him, and reveled in him. Something soared within her.

Moments later a starburst of passion blossomed in her breast as Anthony's fingers traced a searing line from her shoulder to her waist. She captured his hand and moved it back, and he cupped her breast, thumb teasing the swelling, sensitive flesh beneath her thin, cotton shirt. Gasping for breath, she pulled her mouth from his.

"Anthony . . ."

"I know. I know. I'm sorry." With all his remaining willpower, Anthony pushed her away. "Forgive me, Harmony. I—"

"No," she interrupted. "You misunderstand. Come with me. Please." She tugged at his hand and pulled him to his feet.

A narrow flight of wooden stairs at the back of the stable led to the small room that had been the coachman's. Harmony climbed the steps and opened the door. She peered tentatively into the tiny room.

It was neat and smelled clean. There was a well-washed, faded coverlet on the small bed. She pulled Anthony into the room. He took her immediately into his arms.

"We don't have to do this, Harmony," Anthony whispered hoarsely. "It's only a matter of days now."

"I don't want to wait," Harmony replied. She didn't think she *could* wait. Pressed against his length, she felt the very positive, physical proof of his need of her, his longing. It seemed the core of her being was centered in that spot. She was no longer even aware of the rest of her body. She was a flame, and only he could quench her heat.

"I want you," Harmony breathed against his mouth. "I love you."

Anthony moaned. He was past all restraint. It was right. The moment was right. They were meant to be together. They always had been.

Harmony had never known such urgency, such intensity. Anthony's body pushed her slowly, carefully toward the bed as his hands fumbled with her skirt and petticoats, lifting them. Harmony's fingers tore at the buttons of her blouse, then at the buttons of Anthony's shirt. A birdlike cry flew from her throat when she pressed her naked breast to his at last.

His skin was smooth and slippery with a sheen of sweat. She felt soft, pliant, feminine against the ridges of his muscular chest and abdomen. She burned. Her hands moved downward.

He throbbed, pulsed. She felt herself quiver in the most secret, private part of her, felt the welcoming, wanting moisture there. Her fingers felt every inch of his manhood, straining against the fabric of his trousers. Then the backs of her legs came in contact with the narrow bed, and she pulled him down on top of her.

There was no knowing, no rational thought. Only passion, desire, hands and lips and bodies. Clothing disappeared as if by magic and they were together, pressed together and suspended in a timeless time. Harmony felt him between her legs, pushing, gently pushing, thrusting his way into her body, her soul. She rose to meet him . . .

Chapter Twenty-five

*H*armony opened her eyes slowly, languidly. Her bedroom window remained ajar from the evening before, and she heard the singing of birds. By the intensity of the sun, and its slant, she knew she had slept quite late. The room had also grown warm. Harmony threw back her covers.

She had been naked under the sheets. Never before had she slept that way. But when she had at last crept into her bed, in the wee hours before dawn, she had wanted nothing to disturb the memory of Anthony's hands on her body. Harmony sighed and closed her eyes again.

She had never even imagined, in her wildest dreams, lovemaking would be like what had passed between them. And it was something she had dreamed of, and imagined, many times. Her parents, deeply in love with one another, had been openly affectionate. Her mother had been open and frank with her about the facts of life, and how wonderful the physical part of a relationship could be between two people who cared deeply about each other. She had taught Harmony to be unafraid when the time came and she knew she was with the right person. Furthermore, she had told her never to be shy with that person, but to ask for what she felt she needed or wanted. Harmony had had to ask nothing of Anthony.

With a renewed thrill, she remembered the ways, and places, he had touched her. Shivering, she remembered the trail his tongue had taken across her body, and how he had used it to raise her to heights that were dizzying. She recalled the feel of him beneath her hands, every inch of him, and the scent of him, musky and electrifying. With a groan, Harmony rolled over and buried her face in her pillow.

Three days. How was she going to wait another three days? She was not even going to be able to see him, much less touch him, hold him. He had told her he had to go into London and finish up his business affairs and make the arrangements for their hasty wedding.

Business affairs. What business? What did he do? Was it truly legitimate, or . . .?

Harmony tried to still her thoughts. She had made her commitment to him. She had vowed to trust him. Besides, she knew with greater certainty than ever that even if he turned out to be England's most wanted criminal, she would still love him and go away with him. Their love was fated, destined. There was no turning back.

There was, however, going to be some difficulty going forward.

Harmony groaned again. But this time it was not with remembered pleasure.

There was no getting around it. She was going to have to tell Agatha. She feared her reaction.

No matter what Harmony might know, or suspect, herself, to Agatha Anthony was still a lord. A wealthy one at that. She had gone so far as to tell Harmony the only way she would ever be free, or have money, would be to marry a man of substance. Did it not stand to reason, therefore, that she would be delighted with the news of the impending nuptials?

Harmony doubted it. It was too soon, too fast. It wouldn't be *seemly*. Tongues would wag. Agatha would hate it. Not to mention the missed attention a large and lavish wedding to an aristocrat would have drawn.

On the other hand, Harmony would be out from under her roof and, in Agatha's eyes at least, suitably wed no matter how precipitously.

Either way, there were going to be initial fireworks. She might as well get it over with. Reluctantly, Harmony slid her bare legs over the edge of the bed and sat up.

In minutes she was dressed in proper attire, although still acutely aware of Anthony's warmth and scent on her skin. Despite her apprehension, she nearly skipped down the corridor.

The dining room was empty. Harmony had not actually expected to find her sister lingering over a late breakfast. But neither had she expected to see the room cleared of every remnant of the meal, including tea. It was undoubtedly done out of spite. No matter. Harmony marched toward the morning room, where Agatha typically spent an hour or two over correspondence.

"Don't expect Cook to prepare anything for you," Agatha said without looking up from her escritoire. "Meals are served at specified times and guests are expected to be prompt."

"So that's all I am to you, Agatha . . . a guest?"

Agatha laid down her pen and turned slowly in her chair. "Do you really believe you have behaved toward me in a . . . *sisterly* . . . way?"

As difficult as it was, Harmony managed to hold her tongue. "I'm sorry if my nature antagonizes you," she forced herself to say. "Do you mind if I sit down?"

"As you see, I am engaged. You may, however, suit yourself." Agatha returned to her letter.

Harmony perched on the edge of a narrow window seat. She felt the sun on her back, but it did little to dispel the chill in the room. She cleared her throat.

Agatha threw down her pen. "You obviously have something on your mind, Harmony. In the interest of conserving time, and my patience, why don't you go ahead and tell me what it is."

It wasn't the best of beginnings. But it was too late now.

"I have something to tell you, Agatha. Something that I think will make you quite glad."

"Oh, really?" Agatha's brow furrowed as her eyebrows arched. "I believe I'll be the judge of that."

"Very well." Harmony folded her hands on her lap. "If you recall, you told me once, not long ago, that it would be . . . advisable . . . for me to marry a man of money."

Agatha's eyes narrowed, but she remained silent. Harmony continued.

"Well, I'm going to do exactly that. I'm going to marry Lord . . . Lord Farmington."

The room became entombed in silence. Even the birds seemed to have ceased their singing. Agatha's features remained perfectly impassive.

"And you've known him how long?" she asked at length, tonelessly.

"It doesn't matter how long we've known each other. We're in love."

Agatha made a rude noise and returned to her letter. "You know nothing of love," she said without turning. "Certainly not in this short a time. Don't be absurd. Go on about your business and let me finish my correspondence."

Harmony had expected many things. She had not expected to be dismissed so summarily. Perhaps, however, it was a blessing in disguise. She rose to leave.

"Where are you going?" Agatha inquired sharply.

"I'm going on about my business, as you so wisely advised."

"Don't be cheeky!" Agatha pushed back her chair. "And you wonder why I refer to you as a guest!"

"Soon you won't have to refer to me as anything at all. I'll be gone."

"You're going nowhere."

"I'm going to marry Anthony," Harmony replied levelly. "He's coming for me in three days."

"Three days!" Agatha pushed to her feet so quickly and violently her chair toppled over backward. "Are you out of your mind?"

"Probably not. But I am in love. And I *am* leaving."

"You will not set a foot outside this house!"

That was more like it. Harmony almost smiled. "What are you going to do, Agatha? Lock me in my room again? What are you going to tell Anthony when he comes for me?"

Agatha's arms were stiff at her sides, her hands curled into fists. A vein throbbed in her temple. "I will tell him exactly what I'm going to tell you now," she said in a tightly controlled voice. "I'm going to tell him that as far as I can ascertain, there *is* no Lord Farmington. And until I find out exactly who he is, and where he comes from, you are going absolutely nowhere with him."

If someone had nailed Harmony's feet to the floor, she could not have been more securely rooted to the spot. She felt her fingers grow cold as her heart ceased to beat and her circulation stopped. With horror, she watched a smile creep onto the corners of her sister's mouth. She had seen that smile before. She had seen it last night when Agatha finally joined them in the carriage. After having spent several minutes talking to Lady Margaret.

"You look a trifle pale, little sister," Agatha sniggered. "What's wrong? Is there something you already know about *Lord* Farmington that you're afraid I'll find out?"

Harmony didn't dare so much as lick her lips. She concentrated all her efforts on keeping her face expressionless. How much did Agatha really know? *What* did she know?

"I know," Harmony said at last, voice cool, tone even, "that he is a good, decent human being. I know that he loves me, as much as I love him. I know that the length of time we have known one another matters not at all. And when he comes for me, I will leave with him."

"How bold, Harmony. How bold. And how foolish." Agatha leaned over in her chair. She let her eyes conspicuously caress the half-finished letter lying on her escritoire. "I must make haste to pen the remainder of this missive so I may have a courier on his way to London with it by late morning."

Harmony knew Agatha baited her; however, she refused to bite. She feared, too, her voice would be unsteady if she tried to speak.

"That way," Agatha went on, "I should have a reply by the day after tomorrow. And we will know for certain just who Lord Farmington is . . . or isn't."

Did she have feet anymore? Was she standing on two legs? Harmony's entire body felt numb.

"Go on. Off with you." Agatha made a shooing gesture. "I have work to do."

Harmony watched her sister sit back and relax in her chair. She couldn't believe this was happening. She thought she might be sick.

"What's wrong with you, Harmony?" Agatha said crossly. Then she brightened. "Or is it that you're afraid? That's it, isn't it? You're afraid!"

The spell was broken at last. With a stifled cry, Harmony whirled and fled the room.

❦

Anthony sat forward on the chintz-covered sofa and gratefully allowed Sneed to massage his shoulders and upper back. He was bent at the waist, arms on his thighs, head hanging low.

"Whatever did you do to—?"

"Don't talk, Sneed. Just keep rubbing."

The massage continued for several minutes. Then Sneed gave him a parting slap on the back and stepped away from the couch. Anthony straightened and leaned back slowly.

"I don't suppose," he said lazily, "that you could sweet talk Maggie into making another pot of coffee?"

"No, I don't suppose. You're the one who does all the sweet talking around here."

"Be that way."

"Thank you. I suppose I will."

Anthony allowed himself to languish another few moments, then pushed up from the soft, inviting cushions of the couch. He yawned and stretched.

"What are you doing, Sneed?"

"Exactly as it appears. Packing."

"But I'll be coming back here."

Sneed looked up from the shirt he folded atop the neatly made bed. "Might I say that would be most foolish?"

"You already told me that staying out all night was foolish."

"A young gentleman needs his sleep," Sneed replied archly.

"And you told me proposing to Harmony was foolish."

"After so little time? Of course it's foolish."

"You're not the one who's in love, Sneed. Besides, I've told you. She's the one. She loves me. She loves me for who I am."

"So you've said."

"And she'll love me when she finds out, well, exactly *who* I am."

"Undoubtedly she will love you more," Sneed commented dryly.

"Don't be sarcastic."

"I apologize," Sneed said with sudden seriousness. "I really do. But you've spent much of your life taking such elaborate precautions. It has stood you in very good stead, I might say. Now you've risked it all for this girl."

"Because she's worth it, Sneed. I'm telling you."

"She may be. She may be at that. I've never seen you like this. If nothing else, however, have you considered the risk you're taking in deceiving her?"

"Yes. I have. But I had to know first if she loved me for me."

"Apparently she does."

"Yes. I'm convinced she can live with the kind of constraints my lifestyle will impose on her. And continue to love me in spite of it all."

Sneed sighed heavily. "I must leave it to your better judgment. But for your future protection, I really must suggest that you move into—"

"No, Sneed." Anthony shook his head vigorously. "I'll be all right, I promise you. I'm going to arrange to have the ceremony in London. As you well know I have good friends there. We can do it quietly, without fanfare. We'll sneak right back out of the city before anyone even knows we're there. When we do, I want to come back here."

"Sentiment? Old time's sake?"

Anthony smiled. "Something like that, old friend."

"A few stolen moments of bliss before she begins her new life?"

"Finally," Anthony said with exaggeration. "You understand."

The ghost of a smile touched Sneed's elongated, sagging features. "Just answer me one thing. Since you are so convinced of the lady's love, why not tell her now? Why wait until you're married?"

Anthony shrugged. He walked over to the bed and idly fingered the shirt Sneed had folded.

"I'm not sure, Sneed," he replied honestly. "I have

actually told her I'm not really Lord Farmington. She had already guessed as much, and it didn't matter to her. I just . . . I don't know." Anthony shook his head. "Maybe I've simply become so paranoid I can't bring myself to do it until we're safely wed."

"But if she loves you as you say . . ."

"All right, all right. Chalk it up to simple foolishness. But I want to do it my way."

"That's how this whole conversation started . . . the topic of foolishness."

"Yes, you're right. And I know you're going to accuse me of it once again, but . . ."

"But?"

"I want you to take my mare, ride north at once. Today."

"Are you mad?"

"I can easily hire a temporary coachman. He'll never suspect a thing. But I need you to take care of things at home for me."

Sneed crossed his arms tightly, and stubbornly, across his chest. He shook his head firmly. "I won't do it. I won't."

"Who's in charge here?"

"Someone other than you as you've apparently taken leave of your senses."

"Everything will be all right, Sneed. I promise you. I'll be careful. But you have to do this for me."

Sneed shook his head.

"Please, Sneed. I want everything to be nice for her. Nobody even knows she's coming."

"What about your mother? Don't you think she deserves a bit of a warning?"

"That's one of the things you're going to do at home. Tell her about all this. She'll be delighted, I'm sure. Especially when she finally meets Harmony. Please, Sneed? You're the only one who can do this for me. For *us*. It's going to be hard enough on her as it is."

Sneed let his arms fall to his sides. "Welllll . . ."

"Thank you, Sneed. Thank you." Impetuously, Anthony embraced the older man. "Now I'm going to go sweet talk Maggie into more coffee."

"Good luck." Sneed's smile lasted only as long as it took for Anthony to leave the room. Then it slipped away and his eyes clouded over with concern.

He had a very bad feeling about how this was all going to turn out.

Chapter Twenty-six

The fawn was young enough to still wear its camouflaging spots. It stepped from the shade of the woodland into the sunlight and stopped. One ear twitched. It bent its head to nibble at the grassy verge that bordered the garden path.

Harmony sat as still as a stone. The slight morning breeze was blowing in her face, so she knew the fawn had not caught her scent. If she made no movement, perhaps the animal would not see her either. It was a special moment, and she wanted to prolong it. It was the first genuine peace she had known in nearly three days.

The fawn lifted its head, large brown eyes searching. It stepped over the brick path and stuck its nose into some mossy ground cover.

Under her tender ministrations, the cover had only begun to grow this week, and now it appeared the deer would eat it. The fawn's mother must be somewhere nearby. But Harmony didn't care. Today was to be her last day under Agatha's roof.

A curious jubilation swelled in her breast. Soon she would be free of her sister, and bound to Anthony, the love of her life, forever. She did not yet know where she would live, or how she would live. But wherever it was, at least she would not have to sneak around. She would not have to worry about running into Agatha every time she turned a corner.

The urge to take a deep breath was almost overpowering, but Harmony quelled it, afraid to disturb the fawn. It seemed she was afraid of many things lately. Afraid, for instance, that Agatha would see in her eyes that she was right; Harmony did fear what they might learn about Anthony. He was not, he had admitted to her, Lord Farmington. So, who was he? He had also said, however, he was genuinely titled, and she believed him. But he had added that although he had told her truths, he had not told her all of them. Would an unrevealed "truth" give Agatha the power to ruin what had grown between them?

It was possible. Anything was possible. Agatha would do anything to destroy Harmony's happiness; she knew it without doubt. She also knew her own patience was coming to an end. Another reason to avoid her sister was the likelihood that she just might wrap her hands around Agatha's throat. How could anyone be so vicious? Especially to a member of one's own family, the only family they had left in the world?

Harmony didn't know. She no longer cared either. She only wanted to be away, away with Anthony, away from Agatha. Even should Anthony prove to be the bandit he had initially claimed to be, she would marry him. She didn't care. Her only fear was that if it did, indeed, prove to be the case, she had gotten away with Anthony before Agatha found out and tried to stop them.

Perhaps the situation was, in a way, a blessing. If her love had to be put to a test, this was a good one. She hadn't the slightest uncertainty about loving Anthony, marrying him. The moment he arrived she would fly into his arms. She would leave this cursed house, leave her sister, without a backward glance or a single pang of regret.

Harmony took a deep breath, forgetful of the fawn. Its head snapped up and an instant later it bolted back into the sheltering shade of the trees. Harmony watched it go and rose from her bench seat. She was almost entirely packed. All she had to do was change into her traveling suit and fold away what she had on at the moment. She smiled to herself.

The suit was the blue one Anthony had first seen her in. She would be, truly, his Lady Blue.

❧

Mrs. Rutledge stood in the doorway of the morning room and cleared her throat. "Excuse me, Miss Simmons. I hate to disturb you, but—"

"Then don't," Agatha snapped. "Can't you see I'm busy?"

"But a courier has arrived," Mrs. Rutledge went on implacably. "He says he has a special delivery message for Miss Agatha Simmons."

"Why didn't you say so at once?" Agatha rose in a swirl of pale gray silk and brushed past the housekeeper, who calmly moved aside. She followed her mistress down the corridor to the foyer.

"Where is it? Give it to me," Agatha demanded of the middle-aged, wiry man dressed in nondescript livery. He produced an envelope she snatched from his hand and immediately ripped open. She scanned the lines of the enclosed letter almost greedily. An uncharacteristic smile temporarily brightened her generally saturnine expression.

"I knew it!" Agatha exulted. "Here's my proof!"

"Proof?" Mrs. Rutledge echoed.

"Never mind. Get the coachman. Have him bring round my carriage at once."

"Have you forgotten, Miss Simmons? He turned in his notice and left several days ago."

"What? Oh . . . oh, yes." Agatha turned to the

wide-eyed man lingering in the doorway. "You came in a coach, did you not?"

"Y-y-yes," the man stammered.

"Good. You're hired. Come with me."

Mrs. Rutledge stood in the foyer and watched her mistress sail through the doorway, down the front steps, and along the front path, the driver in tow. She shook her head.

Whatever had given her mistress such cause for excitement did not bode well for the younger Miss Simmons. Hopefully, her stay would be coming to an end sooner than expected. There had scarce been a moment's peace in the house since the young strumpet had come to stay. Mrs. Rutledge gave a disapproving sniff and closed the front door.

Several days of pushing the window open a little wider each time had finally loosened the ivy's grip on the glass. Harmony was able to open it nearly all the way, which she did the moment she returned to her room. The sun climbed high toward noon and the day had grown almost stiflingly warm. Harmony leaned a way out the window to catch the breath of a passing breeze. And saw the coach standing in the drive.

Her heart lurched. He had come.

But no. It was not Anthony's shining black coach, nor the four elegant horses that pulled it. Who could it be?

Even as she wondered, she saw her sister emerge from the house. A small, thin man hurried in her wake. Agatha climbed into the coach without waiting for the driver's assistance. She appeared to be in a hurry. It wasn't like her.

Harmony withdrew from the window, a sickening feeling blooming in the pit of her stomach.

What was Agatha up to? Where was she going? The sickening feeling rose to the back of her throat.

Agatha had said she was writing to someone in London, sending the letter by special courier. She had said she expected her answer by . . . today. An answer about Anthony's true identity. Had it arrived?

Harmony bent over suddenly, arms wrapped protectively around her midsection. She felt as if she had just received a blow to the abdomen.

"Anthony," she whispered. "Please come. Please come soon."

Lady Margaret held her pince-nez up to her eyes and read the letter Agatha had handed to her. She drew in her breath sharply and dropped the pince-nez to dangle by the chain around her neck. The piece of paper fluttered to the floor.

"Agatha," Lady Margaret said on an exhalation. "This is most shocking."

"It's positively scandalous." Agatha's expression was grim, but her eyes glittered.

"What are we going to do?"

"That's why I came to you, Lady Margaret. It was your good advice, and your husband's connections, that helped to expose this . . . this evil *charade*. I must defer to you once again."

"Quite right. Quite right." Lady Margaret paused for a moment in thought, then pressed a hand to her heart. "To think I had him as a guest of honor in my home!"

"To say nothing of the fact he is affianced to my sister!" Agatha pulled a lacy handkerchief from inside the cuff of her sleeve and dabbed at her face with it.

"My reputation as a hostess, as a woman of good character, will be ruined!" Lady Margaret reached behind her and yanked on a bell rope hanging to one side of the portrait of a nobleman standing beside a saddled horse. A uniformed servant appeared a scant moment later.

"Bring me my fan and my salts," Lady Margaret commanded.

"I will never be able to hold up my head in the

community again!" When the maid reappeared with the requested items, Lady Margaret snatched them from her and vigorously began to fan her face.

"This is devastating, Agatha. We must *think*."

Agatha nodded gravely. "We must think, and we must act. Quickly. The charlatan is coming this very day to take Harmony away."

"No!"

"It's not to be borne, Lady Margaret. I must stop it. But how?"

"Be quiet a moment. Let me think." Lady Margaret closed her eyes, laid the fan and her salts aside, and pressed her hands to her temples. "The most important thing," she said at length, "is to keep the entire thing hushed up."

"How is that possible?" Agatha mourned. Her initial excitement had turned to genuine distress. The ramifications were truly terrible. "If we expose him as an impostor, as we must, everyone will know. We really *will* be ruined! *Both* of us have had the wool pulled ignobly over our eyes," Agatha finished. She thought it quite clever that she had inextricably bound Lady Margaret to her dilemma.

Lady Margaret grew thoughtful. She pursed her lips and folded her hands in her lap. "The letter says only that there is no Lord Farmington, correct?"

Agatha nodded. "Not living, anyway. The last to

hold that title passed away eleven years ago. Childless."

"Why would this . . . Anthony Allen . . . need to hide his true identity, if not for some nefarious purpose?"

"You . . . you mean you really think . . .?"

"What else can I think?"

Agatha's eyes were wide. She hugged her arms to her breast. "He might really be the . . . the jewel thief?"

"If it sounded plausible three days ago, why not now?"

Agatha shivered. "It's just so . . . so *horrible* to think of it. A thief among us in our very homes!"

"Do not distress yourself, Agatha," Lady Margaret said firmly. "He will not be among us much longer."

"Why? What are you going to do?"

"The local authorities have been quite vexed about their inability to apprehend the criminal in our midst, operating right under their noses. I should think they would be most glad of information that will lead to his immediate arrest."

"But . . . but won't that be worse for us? It's bad enough if everyone finds out we had been taken in by, and harbored, a simple impostor. But a jewel thief!"

"Calm yourself, Agatha. Please. You forget who you are dealing with."

Agatha squirmed in her seat. "I apologize, Lady Margaret. Still, I don't see . . ."

"Angus has some very powerful connections. I thought that had been proved to you."

"Well, yes, but . . ."

"And we are the very pillars of this community, are we not?"

"Oh, certainly. Yes, Lady Margaret."

"Then I beg you to have some forbearance. Many things can be accomplished by people in . . . our position."

"Of course . . . of course, Lady Margaret!"

Lady Margaret once again reached for the bell rope and tugged it. The maid appeared with familiar alacrity.

"Have the coach prepared, Cynthia," Lady Margaret ordered. "And inform my husband I have need of him. Hurry up, now. Off with you!"

"Where . . . where are you going?" Agatha squeaked.

"To the authorities, of course. Angus and I must inform them that the perpetrator of the monstrous villainies that have taken place in our fair village has been unmasked. We must arrange for his capture."

"But . . ."

"The whole sordid affair will be kept quiet, I assure you. *Lord* Farmington is going to disappear as quickly and mysteriously as he appeared. I have a plan . . ."

Anthony stood outside the rundown livery stable and glared at the fat, balding man who had professed to be able to drive a coach and four. That had been inside the musty stable where Anthony had found him. Now, looking at the carriage and the horses standing outside his establishment, the man seemed less sure of himself.

"Well," Anthony said impatiently. "Either you can drive it or you can't. Which is it?"

"I dunno." The man scratched his naked, pink scalp. "Them be some pretty fancy horses. What they be called?"

Anthony sighed with impatience. "They're Hackneys. Hackney horses."

"Hey!" The man brightened. "I heard o' them. High steppers, ain't they?"

"Yes. Yes, they are. Can you drive them or not?"

"Where you git 'em?"

"I breed them, actually. Not that it's any of your burning concern. Can you *drive* them?"

"Guess so."

"Good. Wonderful. Let's get going."

"Wait there half a minute, Mr. Fancy Pants. There's a little matter of me pay."

Anthony reached into his coat pocket and pulled out a small leather sac. He bounced it once on his palm, then tossed it to the driver. "I believe this will do."

The man hefted the bag's weight, eyes bulging. "I guess it will."

"Can we get going, then?"

"After you, young gentleman, sir." The man made

to open the coach door, but Anthony stopped him.

"I think I'll ride up beside you," he said. "For a way, at least. Just to make sure you're as . . . proficient as you say you are."

"Have it your way."

The two men climbed up on the bench seat. The driver took the reins and shook them. Nothing happened.

"The brake," Anthony growled, exasperated. "You have to release the brake!"

"Oh . . . oh, yeah." The driver pushed the handle forward and shook the reins again. The team moved forward onto the main roadway.

The stable Anthony had found was on the outskirts of the city, and within a few minutes they had left the London traffic behind. The horses trotted smartly along on the open road.

"Let them have a little more rein," Anthony advised. "They can move out at a much brisker pace."

The driver gave the lines another modest shake. It was more than Anthony could stand. The urgency growing within him had reached an intolerable pitch. He grabbed the reins from the startled man, pulled the carriage whip from its holder, and snapped the lash sharply. The coach surged forward.

"Hang on!" he yelled to the driver. He snapped the whip again and the horses broke into a gallop. He knew suddenly, inexplicably, he had no more time to waste.

For the hundredth time that afternoon, Harmony walked to her bedroom window and looked out over the drive. It remained empty. No sign of a coach. Not since Agatha's return. Harmony turned her back to the window.

Where had Agatha gone? She had thought, surely, that upon her return Agatha would be bursting with news of some kind. But there had been nothing. Something had to be afoot. But what? Not knowing was almost worse than whatever horrible thing Agatha might have to tell her.

Please, Anthony, Harmony prayed. *Please hurry.*

Hands clasped tightly together, Harmony crossed to her dressing table. Also for the hundredth time that day, she nervously inspected her reflection. Anthony would be pleased, she was certain. She forced a smile to her lips.

The sapphire blue of the suit matched her eyes to perfection. She had pulled her hair back from her face and curled it into ringlets that tumbled down her back. She had her gloves ready, and her jaunty little traveling hat. All the bags were packed. She was ready to go. *More* than ready to become Anthony's wife.

A thrill of pleasure coursed through Harmony's limbs. It intensified when she heard the familiar crunch of carriage wheels on the gravel drive.

Her first instinct was to run to the window and make sure it was Anthony's coach. But it had to be him. Of course it was him!

Harmony flew from her room to the corridor. She picked up her skirts and ran to the stairs and took them, dangerously, two at a time. One more length of hallway, one more turn . . .

Harmony rounded the corner into the foyer and stopped dead in her tracks, panting.

"Mr. Henry!"

"Miss Simmons." The constable nodded gravely.

Harmony looked past him to the two younger, but equally grim-faced men who stood behind him. "What . . . what are you doing here?" she stammered.

Agatha took a step forward. "They've come to arrest a jewel thief," she announced jubilantly.

"What?"

"You heard me. They've come to arrest your . . . *fiancé*."

"No." Harmony shook her head slowly from side to side in denial. "No . . ."

"Yes," Agatha said tartly. "Thanks to the aid of some highly placed people, we have uncovered the fact that Anthony Allen, Lord Farmington, is no lord at all."

"But that doesn't mean—"

"The thefts began when he first made himself known in this community," Mr. Henry interjected. "And let us not forget that it all began with your sapphire ring."

Harmony couldn't speak. An abyss had opened beneath her feet. At any moment she was going to fall into, and through, the earth.

"Yes," Agatha echoed smugly. "Let us not forget. He *claimed* to have found your ring. *I* maintain that he stole it. Then used it to gain entrée into my home, into local society, in order to perpetrate more of his iniquitous crimes."

Stunned, Harmony felt her jaw drop. Could it be true? Could it?

Her doubt lasted only an instant. A thief Anthony might be. But he had not used her. He loved her. She knew it beyond doubt.

"You just want to ruin my life, Agatha. Admit it!" Harmony cried.

"I want to *save* your life, you foolish girl. Not to mention your reputation."

"You mean *your* reputation!" Harmony spat.

"How dare you?"

"Now, now." Mr. Henry stepped between the two women. "There's no point in denying it, Miss Simmons," he said to Harmony. "We have all the proof we need.

I'm sorry, but your . . . friend . . . is definitely the man we've been looking for."

The full impact of the reality hit Harmony with the force of a blow to the abdomen. "No!"

With all her strength, Harmony pushed Mr. Henry aside and bolted for the door.

"Stop her!" the constable shouted.

Harmony felt rough hands grab her arms. She struggled, but the two other officers held her tightly. She kicked one of them and was rewarded with the sound of a grunt.

"Take her to her room," Agatha ordered. "The vixen! Mrs. Rutledge, show them the way. Lock her in!"

"Nooooo!" Harmony screamed. She tried to kick again, but the two men simply lifted her off her feet.

Thus suspended, she was carried through the hall-ways and up the stairs to her room. Mrs. Rutledge opened the door and the men carried her inside where she was deposited unceremoniously on the floor. The men left, closing the door behind them. Harmony heard the sound of a key turning in the lock. She flew at the door.

"Let me out! Damn you, let me out!"

Harmony balled her fists and banged on the door until her hands were raw. She kicked. Futilely. Once again, she was a prisoner.

Sobbing hysterically, helplessly, Harmony sank to

the floor in a pool of sapphire silk.

Anthony drove until they reached the turnoff into the wood that surrounded Agatha's home. He hauled his team to a stop.

"You drive from here," he told the coachman. "And remember. We're picking up a lady. Please treat her like one. And say as little as possible."

The man nodded, a serious expression on his round face, and pressed a finger to his lips. Anthony climbed down and into the coach. He tapped on the front wall, hoping the driver would know what it meant, and was gratified when the carriage rolled forward.

Only a few more minutes, he told himself. Only a few more minutes and he would have Harmony safely away. Another hour to return to London and the small, private chapel where a few of his closest friends awaited. Then they would be united forever. His every prayer would be answered, his every dream come true.

Anthony tried to relax for the remainder of his journey, but it was difficult. He found himself on the edge of his seat, literally, when the coach finally pulled into the gravel drive. He was surprised to see another vehicle, a rather shabby one at that, already parked in front of the house. A prickle of apprehension traveled down his spine.

Not waiting for the driver to climb down from his box, Anthony opened the door himself. He had one foot on the ground when the front door to Agatha's house opened and three men emerged. The one in the lead raised a pistol and aimed it squarely at Anthony's chest.

"Put your hands up," the man ordered. "You're under arrest in the name of the Queen."

Time came to a halt. This was incomprehensible. Slowly, Anthony raised his arms. He saw Agatha appear at the top of the front steps. She squinted in the bright sunlight. And smiled.

While the one man held the gun on Anthony, the other two came around to flank him. One of them pulled his arms down and pinned them at his back; the other slapped on a pair of handcuffs.

"And to what," Anthony drawled sarcastically, "do I owe the pleasure of your company?"

"Jewel theft," Mr. Henry replied promptly.

"You're out of your mind."

"No, Mr. Allen, I am not. It was you who was out of your mind if you thought you'd get away with your thievery indefinitely."

"This is outrageous!"

"Shut up!" Agatha, who had been watching from the top of the steps, hurried down the path to stand behind Mr. Henry. "Shut up, you . . . you scoundrel.

You fiend!"

Anthony forced himself to recover a measure of calm. "Miss Simmons, I'm afraid there's been a great and terrible misunder—"

"Don't you 'Miss Simmons' *me*!" Agatha shrieked. "Gag him! *Gag* him!"

"Don't you worry, Miss Simmons," Mr. Henry soothed. "We've been warned about his silver tongue. We're ready."

"What are you—?" It was all Anthony got out before a strip of linen was clapped over his mouth and secured tightly at the back of his head.

It couldn't be happening. It simply couldn't be happening.

"All right," Mr. Henry said. "Take him to the wagon."

There was no point in resisting. The two young officers hustled him toward the other vehicle. He was shoved rudely inside and stumbled with his hands secured behind him. Quick as a cat he turned over on his back, not trusting the two officers. As he did so, he chanced to look up. His heart froze within his breast.

"Anthony!" Harmony screamed. She thrust her window all the way open and leaned precipitously over the sill. "Anthony!"

The coach door slammed shut. Harmony was lost from his sight.

Harmony did not think she would ever sleep again. She had lain down on her bed out of sheer, physical exhaustion. She had paced the floor, pounded and kicked on the door, and screamed herself hoarse. She had carried on until sheer exhaustion had felled her. Never had she actually expected to fall asleep. But she awoke, with a start, to realize darkness had fallen. Harmony scrambled to her feet.

"Anthony . . ."

Where had they taken him? To jail?

Was she still sleeping and tangled in the fabric of a nightmare?

Not bothering with a light, Harmony hurled herself at the door and raised her hands to begin pounding anew. It opened so suddenly she lost her balance and nearly fell into her sister's arms.

"Agatha!"

"Who else did you expect? Your charming fiancé?" she inquired cruelly.

"Where have they taken him?"

"To jail, of course. Where he belongs."

"You can't do this. He's innocent!"

"Oh, yes I can. And no, he's not."

"You can't prove it! You can't prove any of it," Harmony said desperately. "There'll be a trial and—"

"Oh, no, there won't be." Smiling, eyes fixed on Harmony, Agatha shook her head. "That's what I came to tell you, as a matter of fact. So I could spare you needless suffering and worry. There will be no trial."

Harmony's arms suddenly felt so weak she didn't think she could raise them if she wanted to. "What . . . what do you mean there won't be a trial?"

"Just what I said." Agatha's smile never faltered.

"But you can't . . . it can't happen that way. It's not—"

"It's what some very powerful people want," Agatha interrupted. "And so that is the way it will be."

"People? Lady Margaret, you mean." Harmony's tone had subtly hardened.

"Lady Margaret's husband will never let it be known they hosted a common criminal in their home."

"He's *not* a—"

"The scandal would be ruinous," Agatha went on blithely, ignoring her sister. "There's our family name to consider as well. And *your* honor, Harmony."

"I don't care about my honor!"

"No," Agatha agreed. "You obviously do not. I, however, do. Furthermore, I still hope to see you respectably married one day. No decent man will have you should it become known you were involved with not only an impostor but a criminal."

Harmony's fists were clenched so tightly her

fingernails cut into her flesh. Unnoticed, a drop of blood fell to the floor. "He is *not* a criminal," she said through gritted teeth. "And you cannot deny him a fair trial."

"*Au contraire*," Agatha replied lightly. "There will be no scandal because there will be no trial. Anthony Allen will simply disappear. The story will be put round that you and he had a lover's spat, and he moved on."

"You can't make Anthony 'simply disappear.'"

"Oh, no?" Agatha's smile was almost feral. "You underestimate the power of the people who are my friends. Anthony will be hanged at dawn, secretly. Even now, as we speak, a scaffold is being erected within the confines of the Millswich jail."

Horror clutched at Harmony's heart. Icy terror held her in its grip.

But her anger was growing. And it was white-hot.

"You *witch*," she hissed.

"Call me all the names you like, sister dear," Agatha snarled. "There's nothing you can do to save your precious Anthony now. I've *won*. I've beaten you!"

"And it's what you've wanted all along, isn't it, Agatha?" Harmony said with quiet menace. "It's what you've wanted all your life."

In response, Agatha laughed, a sharp, bitter sound like the bark of a dog.

Harmony smiled grimly. "Well, Agatha, this is

what *I've* wanted."

Harmony put all her strength, all her anger, all her desperate fear for Anthony into the punch. It caught her sister squarely on the jaw and lifted her from her feet. She flew backward and slammed into the door-jamb. Her expression registered momentary surprise. Then her eyes rolled up in her head and she slipped to the floor. Something fell from her pocket.

It was a key. Harmony had seen it before. It was the key to Agatha's safe.

Her thoughts whirled madly. There was money in the safe. Enough money, perhaps, for she and Anthony to get far away. If she could save him, rescue him. If . . .

The idea formed even as Harmony dragged her sister inside her bedroom. She slammed the door behind them and turned the key that Agatha had left in the lock. Then she raced down the hall to her sister's room.

It was a daring plan. Risky. With very little chance of success. And a very large chance of failure . . . and death.

But she had to try. She had to.

Chapter Twenty-seven

Harmony waited for a rush of fear, guilt, anything. But the only thing she felt was power. Power and strength and determination. She ran into Agatha's room and fell to her knees in front of the safe. The key turned smoothly and she yanked the door open.

It seemed the money almost leapt into her hands. She had no qualms whatsoever about taking it. When she had grabbed as much as she could hold, she jumped back to her feet. And realized her terrible error.

Everything she needed was locked in her bedroom with Agatha. Furthermore, Mrs. Rutledge would certainly be coming 'round soon to see her mistress safely tucked into bed. Teeth bared, hands fisted around the money, Harmony knew what she had to do.

Holding up her voluminous skirt, Harmony took the stairs two at a time. At the bottom, she temporarily shoved her wad of bills into the potting dirt of a spindly potted palm. Barely in the nick of time. She heard footsteps approaching from the direction of the dining room and kitchen.

Her worst fear was not realized, however. It was not Mrs. Rutledge who appeared moments later but Sophie, the cook. She carried a tray with a pot of tea, a cup and saucer, and a small plate of biscuits.

"Sophie!" Harmony exclaimed, surprised and grateful.

"Miss Simmons. I hope I didn't alarm you. Mrs. Rutledge has gone off to bed and I'm bringing the mistress her nightly tea and biscuit."

"How kind of you. But here, let me help you. I was just going upstairs myself."

Harmony held her breath for a moment, but Sophie willingly surrendered the tray.

One hurdle leaped. Balancing the tray carefully, Harmony retraced her steps to the bedroom. Agatha had apparently regained consciousness. The pounding and screeching began almost the moment Harmony reached her door. She set the tray down, inserted the key in the lock, and prepared to do battle.

Agatha was on her the instant she crossed the threshold.

"Bitch! Whore!"

Agatha's eyes were nearly as wild as her hair. Her arms pinwheeled as she tried to strike Harmony, fingers curled into talons. Spittle flew from her lips as she spewed her imprecations. What Harmony knew she had to do did not bother her in the least.

This time her blow was not spur of the moment, but well planned and precisely aimed. Harmony hadn't grown up rough-and-tumble on a cattle ranch for nothing. She knew where to put her fist to obtain maximum results. When she connected with her sister's left temple, Agatha went down like a marionette whose strings had been severed. She would be out for a good, long while.

Mrs. Rutledge safely tucked away for the night, Sophie undoubtedly on her way to bed, and Agatha out cold, Harmony set to work with a vengeance. The first thing she did was strip to her chemise and petticoats, then pull open the lid to her recently packed trunk. Rummaging madly, she finally found what she was looking for at the very bottom, wrapped in a split riding skirt.

Triumphant, Harmony laid the bundle on the floor and carefully unwrapped it. A surge of something fierce and primal surged through her breast. Without further thought she stepped out of her petticoats and pulled on the riding skirt. It took only moments to locate a cotton blouse, and her fingers did not even fumble when she fastened it. Her eye was on the prize; she would not falter.

Black gloves and riding boots almost completed

the ensemble. There was only one thing left to do in the house. Bending down, Harmony picked up the holster and fastened it low on her hips. It felt wonderful, powerful, liberating to slip her revolvers into place. A brief test of their proper placing for a quick draw and she was almost ready to leave.

The seeds of a plan had germinated in Harmony's head and she hastily packed a smaller bag with some items she ticked off in her fevered brain: riding breeches, a Stetson, one of her looser fitting gowns, and a matching bonnet. Feeling as if it might be an omen, she noted the gown she had selected was blue. It was time to go at last.

It gave her grim satisfaction to once again lock Agatha into the room. At the bottom of the stairs she retrieved the bills, shoved them into her pockets, and buried the key in the dirt. Mrs. Rutledge had her own set, of course, but maybe the action would set them back just a little. An instant later she was out the door and on her way to the stable.

Harmony blessed her father for his insistence on her learning to drive a team. It took only a scant few minutes to take Agatha's horses from their stalls and set their harness. Even amid the turmoil of thoughts spinning in her head and the adrenaline pumping through her veins, she felt sorry for the underfed, ungroomed beasts. In that moment she decided she would do whatever she had to do to keep them with her and never return them to her sister. If she survived.

The coach was heavy, but Harmony managed to haul it by its shafts out into the open. The docile horses were quickly and easily hooked, and Harmony climbed up onto her driving seat. She had already stowed her bag inside.

The first thrills of absolute fear began worming their way through Harmony's body. How late was it? How close to dawn? How much time did she have left? Then the next problem asserted itself, and she put aside the tormenting questions.

The solution occurred to her almost as soon as the problem presented itself and Harmony turned her team down the road to the inn. When she arrived she kept the coach in the shadows of the attached stable and slipped into the fragrant darkness unnoticed.

It was a good night for Maggie. The inn must be full. There were several mounts to choose from.

A clean-limbed bay gelding was swiftly tacked. Having already assessed the animal, it was relatively easy to judge its worth, and she threw a number of bills into the now empty stall and led the horse out of the barn where she secured the reins to the back of the coach. Within moments she was off again, in a race with the dawn.

The long night was almost over. Anthony knew because of the barest lessening of the darkness in his cell. Dawn approached. What did it bring with it?

He feared the worst. Something was very wrong. And not just the fact that he had been arrested. It was the way he was being treated.

Painfully, Anthony drew his knees up under him. Back pressed to the damp, moldy wall, he pushed to his feet. It was difficult with his hands still cuffed behind his back. The gag remained in his mouth as well, and his tongue was as dry as a desert. He had a powerful thirst. He had a powerful fear, too.

He had never heard of anyone under arrest being treated this way before. Of course, he wasn't privy to the law's deepest, darkest secrets. Was he about to become one of them? It was possible, he had to admit.

He also had to admit that Sneed had been right. He had taken the biggest risk, and made the biggest mistake, of his life. He should have been truthful from the very beginning. But would she still have loved him?

Yes. Having come to know her as he had, he could not deny that her love for him was honest and true. It had nothing to do with what he was or wasn't. It would have been a little harder to win her, perhaps, at first. But their love, it seemed, had been destined. Nothing could stand in its way.

Or could it?

Had he achieved his final destiny? Had he reached the end of his life?

It couldn't be. It simply couldn't be. He had it all now. How could it be over?

Anthony shook his head as if to free himself from such horrific thoughts. He walked over to the tiny window of his cell, the one through which the first faint rays of light were entering. Approximately three-quarters of the jail cells had been constructed belowground, and he had to stand on tiptoe to see outside. He was eye level with the street that ran in front of the jail.

Someone would come along soon. And when they did, he would . . . what? Yell? How would he accomplish that, gagged as he was? He could ask for no aid.

Nor could he plead his innocence. Or tell someone in authority who he really was, and tell them whom to contact to verify it.

Something cold and hard lodged suddenly in the pit of Anthony's stomach.

Was that why he had been gagged . . . to silence him? But why? And for how long? This state of affairs couldn't persist. It was against all common procedures of English law.

It seemed he was about to get his answer. Anthony heard footsteps in the corridor. He turned to his cell door to face his jailer.

There were three of them again. The two younger men from the previous day, and a third he had never seen before. The man was squat, muscular, and had a balding head patterned similarly to a monk's tonsure. He had hard, dark eyes set close together, and they seemed to gleam with a strange and unfathomable passion. Gooseflesh rose on Anthony's skin.

The short man unlocked the cell door. "Bring him out."

The other men flanked Anthony. Each took one of his arms. They marched him out of his cell and down a narrow corridor, the shorter man in the lead. At the end of the hallway he opened another door and they all proceeded through it into the pink glow of dawn.

They were in a courtyard, shielded on three sides by the U-shaped jail. A fence with a padlocked gate closed off the fourth side. In the center of the yard stood an erection whose familiar shape caused a temporary blackness to pass in front of Anthony's eyes.

It was a gallows.

Chapter Twenty-eight

The first faint lessening of the darkness gave Harmony renewed strength, strength born of fear. Agatha had said Anthony was to be hanged at dawn. Pulling the coachman's whip from its sheath near her right hand, Harmony sent the lash whistling over the horses' backs, and their speed increased immediately. The ground seemed to shudder beneath their pounding hooves and Harmony rose to her feet, all four lines being manipulated in her left hand, the better to wield the drop-lash whip in her right. It vaguely occurred to her that she must very much resemble a stagecoach driver trying to outrun a band of marauding braves.

It was only a few miles to Millswich. Her horses ate up the ground, and she soon saw the village ahead. It was early enough that no one was about yet, and she was grateful. Nevertheless, to be as cautious as possible, she halted and pulled out the blue scarf she had tucked into a pocket. Harmony folded it into a triangle and tied it over her face, leaving only her eyes exposed. Then she picked up the reins again and looked for a place to park the coach out of sight.

A copse of trees on the outskirts of town would do nicely. Harmony drove her team into the deep shade, then beyond into a clearing a good way back from the road. She put on the brake, wrapped the reins around it, and climbed down from the coachman's box.

The bay gelding was none the worse for wear. Harmony detached his reins from the coach and mounted. Heart hammering painfully, she noticed that dawn pinked the eastern horizon when she left the shadows of the trees. She urged her horse into a gallop and headed straight for the Millswich jail.

❦

It couldn't be happening. But it was. Somebody wanted him dead.

Although he apparently walked to his execution, the irony of the situation did not escape Anthony. He had lived his life in secrecy. Now he was going to die in secrecy.

But why?

It was Agatha and Lady Margaret; it had to be. They must have discovered he had "borrowed"

Farmington's lordship. All the jewel thefts, coincidental to his arrival in the area, would be difficult to ignore. There was also the incident with the sapphire ring he had "found." They had attempted to add two and two. With a sum of four, their reputations would be at stake. They couldn't allow such a thing to happen. Society could never possibly know they had harbored a thief. Féted him. Allowed and embraced his engagement to one of their own.

So there would be no trial, no fanfare, scandal. A jewel thief, a bounder, a rogue, would simply disappear. Perhaps he had simply moved on, some would say, to practice his talents in another location. Maybe he had met with a more fitting end. Either way, it didn't matter. Life would go on as usual. Only a very few would know what had really happened to him. Or care. He had a brief vision of his mother's face and felt a stabbing pain in his heart.

Sneed had been so right, Anthony thought as he climbed the steps to the platform. And he would not even get the chance to say "I told you so." Pity.

The greatest pity, however, was the death of a love newly blossomed, cut down at the height of its bloom.

The short, muscular man slipped a black hood over his head.

Fear nearly unmanned him. He felt his bowels turn to water and had to fight for control. His heart raced at an impossible speed and his knees threatened to buckle. He was about to hang. About to die. He forced his thoughts from a glimpse of hell to a vision of heaven.

I love you, Harmony. I will always love you.

He felt the noose being slipped over his head, around his neck.

I am so very sorry for the mistakes I've made. For the pain you will suffer.

I love you.

❧

Dawn. It had arrived. Harmony leaned low over her horse's neck, urging him to greater speed. When she reached the jail, she pulled him to a sliding stop and threw herself from the saddle. She landed on her feet, already running.

There was no time for thought or finesse. Harmony burst through the first door she came to, pistols drawn.

A uniformed man behind a desk leaped to his feet. "Wha—?"

"Hands in the air!" Harmony ordered. Had her business not been so deadly serious, she might have giggled. This was England, not America, yet the scene was right out of a dime Western novel. As it was, with Anthony's life hanging in the balance, she grimaced behind the blue kerchief.

"You heard me." Harmony poked at the man's chest with one of her pistols and his arms shot skyward. "Now take me to the prisoner who's supposed to hang this morning."

The man opened his mouth to speak. Harmony backhanded him across the cheek with the revolver in her left hand, leaving an instant welt and several bright spots of blood. He scurried for the door.

They were headed toward what appeared to be a door to the courtyard. The notion was confirmed when it swung wide and two guards entered. Harmony had a brief glimpse of a scaffold—and someone on it—before the door closed again and she started firing.

The man in front of her, her guide, dodged sideways, slipped, and crashed into the wall. One down. The other two, coming at her, crumpled to the ground, each clutching a foot.

"Stay down or I'll aim higher next time," Harmony rasped as the raced past them and flew through the door.

It was Anthony standing on the scaffold; she saw him at once. The noose was already around his neck, a hood over his head, and a short, balding man—Mr. Henry, she realized with shock and dismay—had his hand on the lever that would open the trapdoor and send Anthony to his death. There wasn't a heartbeat to lose.

But wait. Was it truly Anthony? The hood made it almost impossible to tell, although the figure was the right height and weight.

"Anthony!" she cried.

"Guards!" Henry shouted. "What are you waiting for? Go get that woman!"

The man on the scaffold tried to twist away from Henry, and the moment he moved Harmony knew it was Anthony.

As the guards pounded down the gallows steps, Harmony shoved the pistol in her left hand into its holster and fanned the hammer of the revolver in her right, peppering the scaffolding at eye level. The two officers heading down the steps reached for their weapons, but they weren't fast enough. Harmony had plenty of time to retrieve the pistol on her left, take precise aim, and blow their arms out of their hands before their fingers could fasten on the grips. She pointed both pistols at Henry.

"Take the noose off his neck, and the hood. Unlock the cuffs."

"Have you lost your—?"

"*Do* it." Harmony fired two more shots, one with each hand, to the right and left of the constable's feet. He removed the rope and the hood but, in his nervousness, fumbled the key to the cuffs. Keeping one pistol aimed at Henry's head, the other on one of the guards, Harmony said, "Anthony, jump down."

She was in front of the scaffold when his feet hit the ground. Still aiming one gun at Henry's head, she spun Anthony around. A single shot freed his hands. A second shot shattered the lock on the gate leading to freedom.

"Miss Simmons," Henry shouted as she and Anthony bolted for the gate, "you can try to disguise your face, but you cannot hide the color of your hair. Give up now before you end up in the cell next to Allen's."

As she raced through the gate and rounded the corner toward the front of the jail where she had left her horse, Henry's final words were lost to Harmony. Undoubtedly it was merely more of the same. And no matter what he said, it didn't matter anyway. She'd be going into hiding with Anthony. She had forever alienated her sister and shot two guards in the foot. There was no going back. Anthony at her side, she continued to run as fast as she could.

They were in perfect synch. As Anthony vaulted into the saddle, Harmony holstered her guns, then reached out her right hand to him. In one smooth motion he pulled her up and in front of him, and they were on their way. Harmony covered the retreat, sending a few rounds into the ground at the feet of the two pursuing guards. Mr. Henry, no doubt, was still standing, dazed, on the scaffold.

Harmony didn't know how long they might have. A little time, surely, before the men managed to get mounted and out of the courtyard. Then they would be after them.

She rode the gelding hard, lashing his flanks with the end of her reins, urging even more speed from the tiring animal. Flecks of foam blew from his mouth to stain her skirt, and her fingers tangled in his blowing mane.

At last she came to the place she had marked at the side of the road. A piece of white material, torn from the tail of her blouse, fluttered from a tree where she had impaled the cloth on the point of a twig. She pulled on the reins, and the gelding left the road and came to an abrupt halt.

"Get down, Anthony, quickly."

He obeyed, then held out his arms to catch her as she slid from the horse. Before she could protest, he drew her into his arms and kissed her. Hard. She pushed him away.

"We don't have time, Anthony. We—"

"There is no 'we,'" he interrupted. "Take the horse. Go on."

Out of breath, Harmony could only shake her head. Anthony caught her face in his hands to still her.

"You can get away. You'll be forgiven for your rash

act in the name of love. I'll see to it. Go back to your sister. Go back to where you're safe. I'll take care of the rest."

"I can't, Anthony. It's too late. I . . . I've done something to her. She'll have *me* arrested, too."

Despite their circumstances, the crooked smile started to twitch at one corner of Anthony's mouth. "What did you do, Harmony?"

"Now's no time to talk, Anthony!" She grabbed the front of his shirt and tried to pull him into the trees.

"Harmony, what—?"

"I have a plan, Anthony. Just be quiet and follow me."

"But they're going to be right behind us! We don't have time for this—whatever it is. We have to get away. We have to keep riding. At least until we get to a place where I'll be recognized, for who I really am, and be safe."

Harmony took a precious moment to plant her hands on her hips. "This is going to be the first and last time you ever underestimate me, Anthony Allen. Or whoever you are. Now, come on!"

Baffled and bemused, and very much in awe, Anthony allowed Harmony to lead him through the trees. Before long they came to a small clearing. Anthony's jaw dropped.

"How . . . how did you . . .? I mean . . .?"

Anthony, still numb and somewhat dazed by the swift succession of life-altering events, not the least of which was watching the love of his life rescue him from certain death with guns blazing, could only continue to stare, uncomprehending.

"Anthony. *Please.* We haven't much time." Exasperation turning to fear, Harmony pulled open the coach door and yanked out her bag. She pawed through the contents until she found the gown and bonnet and thrust them at him. "Here. Put these on."

"You are amazing, but . . . but won't we be recognized anyway? They know who we are. And they're looking for a man and a woman, no matter how they're attired."

"Not this man and woman," Harmony said tartly.

Anthony finally realized what he held in his hands. "Oh, my God. You've got to be kidding."

"Just hurry up, my darling. There is no time for complaints."

The fog in Anthony's brain began to lift and clear. Harmony had just risked her life for him, and they were not out of danger yet—not until he could get to a place where people knew him—where he would be safe from re-arrest. The beauty and simplicity of Harmony's plan became immediately clear to him, however, and he pulled the gown on over his clothing.

Her plan just might buy them some more time should they be stopped again before he could get them to a place of safety.

It felt like a corset had been loosened and Harmony could finally breathe again. Heedless of her modesty, she took off her riding skirt and boots and pulled on the breeches. Then she moistened her kerchief with saliva, dabbed it in the dirt, and applied the resulting mess to her cheeks and chin. As she pulled her boots back on she watched Anthony adjust his bonnet and she felt the beginnings of a smile caress her lips with the softness of a butterfly's wings. She wanted to let the smile fly free, but the danger was not behind them yet. She jerked her Stetson from the bag, jammed it on her head, tucked her hair up under the brim, and climbed back into the coachman's seat.

"Get in, Anthony," she ordered, and snapped the drop-lash the instant she heard the door close. The carriage surged out of the trees and onto the road, the team moving at a brisk clip.

Her heart tried to beat its way out of her chest again. They were so close, so close to making it. She had actually pulled it off in a scene right out of one of her favorite novels. And that's exactly what it seemed like: a scene out of a novel. Reality had become totally suspended.

Surely she had not really just broken her lover

out of a jail and saved him from the gallows, six-guns blazing. It must have been somebody else. It couldn't possibly be little Harmony Simmons, her sister's ward.

Reality returned with a jolt, however, when she heard hoofbeats pounding behind the coach.

They had only traveled down the road two or three miles. Was it the English lawmen behind them, or had they traveled far enough and fast enough away? Harmony's muscles tensed, but she willed her features to remain expressionless. She pulled the hat down a little tighter on her head. The mass of her hair, tucked up inside, threatened to dislodge it. She held her head very still as the riders came alongside the coach.

"Halt!"

Harmony recognized Mr. Henry. He looked ridiculous on horseback. She hauled on her lines and the coach rolled to a stop.

"You, in the coach, step out where I can see you."

Harmony made to get down, as if to help her passenger, and prayed Mr. Henry would stop her. Her prayers were answered.

"Stay where you are, driver," he commanded, to her relief, although she did feel a bit nervous when he gave her Western-style hat a curious glance.

Harmony obediently sat back down. She heard the coach door open. She watched Mr. Henry automatically tip his hat.

"Good morning, ma'am," he said politely. "I'm sorry to inconvenience you, but we're looking for two riders on horseback, a man and a woman. Have you seen anyone go by?"

Harmony swiveled her eyes in her head as far as they would go. She watched Anthony raise a hand to his mouth, as if shy—tilting his head downward so the bonnet brim shielded his man-sized hand—and shake his head in the negative. The bonnet skewed slightly to one side. She held her breath.

"Well, sorry to bother you, ma'am. If you do see these two, head in the opposite direction. They're armed and dangerous."

Harmony watched Anthony nod. Mr. Henry put his heels to his horse and the group rode off. She watched Anthony gather his skirts and climb back into the carriage. When he was safely inside, she drove on a little farther to a fork in the road.

From the dust cloud, she could see which way the men had ridden. She took the other road and continued for a mile or two, until she found a likely opening in the trees. Cautiously, she guided the team into the wood. She kept on until the density of the trees made it impossible to go forward any farther, then tied the reins to the brake lever and jumped down. Anthony emerged from the carriage.

Unbelievably, they'd done it. She had rescued her

lover from jail, literally from the gallows, disguised him as a woman, and fooled the law.

Harmony waited for the full, sobering effect of what she had done to come crashing down on her like a load of rubble, but all she could feel was elation. It swelled in her breast until she thought she might burst with the strength and power of it. And then it turned into liquid happiness and flowed through her veins. She looked at Anthony, skirts gathered in his left fist, bonnet askew, and suddenly burst into gales of hysterical laughter.

"Oh, you . . . you'll regret this," Anthony warned, but there were no teeth in his bite. He whipped off his hat and took Harmony into his arms, stifling her laughter with his mouth.

Chapter Twenty-nine

He kissed her for a long, long time. Then he held her at arms' length.

"If this hadn't happened to me," Anthony said, "I never would have believed it. You are the bravest, smartest, most beautiful woman in the world."

"I love you," Harmony replied simply.

"I can't believe you did this, risked your life for me."

"I *really* love you."

"I *really* love you, too." He kissed her swiftly on the tip of her nose. "But we have to talk."

"I know."

"Let's get out of these clothes first."

"Anthony, I don't think we . . ."

"It'll be all right. I promise. I also promise that I cannot talk to you, say what I have to say, dressed like this."

A giggle tickled at the back of Harmony's throat, threatening to send her back into paroxysms of laughter. "I think you look kind of nice."

"You look better, a *lot* better in blue than I do. My Lady Blue."

"The bandit Lady Blue. It does have a certain ring to it," Harmony said lightly. She regretted it the instant she saw the expression on Anthony's face.

"Now, come over here and sit down," Anthony said. "There's something I have to talk to you about."

It was hardly surprising. They were fugitives from the law. They were on the run. They had a great deal to talk about. She sat down beside him at the base of a large and ancient oak tree. Anthony took her hand.

"I mean it, Harmony," Anthony began. "What you just did for me is the bravest thing I have ever heard of, much less experienced. If I ever had any doubts about how much you love me, I certainly don't now."

"Well, that's good. Because in your whole life, no one will ever love you more than I do."

"I believe that," Anthony replied humbly. "I hope you know I feel exactly the same way about you."

Harmony merely nodded. A lump was trying to form in her throat.

"I also have no doubt," Anthony continued, "that you and I will have a long, happy, and successful marriage."

"Oh, Anthony! You mean we can still—?"

"Of course we can still get married," he interrupted. "I think we'll make a great team."

This time it was Harmony's face that fell. She hadn't actually thought about it before. But if Anthony lived the life of a thief, she supposed she would have to also.

"You mean I'll . . . I'll have to steal, too?" She could have bitten her tongue off the instant the words were out. She didn't want him to think she would do anything, *anything*, to remain by his side.

So it was true. Anthony felt something profound happen deep inside of him. They all thought him a jewel thief. Harmony as well. Yet she had risked her life for him, rescued him. Was apparently even willing to live a life of crime for him. The power of her love rocked him.

"No, Harmony. You won't have to steal," he said quietly. "I would never ask you to do such a thing."

She breathed a small sigh of relief.

"Your life is not going to be particularly easy, however. You know that, don't you?"

"I'm a big girl. I knew what I was doing when I strapped my holster on. I've chosen to live my life with you, no matter what that life is." Harmony drew a deep breath and sighed. "I never would have thought I could do any of this, Anthony. I have to admit it. But I did it because I love you with everything I have, everything I am, with all my heart and soul. You are my life. I will share whatever life you live. Willingly and without hesitation or regret."

It was Anthony's turn to sigh. The breath he exhaled was shaky, however, and he realized he was very close to tears. He swallowed and cleared his throat before he was able to continue. "I do believe—no, I *know*—you're perfect for that life, Harmony, my love, my heart."

"Could you answer me just one question, please?"

"Anything, my lady."

"Could you tell me where, exactly, we're going to live? I mean, is there a . . . a *place*? Or do we, you know, have to keep moving? Or . . ."

At last. She had freed him. Her love had freed him. Anthony laughed. Long and hard, as he had never laughed before.

Harmony wasn't quite sure how to take his response to her question. But at least he was happy. She persisted. "What's so funny?"

"Yes, there's a 'place,' Harmony. I never lied to you about that. My home is north and west of Lancashire. I raise horses and cattle, as I said. Among my other pursuits. And my mother lives there, too, as I also said."

"But you . . . you're a . . . a . . . I mean . . . how can you stay in one—?"

"Sssshhhh, my love." Anthony kissed her quickly to still her lips.

Harmony, however, was not to be hushed anymore. She pulled away from Anthony. "You'd better tell me, right this second, what your name is and who you really are, Anthony Allen. Anthony Allen, I *think*."

Anthony sighed again. Everything that had ever happened to him in his entire life was exhaled and expelled forever in that single breath. When he inhaled, it was to absorb Harmony's essence. His gift. His life.

"All right, my sweet." He cleared his throat. It was time. Time at last. "Have you heard of a man named Bluefield?"

"Bluefield?" Harmony tasted the name on her tongue. "Well, yes. Yes, of course. Even in America he's famous. Or infamous, depending on how you look at it."

"What do you know about him?"

"As much as anyone else, I guess. Which isn't much. He's rumored to be the wealthiest man in England, possibly in the world. But very little is known about him in general because he's so reclusive."

"Yes, that's right," Anthony said. "He travels, and does much of his business incognito, so he won't be taken advantage of. He's rather shrewd that way. It's how he made most of his fortune. And because so few people know what he looks like, he can occasionally also dine in a public place without being . . . well, importuned for money, for instance. Or date a girl and get to know her before she finds out who he is and goes after him just for his money."

The world stood still. Absolutely still.

Then it hit her. Full impact.

Harmony scrambled to her feet. Her jaw dropped open. She gasped for breath, heart beating wildly, and backed up against the bole of the aged tree to support her quivering body.

"Anthony Allen Rutherford-Smith, Lord of Bluefield," she whispered, stunned. "That's his whole name . . . I remember . . ."

"Better known, simply, as . . . Lord Blue."

No more charades. No more hiding in the shadows. He had everything. Life was complete.

When Anthony took Harmony in his arms, she was unresisting. He lowered his mouth to hers.

"I love you," he breathed against her lips. He flicked them with his tongue. "I love you."

She leaned into him, totally helpless, as usual, in his embrace.

"Will you still marry me?" he whispered.

"I . . . I'm not sure," Harmony stammered. Pressed against him as she was, she was aware of every inch of his lean, hard body. She snaked a hand downward to the hardest part of all. "You are, after all, armed and dangerous."

Fog swirled around her, dimming her vision and

chilling her bones. The richest man in the world. A man whose burden was so heavy he had to masquerade as someone else, even going so far as to test her love by letting her believe he was a thief. And, in doing so, nearly losing his life.

This man, this incredible man, loved her. Loved her bigger than she had ever imagined love could be. Coupled with the day's events, all they had been through together, it was almost more than she could comprehend.

"Harmony?" Anthony prompted, a tiny worm of fear crawling beneath his flesh. "Harmony, are you all right? Are *we* all right? Will you please, *please*, marry me?"

Her very soul sprouted wings and took flight. Happiness was a living thing in her breast.

If he didn't do something, anything, immediately, Anthony knew he was going to cry. His joy could not, would not be contained. Arms wrapped around his love, he sank to his knees and laid her back on the ground.

"Please, just say yes."

"Yes . . ."

The world went away.

Epilogue

luefield. Harmony let her gaze caress the rolling, green hills of her home. How aptly the land was described with its name. The grass was so green that at some angles, and in some light, it appeared nearly blue.

"Lost in thought, my love?"

Harmony turned in her saddle to gaze adoringly at her husband. For old times' sake he had ridden out with her on the chestnut, while she was mounted on the gray.

"I'm sorry," she apologized quickly. "I simply cannot get over how beautiful it is here."

There was more to it than that. He knew her so well. "And what else, my love?"

How did he always manage to sense her every mood? "I . . . it made me recall something my father once told me."

"About . . .?"

"About a state called Kentucky," Harmony explained. "My father told me it was called the Bluegrass State because the grass was so green it almost appeared blue. He had planned to take me there sometime because so many horses are bred there. He knew I would have loved it. But he . . . he never got the chance."

Anthony reached across the space between them and took his wife's hand. "Then I shall take you," he said. "Although I cannot replace your father, I shall endeavor to make sure none of your dreams are unfulfilled."

A lump immediately formed in Harmony's throat. It mattered not at all that she was now very possibly the richest woman in the world. What mattered was that she was the luckiest. And the happiest. She squeezed Anthony's hand until the tears had loosened their hold on her throat and allowed her to find her voice.

"I never want to leave Bluefield, Anthony," she was finally able to reply. "You, and our home, are all of my dreams come true."

He knew she meant it with all her heart, all her being, and it was his gift, *his* every dream come true.

He had to clear his throat before he spoke. "You mean you don't even want to leave here to accompany me to London when I have to go on business?"

"Oh, don't be silly," Harmony replied tartly. "You know I'm never letting you out of my sight again. But no more secrets. Ever. Tell me where we'll be staying. Do you have a home there?" Memory suddenly intruded and she clapped her hands in glee. "Oh, tell me, tell me. Is it in Mayfair? I *love* Mayfair. Is it near your friends?"

"I am terribly sorry to disappoint, my love, but my London residence is not in Mayfair, but on the outskirts of the city." He watched the merest hint of disappointment touch her exquisite features, and swiftly acted to banish it.

"You've been to my London home, actually. At least to the gardens. Don't you remember it? We strolled there together late one evening after dinner in the city."

Harmony's jaw dropped. She couldn't help it. "Oh," was all she could say. And then she was speechless. She watched her husband's eyes twinkle with amusement.

"Ride back with me now?"

Harmony didn't have to give it much thought. The expression on Anthony's face, in his eyes, said it all. And she loved their huge four-poster bed. "Of course, my darling. Let's go home."

How good that sounded. She would never get tired of hearing it or saying it.

They cantered slowly back to their magnificent manor home, enjoying the sights as they went: grazing herds of Highland cattle with their distinctive horns and long hair; fields of brood mares, foals at their sides. Finally, cresting a last, wildflower-bedecked hill, Blue-field Manor came into sight.

Gooseflesh raised on Harmony's arms.

They rode past his mother's "cottage" first, then the elegant sprawl of the stables and adjacent pad-docks. Halting by the stables' wide double doors, grooms instantly appeared to hold their horses while they dismounted. Hand in hand they strolled across the broad, curving drive to the manse's front steps.

The heavy, intricately carved oaken doors opened as if by magic, although Harmony knew either the liv-eried butler or a uniformed maid would be standing there to greet them.

She was right. And wrong.

"Lady Alice," Harmony exclaimed with delight.

"Mother." Anthony took her hands in his and leaned down to kiss her cheek. "To what do we owe the pleasure of your company at this time of day?" He pulled off his riding gloves and handed them to his butler.

"You have company," Lady Alice replied. "I was entertaining until your return."

"Company?"

Harmony heard the alarm in her husband's voice and tried to read her mother-in-law's expression for a clue to what might be happening. But Lady Alice's demeanor remained serene. Harmony next examined her attire: a morning gown of pale peach satin, complementing her creamy complexion, and black, black hair streaked with white. It was, as usual, pulled into a classic chignon. Her casual dress told Harmony the guests were not of social import. So who could they be?

Guests were infrequent and always invited. Harmony's own alarm bells were beginning to clang. Following Anthony's lead, she pulled off her gloves and handed them to Patrice, one of the downstairs maids.

"I didn't see any horses, Mother, or a coach. Nor do I recall issuing any invitations," Anthony said in a tightly controlled voice.

Lady Alice put a gentle hand on her son's forearm.

"They came on horseback, my dear, and the animals are being cared for in the stables. They were hard ridden."

Aha. A clue at last. "All right, Mother, where did they come from? London?"

"Quite near."

If his upbringing hadn't been what it was and there weren't servants watching his every move, Anthony would have lifted his diminutive parent off her feet in a bear hug. He loved the little games they had always played like this. It was a special way they had developed over the years to convey a great deal of information while saying little. It ensured the privacy they held so dear in a very public world.

Translation: the riders were from Millswich; he wouldn't like it when he learned who they were, but their visit was benign. He glanced at his wife, who was just beginning to learn their language. By her relaxed appearance, it seemed she had gotten the message as well.

"My love?" Anthony offered Harmony his arm. "Shall we go and greet our guests?"

Harmony actually looked forward to discovering what their "visitors" had come to say. Like her husband, she understood they were from Millswich and meant no harm. Would she find out at last what had happened to all the players in their little drama following their precipitous departure from the stage and the revelation of the characters behind the masks?

Simply walking to the salon was an exercise in enjoyment. Harmony let her gaze linger lovingly on all she saw on their journey through the massive entry toward their destination.

The cavernous foyer was a room unto itself. Much like an extremely large hotel, comfortable furnishings were centrally arranged to form several different and intimate seating areas. Numerous side tables were covered with antique collectibles and bric-a-brac from around the world, and hand-painted scenes of historical importance graced the ceiling twenty feet above them. Lambent light was cast over all from an enormous and magnificent crystal chandelier.

At the end of the foyer was a wide, red-carpeted stairway, split into two at the first landing. Along the perimeter of the grand hall were six huge arches, three on each side, leading to the music room, dining room, library, salon, ballroom, and grand salon. Bosworth, the butler, gestured to the salon then followed them into the room.

Although Harmony favored the colors in the grand salon, gold and pale blue, she appreciated the soft green tones and slightly more comfortable furniture in the salon. Her eye was drawn to a grouping in front of the carved stone fireplace and the tall, lean gentleman who rose to his feet when they entered the room. She thought the other two men who quickly followed suit looked vaguely familiar.

"My son, Anthony Allen, Lord of Bluefield, and his wife," Lady Alice said graciously.

The tall man approached, hand outstretched.

"Anthony, my dear, may I introduce Clive Bishop, the new constable of Millswich?"

The two men shook hands.

"So," Anthony began, coming right to the point. "You replaced Mr. Henry."

"Indeed, I did," Bishop promptly replied. "I took the liberty of coming here uninvited to deliver the news to you personally. I hope you will forgive me, your lordship."

"I not only forgive you, I congratulate you, Bishop."

"You are most kind. May I also tell you then, that Henry was not only dismissed in disgrace, but will be prosecuted?"

Harmony could not control the little hiss of breath that escaped her lips. She saw her mother-in-law smile and her husband pressed her fingers lightly.

"You have more news, I'm sure, and I would like to know who the other two gentlemen are," Anthony said.

"Of course." Bishop turned to gesture the men over, but they had already started on their way. Before they could reach the group, however, Harmony's rigid composure dissolved into a bubbling fountain of giggles.

Lady Alice pressed a pale, slender hand to her lips to control her own mirth as she watched her son double over, nearly choking on his laughter. Bishop, totally perplexed, could only watch, slack jawed, until the hilarity had subsided.

"I . . . I'm so sorry," Harmony was able to say once she had control of herself again. "But . . . but when I . . . when I saw the two of you limping, and I realized who you—"

Anthony erupted into fresh gales of laughter.

"Anthony, my dearest son," his mother chided. "Won't you and Harmony share what is apparently your private joke?"

"It's actually not a joke," Harmony said at length on her husband's behalf, sobering somewhat. "These two gentlemen were guards at the Millswich jail. When I helped Anthony escape, and in order to prevent his hanging, I . . . I shot them in the feet."

Lady Alice briefly paled, but then high color tinged her cheeks. "You shot them?"

"She did, indeed," Bishop put in. "And it is the other reason we are here."

Harmony was instantly aware of Anthony's tension.

"Well, what is it?" he nearly barked. "Go on, man, speak."

"We are here to convey our deepest apologies, all of us, for the terrible, terrible troubles that were brought down upon you and your family, even and including the fact that Lady Bluefield was forced to fire on the officers. We are all fully aware that a gentleman in your position could most certainly have brought this entire affair to a legal conclusion, and—"

"Enough said," Anthony interrupted, putting Bishop out of his misery. "There is only one thing I would like to know, if you are privy to the information."

"Anything, my lord," Bishop said quickly. "Anything."

"I'm only guessing, of course," Anthony continued, "but I believe Henry was put up to my arrest on false information provided by Angus and Margaret

Donnelly. Is that a fact?"

Bishop colored, an answer in itself, then drew a heavy breath. "You are certainly correct, your lordship. And although no legal remedies were possible, it may satisfy you to know that the Donnelly name has become so tainted with the resulting scandal of the event that they have been forced to move away."

Harmony could wait no longer. "And my sister, Agatha Simmons? Have you any news of her? She was great friends with Lady Margaret."

Bishop glanced at his feet then cleared his throat. "As far as anyone knows, she has become a recluse. I am sorry I do not have more detailed information."

"That is quite enough. Thank you, Mr. Bishop."

"Is there anything else you would like to ask as long as I'm here?" Bishop offered. "I'd like to help you in any way I can."

"Actually, I do have a question," Anthony replied briskly. "Was the *real* jewel thief ever apprehended?"

"I'm so sorry," Bishop said, pulling at his chin with long fingers. "I should have remembered to tell you immediately. Yes, he was. And he turned out to be your typical, common criminal, roving outside of London looking for easy money. He was arrested, put on trial, and now resides in one of London's less than desirable residences."

Anthony was forced to chuckle.

The interview ended shortly thereafter and the trio of lawmen was escorted back to the entrance by the butler. Once they had exited, Lady Alice embraced both her son and daughter-in-law.

"Well, another mystery solved, as your father used to say."

Anthony guffawed and Harmony giggled. "At least now I know where you get it from," she said around the bubble of another eruption of laughter.

"I shall see you at dinner, then, children," Lady Alice said. "Have a lovely afternoon."

"Good day, Mother," Anthony replied, still grinning from ear to ear. As soon as Bosworth and Patrice retreated, he scooped Harmony in his arms and headed toward the stairs.

"Ah, yes, grandchildren," Lady Alice said in a voice that carried across the vast hall. "My dearest wish."

She finally left with the sound of her favorite music ringing in her ears.

Laughter.

By Honor Bound

Helen A. Rosburg

Bound by fate. Bound by love. Bound by honor . . .

Honneure Mansart, orphaned child of a lowly servant, never dreamed that she would one day find herself at the glittering palace of Versailles as a servant to the young and lovely Marie Antoinette, future Queen of France. Nor could she have imagined the love of her life would turn out to be her beloved foster brother Phillipe, who also served the young princess. Their lives were golden.

But the young princess, Antoinette, has a mortal enemy in Madame du Barry, the aging king's mistress. And Honneure has a rival for Phillipe, a servant in du Barry's entourage. Together the women scheme to destroy both Antoinette and Honneure. Then Louis the XV dies, and his grandson inherits the throne. Marie Antoinette becomes the Queen of France.

Honneuré and Phillipe, their lives inextricably entwined with those of the king and queen, find a second chance together. Yet as France's political climate overheats, sadness and tragedy stalk both couples once again . . . tragedy, and a terrible secret that might lead Honneure to the guillotine in the footsteps of her queen.

ISBN#978-0-97-436391-2
US $6.99 / CDN $9.99
Available Now
www.helenrosburg.com

A PERFECT TEN!

"In my opinion, *BY HONOR BOUND* is a must-read for any romance fiction fan, and assuredly deserves the distinction of a Perfect 10. It's just that good!" —*Romance Reviews Today*

Flight to Freedom

D.J. Wilson

I KILLED MY HUSBAND, A TOWN HERO, and then called the police and turned myself in. "He's dead as a doornail," I said to the officer and then spit on Harland Jeffers' bloody, dead body.

With my head held high, I allowed myself to be escorted to a squad car outside my house. A house which had been more of a prison than the cell I was headed for.

Cameras flashed.

"Why did you kill Harland?"

Because he needed killing. And I, Montana Ines Parsons-Jeffers did just that.

So begins the rest of what's left of Montana's life. Not that she ever really had one.

Now she's headed for prison. There's no escaping it. It was the ultimate destination in her Flight to Freedom.

But one man might be able to help . . .

ISBN# 978-1-93-383637-9
Trade Paperback
US $15.95 / CDN $17.95
Available Now
w w w . d o l o r e s j w i l s o n . c o m

BROKEN WING

Judith James

Abandoned as a child and raised in a brothel, Gabriel St. Croix has never known tenderness, friendship, or affection. Although fluent in sex, he knows nothing of love. Lost and alone inside a nightmare world, all he's ever wanted was companionship and a place to belong. Hiding physical and emotional scars behind an icy façade, his only relationship is with a young boy he has spent the last five years protecting from the brutal reality of their environment. But all that is about to change. The boy's family has found him, and they are coming to take him home.

Sarah Munroe blames herself for her brother's disappearance. When he's located, safe and unharmed despite where he has been living, Sarah vows to help the man who rescued and protected him in any way she can. With loving patience she helps Gabriel face his demons and teaches him to trust in friendship and love. But when the past catches up with him, Gabriel must face it on his own.

Becoming a mercenary, pirate and a professional gambler, Gabriel travels to London, France, and the Barbary Coast in a desperate attempt to find Sarah again and all he knows of love. On the way, however, he will discover the most dangerous journey, and the greatest gamble of all, is within the darkest reaches of his own heart.

ISBN# 978-1-93-383644-7
Mass Market Paperback/Historical Romance
US $7.95 / CDN $8.95
Available Now
www.judithjamesauthor.com

Be in the know on the latest
Medallion Press news by becoming a
Medallion Press Insider!

<u>As an Insider you'll receive:</u>

• Our FREE expanded monthly newsletter,
giving you more insight into Medallion Press

• Advanced press releases and breaking news

• Greater access to all of your favorite
Medallion authors

Joining is easy, just visit our Web site at
<u>www.medallionpress.com</u> and click on the
Medallion Press Insider tab.

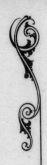

Want to know what's going on with
your favorite author or what new releases
are coming from Medallion Press?

Now you can receive breaking news,
updates, and more from Medallion Press
straight to your cell phone, e-mail, instant
messenger, or Facebook!

twitter

Sign up now at <u>www.twitter.com/MedallionPress</u>
to stay on top of all the happenings in and
around Medallion Press.

For more information
about other great titles from
Medallion Press, visit

m e d a l l i o n p r e s s . c o m